D1296102

THE
WOLF
QUEEN

TABITHA CAPLINGER

THE WOLF QUEEN

TABITHA CAPLINGER

WEST BRIDGEWATER PUBLIC LIBRARY

BLUE INK
PRESS

Copyright © 2021 by Tabitha Caplinger

All rights reserved.

Published in the United States by Blue Ink Press

The Wolf Queen is a work of fiction. Names, characters, places, and incidents are either a product of the author's imagination or are used fictitiously. Any resemblance to actual persons, living or dead, events, or locales is entirely coincidental.

ISBN: 978-1-948449-08-3

Library of Congress Control Number: 2020944363

Cover design by Megan McCullough www.meganmccullough.com

NOR

NORTH KEEP

GRÅLÅS

EAST KEEP

VÄI

SOUTH KEEP

VÄI

KUNNINGSTAD

NAAPURIA

HELIG MOUNTAINS

THLANDS

ASKADALEN

OSTLUND

SKÄMD

JALIL

W   E

N

S

To my daughters, wolf queens in the making;
Always guard your hearts as you follow the Light. Never let the
world define you or tame you.
Be brave. Be strong. Be pure.
Breathe fire.

So many stories begin with once: "Once upon a time…" or "Once there was a girl…". Yet before there was a Once, there was an always. Always has there been Lys. He is the oldest thing, the wisest thing, the strongest thing. He is the mystery that both can and cannot be known. He is pure and good, and He has an enemy.

For nearly as long as Lys has been, so has been Myrkr. They have warred against one another for rule over the realms of men. For the hearts of men are equal parts flesh and stone, light and darkness. Their hearts run cold, then hot—all subject to the waves of whims and desires. The Darkness twists them as the Light pursues them. Even with such power working to bend them, men still hold a power all of their own.

They can choose.

CHAPTER ONE

THE BATTLEFIELD LAY SOAKED with the blood of honorable men. Ylva walked amongst the bodies looking for signs of those still grasping at life. The previous day's fray played in her head as she stepped over the pale corpses of strangers and friends. The sun glinted furiously in a brilliant sky against the swords and axes raised toward enemies. Primal cries arose from dry throats. *It shouldn't be like this*, she thought. The clans had lived from one skirmish to the next for nearly all of Ylva's life—mostly small disputes that arose over farming territories. Occasionally it would be over the broken pride of an insulted chieftain. In any case, neighbors ultimately raised their weapons against one another. Over time, reasons grew shallower and skirmishes more frequent until even Ylva could no longer keep her clan from engaging in these conflicts.

Four days prior, one of her own was found murdered in the forest between their village and that of the Stolthüng. Clan Law dictated that members must avenge any lost brother. When no answer was given for the crime, justice was to be found in a day of war. Ylva despised this ritual. Death upon death did not feel like justice to her. Ylva could recognize that inflicting the same pain on another clan momentarily satiated her bloodthirsty compatriots—until the next crime when their vengeance had all the more increased. She watched as their souls grew darker, thirstier for revenge. Ylva could clearly read this on the warriors's faces—a darkness that first clouded then crept out from their eyes, then lined their faces like unholy masks. There'd been a time when that sight had been peculiar but now it was all too familiar, the glimpse of men losing their will, surrendering it more and more to Myrkr. Perhaps it was merely the naiveté of her youth that had blinded even her to the reality now so plainly in front of her. Perhaps her hope in the goodness of men had been a false one.

Her wolves, Vǫrðr and Shura, barked behind her. Ylva turned around to see them pawing at a body. She jogged over the red-stained grass to reach the source of their interest. She pushed her long braids over her shoulder, away from the blood and mud as she bent down. It was a man…not from her clan but from the Stolthüng. Blood and dirt covered his face. Ylva leaned down close to him and heard a shallow breath from his mouth and nose. She then patted his face with urgency to no avail. She pulled aside his leather armor and found his wound. A large gash slit his right side. The gash's dried blood pulled free when she moved his clothing, causing the wound to ooze. Ylva ripped a piece of cloth from the man's sleeve and held it to the laceration.

"This one is alive!" she yelled across the field toward the others who sifted through the carnage.

A large man, his tanned head bald and covered in the tattooed markings of Ylva's clan, ran toward her. "He is Stolthüng?"

"Yes, Erland," Ylva replied, standing to her feet and looking up at her comrade. The top of her head barely reached his shoulders if she stood on her tip toes. "And the battle is done. He is no longer our enemy. Bring him to his clan."

Erland nodded, then bent down. He picked the man up as

though he weighed nothing at all, then carried him toward the direction of the retreating Stolthüng clan.

Custom dictated that the victor would gain the spoils of war but Ylva did not oblige this. She would allow her warriors to gather weapons from the dead if they had need, but she would only look for the living. She would then return them to their home without incident. She did not do this to receive reciprocation but because she could not stand to do otherwise. War felt rotten in her stomach—even what first appeared as victory on the surface would ultimately be revealed as loss in another form. She could never participate in any celebration after a war. How could she take any delight in violence and death against fellow creations of Lys?

Shura barked at her, letting Ylva know they had made another discovery. Ylva turned toward the gray dog, almost white next to Vǫrðr, whose black fur created a stark contrast between the two lupine creatures. Both wolves growled low at the man who lay before them. The hair on their shoulders stood straight while their stance tensed. Ylva touched the dagger in her belt for reassurance as she approached the twitching body. The closer she drew to the figure, the more it convulsed on the ground. She knelt down, unsure of whether or not to touch the seizing man. She did not recognize him from her own clan, but he also bore no markings of the Stolthüng. Why was he here? For whom had he fought?

The man seized again, his body flailing as if against death itself. Ylva reached out, wanting to somehow soothe his suffering. Before her hand could touch him, his own hand shot up and grabbed her thin wrist. His grip felt so tight that it seemed like her bones would snap. She couldn't break free. Her wolves snarled and snapped beside her. "Shhh now, dogs," she commanded to calm her guardians.

The man's eyes flew open. Horror struck Ylva as she witnessed the display in front of her; one previously only an illusion revealed by her Gift but this time it was no miracle mirage. The bloodshot veins surrounding his irises somehow began to weep an ink-like black liquid, his whole face turning into a sickening shade of gray."The dragon is rising," the man spit out. His lips curved into a wily grin, allowing her to see his red-stained teeth. "He will take the High Mountain and then the realms of men will fall to the priestess, and to Myrkr, one by one." He choked between each word, his breath gurgling in his throat, and then he laughed. "You will die." His last words were a coarse whisper followed by another menacing laugh. He coughed and blood spurted out of his mouth and dribbled off his lips. Then the blood fell onto his chin as a tear trickled down his dirty cheek in one clean line.

Ylva felt his hand go weak before it dropped to his side. She rubbed the soreness from her now freed wrist. This was not Ylva's first brush with angry death. She saw it come many times before and sat beside men as they surrendered to it. She heard more than one set of final words. She listened to the mad ravings of those crossing out of this life and into the next. But she never before witnessed anything remotely similar to this. This man, whoever he was…was more than mad. She looked into his heart and nothing dwelled there but darkness. This…sickness… rejoiced in his pain until fear itself completely overtook the man in his final moments. Vǫrðr pushed his head against Ylva, trying to push her away from the strange corpse. She relinquished as ravens cawed loudly from their circle overhead.

CHAPTER TWO

THE DARK NAVY hues of night replaced the sapphire and coral tints of sunset by the time Ylva and her clansmen returned to their village. The orange glow of the fires and lamps danced in the windows of the humble wooden houses. Ylva could hear the joyous welcomes from each dwelling as her warriors broke ranks upon reaching their own homes. Slowly their numbers dwindled until only she, her wolves and Erland remained in a slow march to their destination. The last cabin at the end of the muddy road belonged to Håkon — the elder of her clan, the Ibharüng.

The old man's robust laughter long proceeded her actual arrival. Håkon sat in his wooden chair with furs draped across his shoulders and legs to keep him warm. A little girl sat in his lap pulling at his long white braids. Another half-dozen children sat in a pack on the floor, all intently listening to one of the elder's fantastical tellings of the old legends.

Ylva removed her quiver and bow and laid them just inside the door along with her trusted axe. "How is it that you have so much time to sit and tell stories?" she playfully asked Håkon. Then she took two large venison bones off the table and tossed them to Vǫrðr and Shura who waited faithfully outside.

5

"These stories are important," Håkon said as he returned the small child to the floor. "I remember when you were young and unable to get enough of my stories."

"I guess that is true." Ylva peered into a large cast-iron pot perched upon the fire. Her mouth watered at the rich scent of stewed meat and herbs.

"Tell us Ylva's story," a little blond boy requested.

"You don't want to hear that," Ylva responded.

"Yes we do. It's our favorite!" said one of the little girls. Her blue eyes were bright, and her rosy lips curved into a wide smile that made her cheeks look even more plump.

Ylva looked to Håkon with a raised brow. "I take it you tell my story often?"

The old man grinned. "They like the wolves."

Shura howled low, causing the children to stir with laughter.

"Tell us the story! Tell us the story!" the children gleefully chanted.

"Quiet, quiet. I will tell you of the girl who came to be raised by wolves," Håkon said. He glanced at Ylva who was now serving herself a bowl of stew, prepared to listen to him regale the children with her history.

When Håkon told her story, it sounded even wondrous to her. In truth, she knew most of it only through what she had been told. She had to admit there was a certain magic to the way he spun her tale, and it made her feel as though she was, or at least could be, more.

"All right children," the old man began, "Ylva's tale begins many, many years before you were even a thought in your parents' minds…"

"Not *that* many years," Ylva interrupted.

"Don't get defensive. They think you are old already, but to me you are still so young. Age is about perspective." Håkon winked at her and asked, "May I continue?"

"Of course," she replied as she sat down at the table.

"On a night just like this," he began, "our warriors had just returned from a triumph on the field of battle. It should have been a celebration—instead, it was marred by tragedy. The war between Lys and Myrkr raged beneath the surface, as it does in most of life's moments. The hearts of men being twisted and tilted in an effort to change fates."

Ylva studied the old man's white, wrinkled face as the firelight danced across it, accentuating the drama in his storytelling.

He continued, "Ylva's father, Magnus, was chieftain of clan Ibharüng, our clan, and my dear friend. He was noble and good, a fierce and courageous warrior. The people, at times, perceived him as something slightly more than human, though he was but a mere mortal. Death would come for him just as it does for all men. Just days before his child was to be born, Magnus and his warriors fought through unimaginable pain until they secured victory. But he did not escape the battle without suffering severe wounds."

"Did he die?" a little boy asked, the one whose red hair was always tangled and face was always a little dirty.

"Of course he did—that's the point," Ingrid replied, an older girl with a tongue as sharp as ever.

"Who's telling this story?" Håkon asked with the shadow of a smile playing at the edge of his lips. The children quickly drew quiet, careful not to disturb him again. "According to our law," he began, "Magnus's child would become clan leader upon his death. But Magnus had a brother. A greedy, prideful man named Ivar. Ivar sought to rule the clan himself. He knew he could not take it from his beloved brother, but he would not give it to an infant. He tried to persuade the elders to allow him to fill Magnus's position upon his death. They were reluctant…as they should have been. And if Ylva had been born just one day following her father's death, then the clan would have fallen under Ivar's leadership. But as Lys would ordain, Ylva was born just moments before her father passed out of this life. This set

Ivar's heart ablaze with jealous fury. With his heart now tainted by the Darkness, he plotted to kill Ylva and her mother."

Mother. The word made Ylva's muscles tense and palms sweat. She had only known her mother, Freja, for moments. Not long enough to remember anything about her. Håkon always told her that she bore her mother's same blonde hair and delicate features. But Ylva could never picture Freja's face or hear her voice whispering in the depths of her memories. Sometimes, in the spring, she would catch the subtle scent of the purple heather growing in the fields—then an unnamable feeling would awaken inside of her. Ylva knew that something was pointing her to her mother, but it felt like grasping at invisible threads. She could never hold onto any meaning. The feeling would pass before she could ever make sense of it.

She didn't know why thinking of the mother she never knew elicited such a stirring within her, whereas she did not feel the same way when considering her father. Perhaps while her mother represented a role she seemed to be missing, her father was the thing she was always trying to live up to. Plus, she had Håkon; he had become like a father to her. He filled at least part of the parental void. Ylva pushed her longing thoughts aside and returned her focus to him.

"Ivar concocted a plan," Håkon continued as he leaned in close, as though he were telling the children a secret. "He waited for night—for the village to all fall asleep. Then he snuck into the home of his brother. He saw his brother's wife, Freja, sleeping with her child still in her arms. He took his dagger and slit Freja's throat!"

The children all gasped. Gaidor, the oldest of the group, touched his hand to another boy's shoulder to calm him when he whimpered. The littlest of the bunch wiped a tear that ran down her chubby cheek. Her older sister, Asta, pulled the mournful child into her lap, holding her in a hug.

"Ivar then turned to the baby. He raised the dagger, now dripping with Freja's blood, ready to offer the baby the same fate he had her mother, when suddenly the infant began to cry. Ivar panicked. He feared that her cries would bring attention to his crime and result in his capture. So he wrapped Ylva in her blankets and carried her out of the house. He made sure to make a mess as he escaped, hoping to create a believable scene. See..." —Håkon leaned back in his chair and stroked his beard— "... Ivar had decided that he could take over the Ibharüng by eliminating Ylva, but he needed to subvert suspicion. He would make it appear as though a rival clan had attacked, all while painting himself as the hero who tried to save his niece. His plan ultimately failed of course."

Then Håkon leaned in closer still. "Though, if you ask me," he said, his voice reaching barely above a whisper, "I think his sudden change of plan to take Ylva elsewhere was the hand of Lys."

"The wolves are coming," Carr whispered to the red-haired boy.

"Yes, the wolves," the elder said. "They are my favorite part as well." Håkon smiled as the two dogs, as if on cue, stepped inside and laid at Ylva's feet. Their large frames took up the remaining floor space. Then he continued, "Ivar ran into the woods with baby Ylva. When he was far enough away that her cry could not be heard, he stopped, set her on the ground, and pulled his bloody dagger from its sheath. He was about to kill her, the last piece of his plot to take her rightful place as clan leader and frame the Fell...when he heard a howl pierce the night's silence."

"The wolves! The wolves!" The children were trying to whisper as they bounced in place.

"Ivar looked up and saw that he was surrounded by a pack of angry wolves. They all stalked around him, growling and howling with fangs bared." Håkon paused. He took the cup that sat next to him and raised it to his lips. He eyed the children over its rim as though he was waiting for them to lose all patience. Ylva chuckled at his antics.

When the children had leaned in as far as they could, twitching with anticipation, Håkon set his cup down and resumed. "Ivar knew he could not take on the entire pack. So as they stalked closer, he began to back away. Baby Ylva began to cry again—it drew the wolves' attention. Ivar thought this was his chance. He could leave the baby to the beasts and return to the village, tell his version of the story and then, just like that, rule our clan. And that is precisely what he did."

"But it didn't work!" Ingrid shouted.

"No, it did not," Håkon replied. "The wolves were sent by Lys. They were not meant to harm Ylva but to save her. That is what *they* did. None of us know exactly how, but the wolves took Ylva, protected and cared for her until she grew strong enough to return to the clan."

Shura and Vǫrðr nuzzled against Ylva's legs. She smiled down at them. Images circulated in her mind of the two wolves as tiny pups. Now these fearsome beasts stood taller than her waist. She didn't understand how she could have flashes of memories as a young girl living with the wolves, yet not remember how they managed to care for her. There was no sense to be found. How does a *wolf* teach a baby how to eat? How to live? Sometimes dizziness would overtake her if she allowed the questions to rise. An itching pulled at her mind, the faintest notion that maybe there had been more than just the wolves—like something, or someone, had been there too. She wouldn't allow herself to think much of it; instead she made it through each day focusing on the fact that she had survived. She told herself that this is what mattered most.

"Finish the story!" the children demanded. Their cries snapped Ylva out of her pondering.

"Here comes the best part!" Carr exclaimed.

Håkon adjusted the fur around his shoulders. "Ivar made the

clan believe his treacherous acts were committed by one of our enemies—the Fell," he said. "Of course our clan sought vengeance. We took the lives of innocent men at his behest. It solidified his place as leader of the Ibharüng. For several years he led us—though nothing like in the way of his brother. Ivar was cold, his heart full of hate. His only concern was power. He would have been our downfall...but for Ylva."

Håkon smiled at her. It wasn't his normal smile. This time it didn't hold its usual mischief. His expression made Ylva feel like he could see something in her that she could not. The smile made her feel stronger.

The elder looked back at the children. "It was dusk, many years later. The sun was setting and a full moon rose in the sky. Men and women were just beginning their evening retreat inside when the wolves howled. I was standing next to Ivar when it happened, and I swear to you—he shivered at the sound. The wolves never drew so near to camp, and yet the howling grew louder. Ivar yelled for the men to gather their weapons and for the children to be brought indoors. But no one moved. We were all mesmerized by the beasts as they prowled into camp. Somehow their yellow eyes looked only at Ivar."

Vǫrðr growled low at the sound of her uncle's name. Ylva patted his head to calm him, her tattooed fingers disappearing in his thick, long fur.

"Amongst the wolves, at the center of their pack, stood a girl. She didn't look much older than ten. She was thin and pale with long blonde hair. She stepped out from their throng."

Håkon coughed. He took another sip from his cup before continuing. When his story resumed, he evenly enunciated each word with careful cadence, so no one in the room could mishear this part of the story.

"The girl walked directly to Ivar. She cast a stare so unmoving that it seemed as though she could see into the depths of his heart. 'Who are you?' Ivar asked the girl, a perturbed urgency in his question. 'I am Ylva. Daughter of Magnus,' she replied. When she spoke, it felt like the ground shook beneath our feet."

As Håkon spoke, Ylva felt haunted in knowing that she remembered no such thing. Nothing about this critical moment seemed real to her. Håkon's account of that night clearly brought the wide-eyed children far more entertainment than would her clouded memory.

Ylva did not interject her doubts as familiar questions circled through her mind. How does a little girl raised in the care of a pack possess the ability to move deftly as a human, speak a human language…even know how to complete human tasks like dressing oneself? How did she know her own name? She was sure these questions had been asked upon her return—yet no answers ever came.

She was very much a girl who looked and acted like a girl, yet she slept on the floor by the fire like a wolf. She felt equal parts woman and wolf—but she never understood where the former came from. Why couldn't she remember these critical aspects of her past?

"What did Ivar do?" a child asked.

"He found it impossible. This couldn't be the infant he'd abandoned in the woods. He denied it and called her a liar. When he did, the wolves growled low and deep, their long fangs dripping with disdain. That's where I come in." Håkon's face curved upward into a proud grin. "I had been the only one, aside from Freja's maid servant, to see Magnus's child after her birth. I knew about her distinguishing mark—a birthmark on her left forearm. It bore a striking resemblance to the one her father had. So I took the girl's arm and sure enough, she had the mark. She was who she said she was."

Ylva looked down at her arm. Her shirt and leather bracers covered the skin, but she knew the mark was there. Just an inch or so from her wrist, a patch of darker brown skin that closely resembled a human heart.

"And the wolves attacked evil Ivar!" one of the boys shouted as he came up on his hands and knees and pretended to snarl like an angry wolf.

"No," Håkon scolded. "The wolves came closer, ready to attack, but Ylva stopped them. She peered into her uncle's heart and saw all of its darkness, hate, and greed, but still...she showed him mercy."

"I would have let the wolves eat him," Ingrid whispered. The other children laughed.

Ylva laughed herself.

Håkon's expression grew stern though his constant smile played at the edges of his eyes. "It is for Lys to place judgment," he said. "Ylva was right to offer mercy. Besides, Ivar got what he deserved in the end."

"What happened to Ivar?" a younger child asked.

"He went mad," Håkon replied. "He raved about a woman coming to him in his dreams. He would say that she claimed his brother's child would bring death to our clan and that he must kill her. He was not to be believed, and it was decided he would be offered to the Fell as recompense. They exacted justice."

"And the wolves?" Asta asked.

"All but Vǫrðr and Shura, only pups at the time, left. These two remained as Ylva's guardians. But if you listen closely, under the light of the full moon, you can hear the others howling. A reminder that they are always close, always watching, always protecting."

Just then the calling of the children's mothers echoed down the street and through the open doorway. The children groaned their displeasure but obeyed nevertheless, running out into the night howling like little wolves themselves. Vǫrðr and Shura howled back, causing the children to laugh loudly as they ran home.

Ylva slurped up the last bite of her venison stew, then wiped the dripping broth from her mouth with the back of her hand. She still wondered about the missing pieces of her memory. The older she became, the louder the questions shouted in her brain. It was becoming more and more difficult to quiet them.

"You seem someplace far off," Håkon said, interrupting her thoughts.

"More like someplace long ago," Ylva replied.

"The same queries as always?" the old man asked as though he already knew the answer. "The Light protected you. You are a miracle my dear, in more ways than one. If you *need* the answers, you will find them…but don't be consumed by the questions."

"You are right," she responded. "I should not be concerned with the past when the present has enough questions of its own." She licked the last traces of the hearty dinner from the wooden bowl before setting it on the table.

"What questions do you mean?" Håkon raised his brow and leaned forward, resting an elbow on his knee.

"There was a man on the battlefield today who did not belong to either clan. His heart bore so much darkness—like I have never before seen. He spoke of Myrkr, of a woman, of death." Ylva shuddered at the memory of the man and his blackened soul.

"I have feared this day," the old man said, then gazed into the fire.

The priestess stood very still, staring into the fire. A stale breeze circled the stone room. The blackened tips of her red hair brushed across her face, an unwelcome distraction. She hissed her displeasure, then held up one pale hand. The wind immediately retreated. She closed her eyes. When the priestess' eyes reopened, her view was not of the fire or the cave-like walls, but instead of a village in the northern region laid waste by her warriors. Where homes once stood now just lay piles of soot and ash. Bodies of men, women, and children lay lifeless on the blood-stained ground. Through the eyes of her army, she watched smoke rise high into the sky, blocking the light of the half moon. A last, faint whimper fell silenced by her soldier's sword. "You have done well," she said to the soldier. Then she commanded, "Return to me. We have more work to do."

CHAPTER THREE

"WHAT DO YOU MEAN?" Ylva asked Håkon. "Do you know what the man spoke of?"

"Aye, it is said there would come a time when the Darkness would rise and it would overcome all men. It will take the High Mountain and be the destruction of us all." The old man spoke the words with such confidence, as though he had already seen it happen.

Ylva stood up and paced the dirt floor. "You talk of myths and legends. There is nothing on that mountain but ruins."

"It is not what is on the mountain, but what lies beneath it." Håkon sighed.

"You don't really believe that to be true?" Ylva asked incredulously. She had heard him speak of the dragon who slept beneath the mountain a hundred times before. While Håkon based much of his storytelling upon *their* clan's history, Ylva knew that this account was not one to be believed. Maybe the myth held the slightest thread of truth, but Ylva had assumed its main purpose came in teaching children what is right and good through means of fable. Yet now he continued rambling into the fire about the mountain and its dragon like it *was* more, like it was prophecy.

"Do not think me a lunatic, Ylva—" the old man began but was cut off by Erland bursting through the door.

"I am sorry, but there is someone here who says he must speak with you," Erland said. "He claims it is urgent."

"At this hour?" Ylva asked. She did not give time for Erland to respond but simply added, "It's fine, I will meet him." She turned to Håkon and asked, "Join us?" The old man nodded and they followed Erland outside.

They walked through the village toward the western gate. An Ibharüng guard stood watch at the entrance, a lit torch in hand. Erland held another—the flicker of the two lights now cast a glow upon three figures previously camouflaged by the darkness. Their steeds stood nearby, the horses' breath visibly escaping as foggy tendrils into the frigid night air.

"I am Ylva, leader of this clan. To whom am I speaking?" she asked.

One of the figures stepped closer, coming into clearer view. His pallid skin and hair looked to be covered in ash and blood. "I am Dagr, of the Fell," he said and then bowed his head. "We come seeking shelter."

"You have come a very long way. Why? Shelter from what?" Ylva asked. There were at least three other clans residing in the territory between her clan and the Fell. While no current dispute existed between them, her uncle's deceit had caused a long-lasting tension.

"Our clan came under attack two days ago," Dagr answered. "They came at twilight with no warning and no reason except to destroy everything and kill everyone."

"Who?" Ylva asked.

"We do not know—they bore no clan markings. We don't believe them to be from the Northlands," Dagr replied. "We came here because we know you to be virtuous and just. We know that you can be trusted and would not simply cast us out."

"If your village was attacked, why are you not helping the survivors? Have they sent you to find a place for them all? To ask me to bear the burden of your entire clan?" Ylva asked only a few of the questions running through her mind. It bothered her to consider that an injured people were left without help. She herself would not have left them out in the cold. At the same time, she would not extend the Ibharüng's help simply because the Fell may believe Ylva's people owed service to them. No— her clan's debt had been paid years ago.

"We are the survivors," another of the Fell said as she stepped forward, a shield maiden with long hair stained with the same blood and ash as her comrade. "The *only* survivors."

"This is Solveig, my sister," Dagr said, "and this is Bjorn." He gestured to the third Fell, a young man of ruddy appearance.

Bjorn looked terrified as blood actively dripped down his arm. "We are all that is left of the Fell. No other man, woman, or child remains alive. All that remains of our village is soot and smoke."

"Why would someone do such a thing?" Erland wondered aloud. "This goes beyond the rules of war." Erland had fought by Ylva's side since she was a girl. He usually spoke very little. While typically calm and steadfast, worry now wrinkled his brow.

"There was no rule to it, no law guiding it. It was pure evil wearing men's skin." Solveig's voice trembled as she spoke, tears streaking her face.

"What do you mean?" Håkon asked, now stepping into the conversation to which he had just been a silent bystander up to this point.

"They were unnatural, the men who attacked us. Their eyes were the color of storm clouds, their veins black. Each possessed the strength of ten men," Bjorn replied. His voice cracked with each word.

Dagr placed a hand on the boy's shoulder. "They were inhuman. It was like they were from another world."

Ylva sighed. "We will give you shelter. Erland will see to it. But be careful not to make monsters out of mortals. It will only incite more fear," she said. She looked to Erland who nodded his compliance and began to lead the three Fell survivors into the village.

"Sometimes mortals become monsters," Håkon scolded her quietly once the others left earshot. "There is more at work here than the hands of men. Do you really have such a hard time believing that?"

"I believe in the Darkness, but this...this is..." Ylva was finding it difficult to wrap her mind around such a thing.

"This *is* the Darkness growing stronger," the elder interrupted. "Just as Lys can bestow gifts of power on his beloved, Myrkr can also give a form of power that is really a curse. The former acts to bless and strengthen while the latter only seeks to take. You of all people should understand there is more at play here than just the natural. Think of your own gift... your Sight."

Håkon was right. Ylva knew it. Lys had given her a gift— one that could not be explained. Some even doubted it, but she knew it to be as real as anything she could touch with her hands. What Dagr had seen, the Darkness taking over a man's heart, was what she saw every time she used her Sight. But she had never known it to break the surface of a man's flesh to become visible by all. She couldn't fathom a darkness growing so strong in a man's heart that it would breech his form and will completely.

This all meant more than Ylva was prepared to accept. The dying man, the elder's stories, and now the catastrophe upon the Fell...the Darkness must be growing. This attack perhaps marked only the beginning. "What do we do?" she asked.

"We send a falcon to the North Keep," Håkon instructed. "The dragon is rising."

It was the second time Ylva had heard those words. It was the second time they caused her body to shiver and draw bumps across her pale skin. For most of her life, Håkon told tales of Myrkr and Lys. He spoke of imprisoning the Darkness generations ago and of a time when it would once again come to reign. He recited prognostications of The priestess turning the hearts of men and her dragon devouring those who would not yield. Did she not believe him? It is easy to believe what we can see and experience, but it is harder to bear faith in the things unseen—the things that defy rational thought. Believing solely in her gift, what she could see, was simply not enough anymore. She must decide: embrace the stories told by the elders or find another option. She could no longer avoid thinking about from where her gift came and the implications therein. If Håkon was right, if his stories were actually coming to pass, she must broaden her belief. Ylva wanted to believe fully in Lys; that Lys could be trusted both with what can be understood and what cannot. The war between the Light and the Darkness breeched the surface of their world and so her faith must go beyond the shallows. Her heart had to be ready.

CHAPTER FOUR

ROHAN SPUN his sword and circled his opponent. He watched, waiting for just the right moment to charge. Then their swords clashed in the air. The man stumbled a step backward from Rohan's sharp push but lunged forward in retaliation. Rohan blocked the blow, then spun and offered his own. Metal clanked. This played out again and again with subtle variances, all with the same result: metallic chords and tired muscles. When he had had enough, Rohan lifted his hand. His opponent bowed and lowered his sword.

It had been ages since real war had come to Väljalil. Sparring felt tedious most days. Rohan especially hated it when rains like today made the training grounds slick with mud. While he came from a long line of warriors, the past necessity of sword-training was now merely a custom to be upheld. As a child, Rohan's father taught him that while kings must never desire war, they must always prepare for it. And prepare he did, every day of his life. And Rohan was weary. Three generations of his bloodline had maintained peace. Now, Rohan drew ever closer to the weight of a crown he did not want. Perhaps an actual battle, a taste of war, would provide an escape from his fears and make him feel like this all meant something.

He shouldn't think such things. A century ago the cost of peace had been a high one; rebuilding the Four Realms had not been easy or comfortable for his ancestors. Rohan tried to remember that he was fortunate if all this tradition and ritual was what maintained it. His father never seemed to forget. He and Rohan were so different. The king often brought up the unnecessary risks Rohan would take as a rebellious adolescent—risks his father never would have taken. He would sneak out of the castle walls to gamble or fight in a grapple, all in a blind thirst for adventure. Rohan knew he had deserved his father's admonishments when they came. He desperately wanted to have his father's honorable, warrior heart but often became lost in the disappointment of his unruly and ignoble choices.

Rohan reached his calloused hand into the well bucket and drank a sip of cool water from his cupped palm. "We will go again," he called to his sparring partner. He reached into the bucket again, this time to splash the frigid water against his face. He rubbed his dripping hand over the blonde scruff of his chin and neck, then through his hair. "Don't go so easy on me this time."

"Aye, Highness," his partner agreed.

Once again, Rohan lifted his blade to the ready. Sparring continued, more clashing metal and leather boots slipping in sticky mud. This spar immediately felt more intense than those of earlier in the day. The prince's combatant picked up his pace and didn't pull back his strength. He boasted a few inches taller than Rohan, not to mention a larger frame. Onlookers might think the prince was outmatched. Despite his stature, however, Rohan battled as a quick and strong swordsman. While he may not yet be able to contend on his father's level of battle, he was not weak. He worked ten times harder than most men so as not to allow life of the ruling family to make him soft.

"Highness!" A shout echoed from overhead.

Rohan did not look away from his opponent as he responded. "Can you not see I am in the middle of something?"

"It is urgent," came the reply.

Rohan held his hand up to stop the match. He gazed upward to find his advisor and friend, Tyr, standing on the balcony which overlooked the training yard. He handed his sword off to a young attendant and jogged up the wooden steps to meet Tyr. "What is it?"

"Sir, the clans in the Northlands are at war—" Tyr began.

"The clans are always at war," Rohan interrupted. "I do not have time to intervene in their squabbles."

"I know, Prince. This is different," Tyr said, a punctuating sigh revealing his friend's concern.

Rohan and Tyr had known each other since they were boys running through the castle halls. His friend, who was more like a brother, always proved himself level-headed. Tyr was a thinker. His reason and logic served as a balance to Rohan's more impetuous nature.

"A falcon came to the North Keep," Tyr continued. "The Fell village was destroyed. They say it wasn't by a rival but something else."

"Like what?" Rohan asked.

"Read it yourself." Tyr handed him a small scrolled note.

Rohan unrolled it and glanced through the lines of messy ink. "The dragon is rising?" He read the final words over and over to himself.

"I think it's in reference to an old myth," Tyr replied.

Rohan was well aware of the legends surrounding Lys and Myrkr. "You are not one to believe those old stories, Tyr. You can't really think that is what is happening?" Rohan balled up the message and tossed it back to his friend.

"Something is happening," Tyr said with his dark eyebrows raised. "Some clans may still revere the old ways, but they are not so easily given over to superstition. Besides, the message came from the Ibharüng. Why? They are neither friend nor enemy to the Fell—or to any of the other clans. They keep to themselves. Why would they get involved unless this attack truly needed our involvement?"

Mention of the Ibharüng sparked Rohan's curiosity. He didn't have much to do with the people in the Northlands. They mostly handled their own business. On occasion, representatives from one or more of the twelve clans would come through the gates of the Keep looking to trade for goods. They would talk of skirmishes and battles, regaling the ale-hall with tales of heroism. Every clan that is but one...the Ibharüng. There were whispers that bore their name but only ones shrouded in a sense of reverence and mystery. If they sent the falcon, Rohan wanted to know more. "Send word to all the clans. I will ride out and we will meet at the North Keep in a day's time," Rohan said before walking away.

"Do you think it is wise for you to leave the walls of the city while your father is so ill?" Tyr asked after him.

Rohan replied while still walking, "If my father dies, I will become king whether I am within or without these walls. King or not, I am the one who is responsible for the Four Realms of Väljalil. If there is an enemy amongst us, we must uncover it," he said.

"We could just send a liaison to meet with the clans," Tyr said.

"Friend, don't you think I can handle the clan leaders?" Rohan asked, feigning insult.

"I think you don't know the clan leaders," Tyr replied. He sighed loudly and added, "I'm coming with you."

The interior of the castle was dim compared to the bright outdoors. Rohan squinted against the torch light as his eyes adjusted. At the end of the long stone hall, he reached the ornately carved door of his father's room. It creaked as he pushed it open. "Father?" he called.

There was a cough. "Son, come in." His father's reply was rough and weak.

"How are you feeling today?" Rohan asked as he approached the king's bedside.

His father lay covered in furs, his head against a pillow. His skin shone as pale as his white hair. Dullness tarnished his blue eyes more and more each time Rohan visited him. He coughed again, wheezing in a breath afterwards. "Better today I think," he said. "But you aren't here to check on me."

"No, father," Rohan replied. "There has been an attack in the Northlands. The Fell village was destroyed."

The king struggled to sit up. "That is unlike the clans. They have laws against such things."

"They do not think it was a rival but something else. Tyr and I are riding tomorrow to meet the chieftains at the North Keep. I will find out what happened and who is responsible."

"Are you sure that is wise?" Rohan's father asked.

Rohan searched his father's expression, trying to decipher his meaning. Was he innocently asking? Was this just a father wanting his son to have certainty, or did the king doubt Rohan's abilities to lead? This wouldn't surprise Rohan—he himself had always doubted his own leadership. While he hid his concern behind charm and confidence...it was always there, nagging at him, the voice that told him he would never be as good of a king as his father.

"Rohan, my son?" His father asked, regaining his attention.

Rohan smiled down at the man and took his hand. "If I am to be king someday, I need to take a more active role. I need to meet the chieftains, I need to show them I am capable."

"I agree," his father patted his hand. "Go with Lys."

Rohan nodded, grateful for his father's agreement though it did not rid all of his trepidation for the day to come. Still, Rohan turned and left.

CHAPTER FIVE

YLVA HAD NEVER TRAVELED to the North Keep, nor outside of the Northlands for that matter. Her village sat at the farthest, most northwest tip of Väljalil. Lush forest surrounded the Ibharüng home before giving way to a river birthed from the Helig Mountains. This river wound through their livelihood before pouring into the nearby sea. It was the most beautiful place she could imagine and she never thought she'd have need to leave it...until now, upon the summons of the prince.

Ylva, her wolves at her side, Erland, and the three Fell survivors left for the Keep at dawn. She had told Håkon he was to blame for this journey. The old man only laughed and mumbled something about it being merely the beginning. She didn't know what he meant—nor did she care to. She only wanted to get to the Keep and return to her clan and life as usual.

Vǫrðr and Shura trotted out in front of the horses. Ylva watched them sniff and scamper amongst the wheat and wildflowers. Occasionally they would catch the scent of something, stop in their tracks, lift their heads to sniff the air, only to return to their frolicking a moment later. Their demeanor brought a smile to Ylva's face. She was not so carefree as her wolves. The familiar forests faded from view as the sun rose higher. She didn't like being so out in the open, so exposed. It felt vulnerable. Ylva didn't like feeling vulnerable.

"Are you all right?" Erland asked, riding up beside her.

"Yes, Erland," Ylva replied, adjusting her seat. "I am fine."

"I don't like this...leaving the clan...going to the Keep," he whispered.

"Neither do I, but if it brings us answers and aid, then it will be worth it. Besides, Håkon will take care of home." She knew her words would be enough to reassure Erland, although they didn't quite comfort herself.

Suddenly, Ylva sensed something. It bore no image, nor scent, but she could *feel* it. Her hair rose when the breeze blew but it wasn't the wind...rather something riding on it. The wolves sensed the change. They had left their fun and were jogging just behind her horse. Their ears stood at attention and their noses tilted into the air.

A small murder of ravens cawed overhead. Ylva had the notion that they were watching her. It was silly but she could not shake the feeling nonetheless. The black birds circled above them in a way leaning towards peculiar. But they were just birds. Weren't they? Maybe she was letting the exaggeration of Håkon's stories get to her. Or...maybe his stories weren't exaggerated at all. Maybe nothing was as simple as she had once thought, not even the birds.

"They are ominous," Dagr said, staring into the sky as he slowed his horse to come side by side with Ylva's.

"Yes, that they are," Ylva responded. Dagr didn't say anything further though his countenance remained grim. Ylva tried to imagine what he and the others had seen during the onslaught. Her unique perception always made battles seem darker, more sinister, but to everyone else, they merely viewed these fights as part of life, a bloody part no doubt but nothing much deeper. The attack on the Fell was far from normal. It was beyond even what her Sight had ever discerned. It was like nothing she had ever seen or heard of…and that was terrifying.

Ylva did not have the luxury of fear. Her people needed her to show strength. Fear could be nothing more to her than a catalyst toward bravery. If she humored fear, allowed it to wander around her thoughts, it would taint her heart.

Håkon often told Ylva that Myrkr favored fear over any other weapon. It was what drove most men toward the Darkness. Ylva knew she must fight that unseeable monster or she would have no hope of fighting those made of flesh and bone.

Shura whined beside her. The she-wolf could sense Ylva's moods. She could tell that Ylva's anxiety continued to grow as the ravens hovered overhead. Ylva guarded herself against it deepening further. With the Keep still an hours-long ride away, she must take captive her thoughts and focus on the Light, on the beauty around her. Ylva concentrated on the present, trusting in the wisdom of Lys for what might come.

The sun was big and orange as it set on the western horizon. The sky above and before them steadily darkened into night as the tall silhouette of the Keep's tower came into view. Getting closer, Ylva could see the roughness of its stone walls and its flickering torches. The structure was larger than she imagined. It was also dirtier. The grass underfoot turned to deep mud that pulled on the horses hooves and required more force and energy to take a step. The stench of manure and waste filled her nose, leaving a foul taste on the top of her tongue. It was noisy, too, with all the people shouting and cackling. All of Ylva's senses were overwhelmed in this fortress, which she did not find appealing in the slightest. Ylva could not see its allure though she tried to find something of worth in it. If this was what the whole of Grålås was like, she could do without it.

"Vǫrðr! Shura!" Ylva called to the wolves as she dismounted her chestnut mare near the stables.

"Follow me this way to the Great Hall," Dagr said, leading them through the street toward a building bigger than anything in her village.

Etchings, intricate lines of runes telling the stories of Väljalil, covered the large entry door to the Hall. The impassioned conversation of the other chieftains floated outside the wooden barrier. Ylva recognized many of the voices from negotiations and battles. Erland opened the door, the three Fell entered first and the room quieted to mutters and whispers. Then Ylva stepped inside with her large wolves looming beside her, and the room became silent. She dipped her chin in a curt nod and walked to take a seat in a dim back corner. The Fell sat close by. Ylva ordered the dogs to sit. They swiftly laid at her feet. Erland stood beside her, ever on guard. After Ylva and her group had become situated, the room returned to its previous chatter.

Ylva observed the interactions. The chieftains of each clan sat surrounded by many of their sons, elders, and even a few shield maidens. They all laughed at one another, swapped insults and honors, and occasionally sloshed the contents of their mugs onto the floor or themselves. Murmurs swirled about the contro- versial impetus for their convening. None spoke to the Fell— which Dagr, Solveig and Bjorn seemed to prefer. None spoke to Ylva either but she did not expect otherwise. She didn't fit in with them. They didn't treat her differently, they simply did not appear to know how to treat her at all.

There was a time, as a little girl, when sitting amongst the other clan leaders would have made her feel insecure. She learned long ago to embrace what made her different and with that came a peace these men could not break. The noise however, might. Ylva rubbed her fingers along her temple to ease the coming headache.

Ylva's impatience grew as she anticipated the start of their assembly. She tapped her foot. Her wolves fidgeted. Finally the creaking of the door signaled a new arrival. Two men entered. Some of the chieftains stood while others, like herself, assessed whether or not that was necessary.

The first man looked around the room. He clenched his jaw. Ylva wondered if he was displeased at the less than unanimously warm welcome or was he nervous? Either way, he didn't seem fully comfortable. The second man appeared more confident. He stepped forward.

"I am Tyr, counsel to Prince Rohan of Väljalil," he spoke. "The prince has—"

"I can speak for myself, friend," the first man interrupted. "I am Prince Rohan, son of Vakr."

He did not need to announce himself with such formality. His blonde hair had been shaved on the sides of his head revealing the black-inked runes of his family name. Runes they would all know well—they clearly told of his bloodline with the ruling family. Perhaps he simply liked the sound of his own name.

"I called you all here because the clan wars in the Northlands have broken the rule of law," Rohan said.

At his words the room erupted in a cacophony of angry scoffs.

The leader of the Stolthüng stood. "With respect, Highness, no clan has broken the rule of law."

"Have you not heard of the attack on the Fell?" Rohan asked.

Ylva watched the prince. He was equal parts confidence and apprehension. To be fair, he was much younger than most of the clan leaders who also cared little for the royal family or its authority. It was not that they were insubordinate—they merely had no use for a king. The clans ruled their own lives and had done so without interference for generations. The unification of the realm had its benefits, but did not ensure that all clans felt an obligation to agree on all things at all times. To them, this prince was just a boy looking to prove himself. Ylva wanted to be careful not to judge him too harshly—but this was difficult to do given the unavoidable childishness visible in his demeanor.

"Aye, word has spread like wildfire through the forests. A destroyed clan does not go without notice, Highness," The Stolthüng leader, Garth, replied to the prince. He attempted to be polite but there was a sarcastic bite to his words, particularly the last one. He regained himself and continued, "It was a terrible thing, but I can assure you it was not at the hands of the Stolthüng."

One by one the other leaders echoed Garth's words, each refuting their clan's involvement with growing contempt. The clan leaders did not take kindly to accusations of any kind, regardless of culpability. The prince wounded his first impression on the group by hinting at the involvement of those in the room.

Ylva shifted uncomfortably in her chair as the room's tension mounted. She knew these men and how to read their moods. She knew to notice when their fists clenched and shoulders straightened. She watched the prince glance toward his aid as each chieftain stood in firm defense of their clan's innocence. The aid returned Rohan's concerned gaze. He seemed unsure how to proceed. Ylva knew if the prince allowed his aid to speak for him now, then hope for retaining any respect would be lost.

The prince bowed his head and stared at the ground. Then he inhaled a heavy breath, raised his shoulders before returning his gaze to the assembly. "If another clan did not attack the Fell, then who did?" Rohan inquired, his firmer tone quieting the acrimonious clamor.

There was a spark of something in his voice just then. His question was a simple one but the way he asked it cracked the surface of his facade. There was authority wrapped in a thin layer of humility. It was something true and it changed the atmosphere even if just a degree, causing Ylva to lean forward in concentration as her wolves' ears perked.

All eyes searched the room for an answer, each waiting for someone to step forward and offer an answer of substance.

Finally Dagr stood. "I am Dagr, of the clan Fell," he said. "With me are my sister, Solveig, and fellow clansmen, Bjorn. We are the last of our house. I can tell you in truth that it was no clan from the Northlands who destroyed our village."

Ylva held her breath and tried to will Dagr to stop speaking, to silence the words she knew were about to come out of his mouth, words she warned him about sharing. Once spoken, he would not be able to take them back. She could not be certain as to how the other leaders would react to Dagr's account. She wanted to reach for him, to jerk him into sense, but her actions could not keep up with her thoughts and neither were quick enough to stop his next words.

Dagr continued, "They were not human."

CHAPTER SIX

HAD Rohan heard the man correctly? What did he mean, 'They were not human?'

"Explain yourself," the prince demanded.

The whole gathering anticipated an answer. Some seemed ready to laugh and others looked terrified. Rohan pulled his shoulders back, prepared to take charge no matter the explanation.

"Those who attacked our village acted like…wild animals," Dagr said. "These 'people' didn't speak beyond primal groans. Their eyes like brewing storms. No cause motivated their attack, nor did they concern themselves with any standard of honor. They slaughtered every man, woman and child within reach without flinching. If any humanity once dwelled in them, it was gone."

The other clan leaders stared at Dagr as though he had gone mad. Perhaps he had. The kind of ravaging he witnessed would make a man crazy, drive him to force reason when none existed. Rohan could sympathize with Dagr's position. To experience such unwarranted violence would create a heavy burden to bear, one that seeks to snuff out all that is noble. It causes illusion to become easier than reality.

"Some men are vile and dishonorable," Rohan responded, "but that does not make them anything other than vile, dishonorable men."

"These were not merely vile *men*, Highness," Dagr said. "They were men possessed by Myrkr himself."

His words forced the air out of the room. After a moment, it flooded back, inhaled in a collective gasp and exhaled in agitated whispers.

One of the oldest chieftains stood. The room sat silent with admiration. It was Ull. He had been a friend to Rohan's father and grandfather. His name was spoken with respect inside the castle walls. Rohan had met him only once. He had been a guest at the High Solstice feast when Rohan was just a boy. They gave him a hero's welcome and he sat at the seat of honor. Rohan had been in awe of him simply because of the esteem granted to him by King Vakr.

"Prince," Ull spoke, "in a time long before—before myself and your father—the realm fought together to imprison the Darkness before it could devour the hearts of men. We believed we would never again need to live in fear of its wrath. Others, however, spoke of a prophecy—a vision given by Lys of the Darkness being freed and his weapon, the dragon, rising from its slumber. For this reason, I believe Dagr of the Fell. I believe that Myrkr again works amongst us."

Scoffs and consensus mingled together in a loud garble of voices.

"Men! Quiet!" Rohan demanded. It was the second mention of the dragon rising. It was the reason the clans were meeting though he hadn't wanted to believe it then and still didn't. He wanted to conduct this gathering in a way that steered clear of prophecies and myths. "Men, we cannot give ourselves over to superstition. Something attacked the Fell—if it wasn't a rival clan, perhaps it was a neighboring opposer or foreign army. We should look to real enemies of the Northlands and of Väljalil before another attack comes to lay another village to waste."

"What enemies, Highness," a chieftain asked. "Have the farmers in Ostlund traded their fields for tyranny?" Others responded to the chieftain's jest with loud laughter. "Would the Naapurians dare to cross our borders?"

"Is that harder to believe than unearthly warriors led by a long-dead priestess?" Rohan argued. "Are you all so arrogant you believe the Northlands too formidable to be defeated by anything less than immortals?"

The gathering again erupted in angry argument.

"Careful, Rohan," Tyr whispered in his ear. "You do not want to make these men your enemies."

Rohan turned his head just enough to see Tyr's furrowed brow and twitching jaw. "I know, but we can't secede to one man's delusions."

"True, but be cautious how you dispel them," Tyr said.

Rohan brought his focus back to the clan leaders, shouting over their contention. "Or are you just ignorant of anything outside your very own forests?" His insinuation of course incited more anger—but he preferred their anger over the assembly forfeiting logic altogether. He would not be so easily swayed into chasing legends.

"We are neither arrogant nor ignorant," a voice, equal parts soft and strong, called from the back of the room. It seemed to bind everyone in gags and chains.

Rohan searched the crowd. One by one, the clan leaders resumed sitting until only one person remained standing—a woman. She looked small...almost frail in comparison to the men surrounding her. Her skin was pale and her features plain. Rohan hadn't even noticed her before now. It seemed though that the others were all completely aware of her presence and had been waiting for her to speak.

"Perhaps it is the prince who is too arrogant to believe there could be something greater than himself, or is he too ignorant?" she asked.

"Who are you?" Rohan inquired, trying to ignore the stifled laughter around him.

A large man covered in dark tattoos—matching the markings on the woman's neck and fingers—said from behind her, "This is Ylva, leader of clan Ibharüng, the Wolf Queen."

It felt like the gathering wanted to cheer her but their tribute was held back by an invisible dam. Rohan was fairly certain it was not for his sake as Ylva walked toward him and each man's head dipped in a fleeting bow.

"Do not worry, Prince, I have no desire or intention to take your crown," Ylva said. Rohan couldn't tell if her words were meant to burn or soothe his ego.

"I have no desire or intention of letting you, or anyone else," Rohan replied.

On either side of Ylva stood a wolf, one black and one light grey. They growled low at him, baring their sharp fangs. Ylva slightly raised her hand to which the wolves immediately relaxed their position. "Then you should listen more and speak less. Or are you so afraid of what you do not understand that you cannot?" She spoke softly to keep the conversation between just the two of them.

"You would listen to such stories?" Rohan heard the derision in his own voice. He didn't care. He didn't like her. He didn't like her nerve, the way she spoke to him, the way it made him feel. He had known this woman for less time than it would take him to drink a mug of ale and she had him cut down to the knees.

"Stories can teach us," Ylva replied, "but in this case it is not about the story but the person telling it, Dagr, one of your subjects and a good man. I would listen to *him*."

Rohan didn't like that she was right almost as much as he didn't like her. "Giving life to shadows is folly," he told her.

"The shadows already have life," Ylva responded. "I see them everyday in the eyes of broken men."

"I take it you believe in the old ways, in the wars of Light and Darkness vying for men's hearts?" Rohan scoffed.

"I take it the prince does not believe?" She tilted her head slightly and stared into his eyes like she was searching his very soul.

Rohan began to squirm inside his own skin. He didn't want to look at her, to wriggle under her scrutiny, so he averted his gaze away from her and looked back towards the chieftains.

"I mean no disrespect to any of you or your beliefs. I was raised on the same stories of Lys and Myrkr. I know the comfort these legends can bring, but should we chase fairytales with a real threat amongst us?"

Dagr stood again and said, "The threat of the Darkness *is* real."

Now Garth spoke again. "I am sorry for what happened to the Fell. The Stolthüng is willing to stand against any enemies that might threaten our ways, but I agree with Rohan. Perhaps we should look to what is tangible before consulting fables."

"Fables?" Ull retorted, wobbly as he stood up on feeble legs. "Those fables are the foundation of our law, of our people. They are truth even if you do not believe. The Darkness cares not of your beliefs. It will not wait. Myrkr is on the move—I would wager his priestess has already returned to the High Mountain."

"She is a story we tell to scare children, nothing more!" Someone shouted.

"She is real, and she should scare you," Ull replied. The eldest of the clan leaders faltered, swayed a little and then rested his weight on his walking stick.

"Prince" —Ylva touched Rohan's arm before addressing the whole assembly— "perhaps we can pursue both possibilities. Discover our enemies and dispel rumors at the same time. Have your counsel look inside our borders, to surrounding lands and kings for divisiveness and reports of war. A scout could also investigate the High Mountain."

"No scout, Highness," Ull said. "If the prophecies are true, then you must see them with your own eyes. Go to the East Keep yourself, see if the smoke rises from the ruins on the Mountain— if the priestess' army is gathering. Do it quickly before more men's hearts and wills are turned to the Darkness."

Rohan looked to Tyr, ever a mind of reason.

"It does no harm to go to the Keep, Rohan," Tyr said. "I can begin an investigation into other options in the meantime."

Rohan considered their counsel. His father would not have rushed into action before first evaluating everything and everyone. The king would consider his own beliefs last—but that approach did not feel instinctive to Rohan. A wrong move would forever affect how these men viewed him. Unlike his father, Rohan had yet to know battle—he was not a hero. And what was it about this Wolf Queen that she had already curried the chieftains' respect? When the day came that Rohan must serve as king, he would need their respect and their allegiance. He wanted them to look at him the way they looked at their Wolf Queen. Perhaps she was the key.

"I will go to the East Keep," Rohan said. "I will look with my own eyes for signs of the fulfillment of your prophecy while my counsel looks elsewhere. But" —Rohan paused and looked to Ylva— "I will only go if the Wolf Queen goes with me."

CHAPTER SEVEN

THE GROWLING OF Ylva's wolves was the only sound in the Great Hall as the chieftains awaited her response.

"Well, what say you, Wolf Queen?" Rohan asked. Ylva didn't like the way he addressed her. She could hear the scorn surrounding his words.

Ylva's curiosity and even annoyance could wait. Her suspicions, however, could not. She looked into the prince's eyes. This time, her gaze didn't stop at the blue of his irises. She decided that now would be the time to examine him. It was time to use her Sight. She felt the energy percolate through her being as it always did when she chose to See—not bound by her own power but guided by Lys. She could survey the silent places of his innermost being, a place reserved as home for either Light or Darkness.

She saw memory mixed with joy, desire and pain—all swirling into a color that painted his heart a murky gray.

Ylva was wary of trusting the prince. She also wanted to return home, but she couldn't get Håkon's words out of her mind —that the Darkness would only grow. She needed to see for herself as much as Rohan did.

"I will go with you," Ylva replied to the prince's request.

Vǫrðr whimpered beside her. Her warden did not like the idea any more than Ylva did.

"I will accompany you," Erland spoke from behind her.

Ylva offered him a smile. "You should go back to our village and help Håkon in my absence," Ylva encouraged him.

Rohan stepped closer, inserting himself into the conversation. "No need to worry, I can protect her." The prince's demeanor was cool as he smirked in her direction.

Erland looked less than amused. He crossed his thick arms over his chest and replied, "Ylva does not need protecting, not by me, not by her wolves and not by you." With a turn of his head, Erland dismissed any further comment from the prince. "Ylva, I pledged to always be at your side. I won't dishonor that now."

"All right, brother, join us," Ylva conceded. Erland had been a little older than her when she returned to her village with the wolves. He wasn't born Ibharüng. He had been found wandering the shoreline near the river basin—young, hungry, alone. He barely spoke. One of the older women took him in and cared for him as her own. He grew stronger, taller, but remained silent. Ylva was the first to offer him friendship. She wasn't bothered by the fact he didn't speak. It somehow comforted her. It meant he didn't deluge her with questions as the other children chose to.

At fifteen years old, Ylva heard Erland speak for the first time. The woman, Jorunn, who had become his mother had passed away. On that horrible day, Erland stood over her death bed for the longest time…just staring at her. It seemed like hours had passed in those silent moments that Ylva stayed by his side. Then he leaned down, kissed his mother's cheek and whispered, "Thank you." The sound had startled her. It was more than unexpected—it had felt miraculous. Ylva was never sure why Erland had chosen not to talk for so many years…or if it was even a choice. Had something formerly broken inside of him somehow healed as loss turned to loving gratitude? Ylva never asked because it made no difference in what Erland meant to her.

As they later watched the embers fade on the funeral pyre, Ylva told Erland he would be her brother now. She wanted him to know he wouldn't be alone. Making him her family by all rights was the highest honor a clan leader could bestow. With some reluctance Erland had accepted—then he promised to always fight at her side. His word had never wavered and Ylva could not let it now. She was sure she would be as grateful of his presence as she had always been.

"We would like to accompany you as well," Dagr said. He and the other Fell walked to the front of the hall as he responded. "The Fell are no more, Ylva. We have no home to speak of and choose to pledge ourselves to clan Ibarhüng. If you will have us, we will give you our loyalty in all things."

"Why?" The question just fell out of her mouth. Nevertheless, she decided to continue. "You could assign your allegiance to any clan here. Others are stronger, not to mention wealthier than the Ibharüng."

"True, but none are more blessed by Lys. We have seen the Darkness. It has shown us how much we need the Light. We wish to join you, Ylva." Dagr's voice sounded quiet but certain.

He was also still afraid. Ylva could see it in the quiver of his chin. She could not let Dagr's fear invade her people. It was more dangerous now than ever. Ylva gazed at each of the Fell: Dagr, Solveig, and Bjorn had sadness swirling in their eyes. She pushed further, using her Sight to look deeper. With her Gift she perceived immense anger and fear hovering like immovable shadows over their hearts...hearts wrapped in grief. But she also discerned something beautiful: the Darkness had not claimed these three Fell in spite of the deep trauma done to them. This did not mean, however, that they were free from vulnerability to it. It was then that Ylva realized that her village would be the best place to protect them.

"You may join the Ibharüng, but you may not come with us to the East Keep. Go back to the village. Tell Håkon what has happened here. Help him prepare the others should another attack come to the Northlands. He will need all the warriors he can get."

"Yes, of course," Dagr bowed his head—then he turned to leave with his sister and comrade.

Ylva grabbed his arm and whispered, "Dagr, I know you all remain afraid of what you witnessed, but do not give any more life to those fears. Even if this is the work of Myrkr, we cannot yield to fear. We must instead face it with courage—or the Darkness will grow."

"Aye, my lady," Dagr replied. "We will be mindful of it. May Lys guide you."

"And may the Shadow not overtake you," Ylva responded.

She watched her adopted clansmen exit with the others as the gathering dismissed itself. The prince coughed beside her. He fidgeted in his place. "Apologies, Highness," Ylva said, "we should leave for the East Keep at once."

"It might be better for us to wait until first light," Rohan said. "You have traveled a long way. I am sure you and your horses need rest. There is an inn where we can stay for the night."

Ylva nodded her consent.

"There is also an ale-hall, if you are hungry," Rohan said, leading the way out into the street.

"I would prefer to eat alone," Ylva replied. She had spent enough time in crowded loud rooms for the day and now needed some quiet. She also had no desire to engage with the prince further.

"Tyr will make the arrangements for you then," Rohan replied without a glance in her direction. "We will gather supplies and depart at dawn."

CHAPTER EIGHT

Y<small>LVA'S</small> <small>DINNER</small> consisted of a piece of stale bread and bone broth. She drank the soup from the bowl then used the bread to sop up any last drops. The broth did not taste nearly as good as Håkon's stew but it was satisfying enough after the long day…a day she was glad to be over. Her head hurt behind her drooping eyes. Politics were more exhausting to her than battle. Her mind needed to settle as did her body if she was going to be ready for another long ride in the morning.

As her sore muscles cried out for sleep, Ylva thought twice about removing her armor, wary of allowing detrimental vulnerability in an unfamiliar place. But her wolves lay at her feet while Erland slept outside her door. For once, Ylva opted for comfort. She unclipped her fur shawl and unlaced her leather corset. She ran her fingers over its embossing, a patterned outline of wolves that ran back and forth over the hard leather. She laid the corset next to her axe, which bore the same pattern of wolves etched into its metal. She then removed the bracers from her wrists.

Ylva pushed up the sleeve of her tunic to reveal her birthmark. She traced the dark blotch with her pale finger. Håkon told her it looked just like her father's. She certainly wouldn't know.

Although, she did feel close to him every time she considered the possibility that they both carried the same mark. Stories of Magnus were told with reverence and honor. Håkon spoke of him often—her father the great warrior and a noble clan leader. While the elder had filled the void of Magnus's absence, she still wished to have known him herself. She didn't want to know the chieftain side of him though—no, she wanted to know the man others didn't see. Ylva wanted to know what stories he would have told her each night as he wrapped her in furs and tucked her into bed. She wanted to know what made him laugh with friends and see how he loved her mother.

They were just dreams. Ylva shouldn't hold on to such futility. Wishing for things she could never have served no purpose. Those longings only grew hungrier and more dangerous the more she fed them. She could not change her past. Ivar stole her family away, her childhood and all the love and security it should have held. She told herself that she must accept this reality and consider these unattainable longings no more.

Shura grumbled beside her, nuzzling her cold nose against Ylva's hip then resting it under her palm.

"I am sorry, Shura." Ylva smiled at her wolf. "I know you and Vǫrðr love me." She scratched behind the dog's ears.

Ylva laid down, tossing and turning in search of a comfortable position before pulling the blanket over her. Vǫrðr and Shura each curled up on the floor next to her, ever by her side. Ylva's only childhood memories involved her wolves. The wolves were her gift from Lys, a family when she had none. She missed the parents she never knew but she owed the woman she became to the wolves. For so long they had been everything— hadn't they been enough?

Ylva yawned. Fatigue pushed her wonderings to the back of her mind. Sleep drifted in.

The room felt cool as sunset drew closer, the sun's beams of light sliding down the cavern walls. A dark wolf stepped inside the room to shake the snow off its back. Three pups followed behind. They yawned and wobbled as they made their way to a warm corner to lay down. The she-wolf then situated herself beside them so they could nurse before falling asleep. Another wolf nuzzled a much younger Ylva. She kissed its head and then laid down on a pile of furs. The wolf laid next to her. Ylva yawned and snuggled closer to the canine, her head using the dog as a pillow. She could hear its heartbeat pulsing softly in her ears.

The crackling of a newly lit fire caught her attention. Between the fluttering of her drowsy eye lids, Ylva watched the flames flicker and dance, casting shadows on the walls to replace the now absent sun. Then the humming began. It grew into a lullaby that echoed around her. The voice resounded soft and deep. Ylva felt a serenity that lulled even the wolves.

Ylva tried to keep her eyes open. She could make out the fuzzy edges of a silhouette. It was a man…he sang as he stoked the fire.

He reached out to pet the she-wolf. "Sweet girl," he said, then went back to his singing.

He didn't seem real but Ylva knew he was there. He pulled the furs over her and kissed her forehead before returning to his seat by the fire. She couldn't see his face. He was just a blur at the edge of her memory. She tried to pull him closer, to bring him into focus…but he remained just a haze. Then a light sparked, it grew brighter and brighter until everything else dissolved. His song faded and the wolves howled.

Ylva could feel something wet against her cheek. She blinked until her eyes adjusted to the emerging sunlight as it peeked through the small window and into her eyes. Shura licked her face. "Good morning, sweet girl," she whispered to the wolf.

Ylva sat up and stretched in unison with Vǫrðr. She noticed that her fire still burned. She wondered if Erland had snuck in and kept it stoked for her—although she was sure she would have heard him. It reminded her of her dream. Was it a dream? It felt more like a memory long forgotten. It was all so very familiar. She knew the cavernous room, the wolves. Who was the man? She didn't know *him* but his presence felt known. She couldn't place why, couldn't fit it neatly together, but while she couldn't remember the facts...she did remember the feeling.

She felt safe.

CHAPTER NINE

ROHAN LEANED against the outer wall of the inn with an apple in hand. He was ready to be on his way and losing patience with the Wolf Queen's tardiness. He took one last bite of the fruit, wiped the juice that dripped down his chin with the back of his hand, then tossed the core in the street as he looked up into the window. He yelled into the building, "Are you coming any time this moon cycle? Or perhaps we should reschedule until a time that is more convenient for you?"

"Who are you talking to?" Ylva's voice came from behind him.

Rohan turned to see Ylva, Erland and Tyr leading the horses toward him. "I thought you…it doesn't matter. Are we ready to go?" he asked. Ylva's wolves, beside her as always, curled their lips baring teeth at him.

"Have been for a while but didn't want to rush your breakfast." Ylva smirked and kicked his discarded apple to the side.

"Well, let's get to it then." Rohan mounted his stallion. "It will be a long ride to the East Keep."

The others followed suit. The four rode out of the gates in the direction of the rising sun. If they rode through Grålås they could possibly save a few hours but Rohan didn't want to be interrupted in the city. Really he didn't want to be seen there with Ylva. He wasn't sure why. It's not like anyone would know her. He didn't want them to know either. This woman made him feel inadequate, like she was analyzing his every word and move—constantly weighing him on scales to determine his worth. He didn't need Ylva invading his home and judging him along the way.

One of the wolves yipped. Rohan looked up to see both wolves staring up at the sky.

"They don't like ravens?" he asked Ylva who rode beside him.

"Not as of late. I can't say I disagree with them," she replied.

Rohan didn't understand what she meant. She stared at the small flock of birds that migrated ever closer. He couldn't tell if it was distress or simply distaste that clouded her features. She obviously wasn't going to offer further explanation if there was one. Rohan doubted she would offer any conversation at all. It bothered him, riding in silence. He needed to pass the time, to keep his own mind from twisting in knots.

"Erland called you the Wolf Queen. Why?" Rohan asked, watching Ylva. "Is it because you keep them as pets?"

"Vǫrðr and Shura are not my pets," she replied without even a glance in his direction. For a moment Rohan thought she was going to ignore the rest of his question. Then after a sigh she continued, her words sounding like a practiced recitation. "My uncle Ivar sought to rule our clan. He killed my mother, then left me for dead in the forest. The wolves found me, raised me and then returned me to the Ibharüng. They still watch over me and they obey me. That is why they call me the Wolf Queen."

"So, the stories are true." Rohan's fascination pushed through the surface as he spoke. An amused laugh escaped him. Perhaps too much laughter. When Ylva looked at him now, he thought he caught a glimpse of something like hurt feelings flick across her face. She broke their eye contact and bit her lower lip. Rohan felt like a fool. His curiosity had gotten the better of him. "I'm sorry," he said, "it must not've been easy having such a start in the world. It's nothing to jest over."

"It is fine," Ylva replied, her tone of voice lightening. "You're not the first to find entertainment in it. Besides, while it's not without pain, there is also a touch of the miraculous."

Miraculous? The way she said the word, the slight upward curl of her lip at the thought piqued Rohan's interest even more. There was more to this woman than what anyone could see. He was sure of it and, though he didn't fully understand why, wanted to uncover each and every clue until the mystery of her was fully revealed.

"What about your childhood?" Ylva's question halted Rohan's thoughts.

"There's nothing so interesting as wolves. I am just Rohan, son of King Vakr, Prince of Väljalil. I am part of a grand legacy that preserves freedom for everyone...but myself." In truth Rohan hadn't intended for his last two words to be spoken out loud but he lacked his usual self-control to silence them. He heard the cynicism in his answer and would normally regret it. Now though he was losing the energy for such things.

"Are you not happy for the advantages your life has afforded you?" Ylva asked.

"For every advantage there is a sacrifice," Rohan scoffed. "I'm not sure the former outweighs the latter."

"You will lead the Four Realms. Such a thing is a great honor," Ylva replied. "Yes, there are sacrifices, but are they not worth it for the people you serve?"

Rohan stared at her. Her head was tilted just a bit. He thought he might see condescension. He looked for it, but couldn't find it. She didn't strike him as naive but leading a small clan in the Northlands was a far cry from being next in line to the throne of the Four Realms. She was out of her depth. "Maybe for you, Wolf Queen" he said, "but we can't all be so perfect."

"Perfect?" Ylva laughed. "I am not perfect. I am far from it and don't attempt it. I strive to be good, to be brave."

"Brave? Really?" Rohan responded.

"What?" She raised an eyebrow at his scoffing.

"I thought you'd say humble, noble, wise, selfless…"

"You think I'm those things?" Ylva asked.

"I didn't say that."

"If *anyone* is those things," Ylva said with a smile, "they are mere extensions of courage."

"Do you not think me brave?" Rohan asked her.

"I didn't say that," Ylva said with a wry smile spreading over her face as she returned the prince's wit in-kind.

For the smallest fraction of a second, Rohan saw her blush. It was too fleeting to be sure.

"I don't know you well enough to say if you are any of those things," Ylva continued.

His stomach clenched, starving for validation she didn't offer. He hated that she created doubt in him or that he cared what she thought of him. He cared what everyone thought of him—his father, his friends. He even cared what her wolves thought of him. Wasn't that what a prince, a leader was supposed to do? To care about how others viewed him? Or was it just easy to believe that was the same as caring about them?

Rohan didn't like the direction in which these questions led him. They pointed out his selfishness. They revealed how little he was like his father and how far he had to go to live up to Vakr's image. Rohan may never back down from a fight but if courage was the root of honor, then he was anything but brave.

Rohan glanced at Ylva, then looked away quickly when she turned toward him. How did this woman seem to highlight all of his insecurities and flaws with so little effort?

"Why did you want me to come with you?" the Wolf Queen asked, breaking the thickening silence between them.

Rohan thought of at least three different answers he could give her that would sound charming, indifferent or wise. He inhaled and exhaled slow enough to give himself time to decide on his response. "I find you intriguing," he said. "I wanted to know why the others respect you." His choice for honesty surprised him as much as anyone.

"You think they respect me?" Ylva jibed. "They fear me, the strange girl with the wolves."

"They don't fear you, not like that," Rohan replied. "They revere you. I saw it on their faces last night."

"Fear and reverence can be easily confused," Ylva said. "Why does it matter? You think allying yourself with me will garner some of that supposed respect for yourself?"

He saw Ylva fidget with her reins and adjust her seat. Was she nervous? Had this conversation taken a turn that made her uncomfortable? Was it the notion of how other's perceived her or talk of alliances? She first struck him as arrogant, with a self-righteousness that gave the illusion of noble piety. Now he wasn't so sure. Did she really not see the awe in the assembly when she walked through?

Rohan didn't like thinking he had misjudged her. He discerned a tiny crack crumbling in the wall between them. "I don't need an alliance," he answered her question as he looked away from her. He stared into the horizon.

"Good," Ylva said, "because I don't plan on offering or accepting one." She tapped her heels against her horse's side and trotted ahead of him.

There was the arrogance again. With it came a headache. "Of course not," Rohan muttered to himself. "The Wolf Queen needs no one."

"She doesn't need you," Erland said, riding past Rohan to join Ylva.

Rohan concealed his embarrassment that Erland had over-heard his muttering. Then came the familiar chuckle of his friend coming up behind him. "What?" He asked Tyr.

"Oh, it's nothing." Tyr's mouth curved into a wide grin. "It's been a while since I've seen your charm lost on a woman. It's kind of amusing."

"I was not trying to charm anyone," Rohan said. "Certainly not her."

"Certainly not." Tyr chuckled again.

"I know what you're thinking and you're wrong." Rohan felt heat rise up his neck. "That woman is exhausting, not to mention arrogant."

"Of course, my lord." Tyr sat up straighter and forced the smile off of his face. "I would never suggest otherwise. It would be ridiculous to think you could find such a woman attractive."

"That it would," Rohan agreed. He looked ahead. Ylva's wolves bounced around her in play. She laughed at their antics... it sounded like music to him. Rohan shook the notion from his mind. He glanced to his left hoping his friend hadn't been paying attention to his momentary lapse.

Tyr stifled another laugh.

"Don't," Rohan bid his friend to stop the conversation.

"I wouldn't dream of it," Tyr replied wearing a sly smile.

CHAPTER TEN

THE PRIESTESS WALKED into the village, slinking past the havoc her soldiers caused without a flinch. She relished the scent of destruction, its earthy aroma of smoke and flesh were a fine accompaniment to the screams of the weak. A man fell into her path. She looked down at him, tilting her head in consideration of his wrinkled brow and the tears and blood streaking his face. He raised a hand to her. Some attempt at speech gurgled from his lips. She lifted the skirt of her black dress and stepped over him.

She glided through the chaos like a ghost until coming to a stop at the village's center. She lifted her black-stained fingers and everything fell silent. The violence didn't cease—it merely lost all sound...a noiseless choreography of carnage on all sides. "I am Senka," she spoke, "Daughter of Darkness, Priestess of Myrkr. I have come to offer you glorious power. Yield to me and live."

The scene's volume returned at her proclamation. The adoring roar of her monstrous army reverberated out from the village and shook the branches of nearby trees. It was followed by the quiet cries of the dying. Some villagers fought all the harder upon hearing her words—only to be killed that much quicker. Others fled. A few cowering souls crawled on weak limbs to fall at her feet.

Senka offered her hand to one such man. He used it to pull himself up to stand before her, trembling. She touched his warm wet cheek. "Now, now...the fear will be gone soon," she cooed. "Myrkr will replace it with strength."

The priestess stepped even closer to the man, her body nearly touching his. She placed the tip of her finger to his chest and traced a circle before pressing her entire palm against the spot. She could feel the rise and fall of his heavy breathing along with the rapid beat of his heart. She licked her bottom lip then dug her long nails into his tunic until they ripped into his flesh. Blood trickled down his shirt. Senka inhaled. The Darkness began to race down her arms' veins, through her fingers and into the man's body. She stood back and watched it take hold of him, spreading across his own veins like charcoal snakes that slithered out from his heart and across his face until they covered his body. His bright blue eyes dimmed, then veiled by a cloud of grey. The man growled low. Then he bowed before her.

"Join the others," she commanded to her newest recruit. He obeyed, entering the violent attacks against his own people as though he had never known them. Senka continued her work amongst those giving themselves over to the Darkness she served. When she finished, she turned to address her general before a pair of ravens interrupted them. They circled above for a moment. Then one came to land on her hand and the other on her shoulder.

Senka petted the bird. "Speak," she said. The raven answered her with a series of babbling croaks and caws. "She is alive," Senka seethed.

She thought she had done away with the girl years ago. In the early days of her rising, Senka plotted and planned every move to ensure victory for Myrkr. She should have known better than to trust a mortal man with such an important task. She should have killed the infant herself. It was no matter now. Her plans would succeed. She stood too close to victory to be stopped. She would not be stopped.

"The prince and the shield maiden are at the East Keep," Senka told her general. "Go dispose of them and anyone with them."

The general brought a fist to his chest and nodded his head.

"Do not disappoint me," she added. "Burn it all."

CHAPTER ELEVEN

IT WAS WELL past dark when Ylva and the others arrived at the East Keep. She wasn't sure whether entering these fortresses in the dark was a blessing or a curse. On the outside, it was the same stone and mud as the North. Ylva wrinkled her nose. The same awful smell surrounded the grounds, too. She would be happy to finish this mission and return home. There the subtle scents of the forest accented the air. It was not tainted by filth and refuse. She sighed.

"I take it the *queen* is not impressed," Rohan said almost with an eyeroll, riding up beside her.

Ylva's shoulders tensed. She was becoming more and more annoyed with his snide behavior. For a moment on their journey she thought there was more to the prince— something beyond his defensive facade. But now her doubt returned.

"The scale of this place, of man's ability to build such a fortress, that is quite impressive," she said. "It also makes me miss the simplicity of home."

"I guess not all of us are cut out for more than hovels in the woods," Rohan taunted.

She watched a smirk curve his lips. "No, I guess not," she

replied. "But some of us also prefer not to smell like manure and rotted food."

The prince's wry smile quickly fell. Ylva giggled, echoed by Erland and Tyr, who were trying ever so hard to stifle it. Even the wolves, tails wagging, seemed to smile at her jibe. While she awaited the prince's rebuttal, the Keep gates parted with a loud creak. A heaviness pressed on them as they rode across the threshold. Vǫrðr and Shura stiffened. Their tails straightened and ears twitched. Ylva felt her own chest tighten. While by appearances this place resembled the North Keep, the mood was completely opposite. No music or laughter filled her ears. No pedestrians casually strolled about. There were only the quiet whimpers of those huddled in darkened alleys. A fear lay over the air. It didn't take Ylva's Gift to see it written on the faces of the assaulted villagers, their eyes glassy and cheeks sullen.

The group dismounted their horses and passed them off to a stable hand as the Keep's military commander came to greet them.

"Your Highness," he said to the prince, "we did not expect a visit. Though I am glad for the surprise. We were about to send a falcon to Grålås."

"What happened here?" The prince asked. Ylva noted the concern that etched the edges of his eyes. The constant trace of mirth she had come to recognize and dislike, had disappeared.

"Follow me." The commander led them up a set of stairs to the top of the Keep wall. "It started about a week ago. People from outlying villages have arrived seeking refuge."

"From what?" Tyr asked.

"That," the commander replied, pointing into the distance toward Skämd, the High Mountain. "Whatever is out there… those traveling to the Keep are afraid of it. Very afraid."

Ylva looked out into the night. A nearly full moon hung amid bright stars in a black sky. On the ground below them, almost like a mirror reflection shaded red, blazing fires speckled the landscape. They littered Askadalen. They shouldn't be there. The Valley of Ash had been desolate for generations. It was nothing but ruins. Who would encamp there now? Ylva could swear she heard a screech echo in the distance. Could Håkon have been right?

"The dragon is rising," Ylva muttered the words. She hadn't meant for them to be spoken aloud; still, they broke out of her mouth and into the night air with a puff of visible breath.

"Something is there…but that doesn't mean it's sorcery," Rohan responded to her accidental utterance.

"You're right, it doesn't—but then what does it mean?" Ylva replied. "You doubt the old prophecy as did I, but everything seems to be pointing to its truth."

"Those fires could just as easily indicate a very ordinary, human enemy hiding in the valley." The prince placed his hands on the stone of the wall's edge. It seemed liked he was looking for something—something concrete, something certain. Ylva was beginning to understand that Rohan lived as a man of sight rather than faith. She tried not to fault him for this. Faith came easier for some than it did for others.

"Those fires could also represent the beginning of something far more sinister," Ylva said.

"I'll not entertain talk of monsters and witches without proof." Rohan turned to the commander. "Send a scout to the valley, someone with enough good sense not to fall victim to wild imagination." His eyes met Ylva's. "You can believe in magic all you want, but I won't let fairytales cloud *my* judgment."

Ylva's spine straightened. She bit the inside of her cheek in an attempt to silence her indignant rebuttal. She wasn't sure if she felt more insulted by Rohan's dismissal of a magic she knew firsthand was very real, and very much a part of her, or at his insinuation that she wasn't thinking clearly. Both felt like an attack on her character. She wanted to slap him. She wouldn't. Wisdom dictated that was not the right response, though it might feel good for a moment. Instead she chose to return her focus to the distant view. She inhaled a deep breath of the cool air, allowed it to freeze inside her lungs where she held it for a count of three.

"I hope you're right, Prince Rohan," she said. "I pray it's a mortal enemy in that valley. But what will you do if it is not? I suggest you find at least a little faith just in case."

"Faith is for the weak," the prince replied.

Ylva turned back to Rohan. He clenched his jaw while keeping a rigid posture. He seemed on guard, as if expecting a sharp response. But she was too tired for an argument, especially a futile one. Faith cannot be argued into someone. Was there even soft enough soil beneath the surface of his uncompromising attitude for faith to be planted? Ylva gazed beyond the reflection of torch light in Rohan's eyes, using her Gift to peer into the hidden places of his soul once more. What was she searching for? Darkness twisting him? A glimmer of light breaking through? She still saw only a mix of gray.

Rohan squirmed and averted his eyes from her.

Ylva sighed. "Erland." She spun round to address her clansman. "I'm tired."

"We will find lodging for the night," Erland responded.

"Goodnight Prince, Tyr. We will retire and await word from the scout before returning to the Northlands," Ylva said before descending the stairs with her brother in front of her and the wolves at her heels.

They found a guest house. Erland refused his own room as always. He instead unrolled his fur mat to make camp outside her door. Ylva sat inside, stoking the small fire, trying to quiet her mind. She missed her own bed...her "hovel" as the prince had called it. "Rohan, Son of Vakr, Prince of Väljalil...impertinent man," Ylva grumbled under her breath.

Vǫrðr and Shura lifted their heads, staring at her.

"Don't give me that look," she said to her guardians. "He is exasperating to say the least. I will be glad to return home, away from him."

Shura tilted her head in response. Vǫrðr exhaled a gruff breath and laid his head back down.

"There is nothing else to it." Ylva wasn't sure if she was trying to convince the wolves or herself. Why was she even giving this man more of her mental energy?

Rohan had gotten under her skin. She couldn't read him and she hated that. Seeing the truth of people's souls was a comfort to her. She couldn't read their minds but she could know the foundation of their motives—not the prince. But one day this ambiguous and perplexing man would be king and Ylva wanted to trust his rule. That was the sum of her ruminations about Rohan. Wasn't it?

Ylva suddenly heard the wail of a signal horn blowing outside. Her wolves jumped up with ears perked. The horn signaled again—then she heard a scream.

"Ylva!" Erland threw her door open in alarm. "The Keep is under attack."

Ylva grabbed her axe and shield then followed Erland outside. They made their way up onto the wall where Rohan and Tyr spoke with the commander.

"What's going on?" she heard Tyr ask.

"Someone is trying to breach the gate," the commander replied.

"Who?" Rohan asked.

"We don't know," he answered. Then he barked orders at the scurrying soldiers before joining them at the entry. "Archers!" he yelled. Within seconds they lined the wall with arrows ready. "Fire!"

Ylva joined Rohan at the edge of the tower wall. They peered over the side to see at least fifty men with a battering ram charging the heavy wooden gate. They did not relent, each crash against the door caused the ground to shake and echoed through the walls. Ylva felt it quake in the stone under her feet.

Arrows whizzed through the air, finding their mark in the flesh of the Realm's enemy. Ylva watched their points sink into backs and shoulders—yet their aggressors continued as though they were but bee stings.

"How is that possible?" the prince wondered aloud.

The wood of the gate began to crack under the siege. Their enemy roared. Those inside the Keep—including Ylva and Rohan—stood waiting, silent and still. Vǫrðr and Shura remained on either side of Ylva, the hair on their backs raised with their ears flat.

Wood continued to crash into wood—again the gate splintered. Soldiers worked to create a brace with no success. Finally, the ram brought the gate down into a shuddering heap of debris. Keep soldiers were thrown backwards as the opposition began to rush through the break.

A melee followed. Warriors of Väljalil rushed toward their attackers only to be flung off with the ease of a cat swatting a gnat. No sword or axe seemed capable of thwarting this enemy who's blood would run black down their arms and chests and seemed to feed their strength.

"We must do something," Ylva told him.

"Aye," Rohan replied with a nod. He drew his sword and rushed down the steps to join the fray. Before reaching the bottom, the prince leapt forward, landing in front of a young soldier in the way of a savage blow.

Ylva followed. She held her round shield in one hand with her axe raised in the other. She came round the prince to slice her axe through the air, making contact with an enemy's back. Her opponent let out a sound—more of a visceral growl than a human utterance—then turned to face her. Ylva could hardly believe what she saw. His eyes seemed like the sky before a storm; milky, murky and foreboding. His skin looked the same stormy gray with black veins running like streams over his entire body. The appearance was so close to one of the visions her Sight would allow her of men who leaned toward the Darkness, but this was no vision and this was no man, not any longer. Dagr had been right. Mortals had become monsters.

"Ylva!" Erland's shout snapped her to attention.

Ylva raised her shield to block the monster's heavy fist. She spun, her axe cutting him again, followed by a blow from her shield against his head. Dark blood oozed down the creature's forehead, over its eyes and gnashing teeth until it dripped from his chin. Ylva backed up slowly. Had this been any normal sort of warrior, these wounds would be more than enough to have him dying on the ground. How could they defeat something that couldn't be killed?

Ylva retreated further back. She needed to think, needed a clearer perspective. Around her, children cried in the arms of their mothers. The soldiers fought valiantly—but the monsters continued to attack without a hint of fatigue or weakness. Vǫrðr and Shura had charged one of the inhuman creatures. They growled and snapped while circling the unholy thing. Then it reached to grab the grey wolf, but she bit into its arm, pulling it downward. The black wolf leapt up onto its hunched back and sunk his teeth into its neck. The monster shook Shura loose. It then reached back, pulling Vǫrðr off of him and slinging him to the ground. The wolf yelped.

"No!" Ylva screamed. Without thinking, she dropped her shield and ran toward the creature, pulling her knife from her belt. Ylva slid in front of Vǫrðr as the savage man charged at her guardian. She lifted the dagger and drove it into the monster's chest, piercing its heart.

The monster roared in pain as it stumbled backward. Ylva stood to her feet with her axe ready...but there was no need. The monster fell to the ground, twitching and writhing. Black liquid flowed from its chest, staining the ground. The creature stopped groaning. Then it stopped moving altogether. Ylva retrieved her blade from its body. The fire in its eyes flickered one last time as the Darkness drained from its veins. The skin returned to a warm flesh tone before cooling back to the paleness of death.

The heart. "You must pierce their heart!" Ylva called to the others. Her eyes met Rohan's. He nodded firmly after glancing toward the corpse at her feet.

"Aim for their hearts!" The prince ordered, plunging his sword into the chest of the monster before him.

As the word spread through the chaos, the tide of the battle turned. Then Ylva saw another of the creatures stalking through the crowd like it was looking for something or someone specific. It made to lunge at Rohan, but she sprinted toward it. Her axe severed its hand. The monster roared then fiercely kicked her forward. She felt the impact, heard the crack of her ribs. She couldn't breathe for a moment. When air finally sucked back into her lungs, a sharp pain filled her chest. She gasped. Everything began to spin. She clutched one arm against her side and gritted through the discomfort so she could lift her axe with her other arm. She thrust the axe into its chest with shocking force. The monster fell, as did Ylva; she dropped to her knees. Everything started to go black.

"Ylva." She heard Erland's voice mingled with the whimpering of her wolves.

Then nothing…just silence and darkness.

CHAPTER TWELVE

THE TREES BUDDED with the bright blooms of springtime. Most of the snow had melted but the air remained crisp. Ylva stepped through the wooden doorway that led out of the cave and into the warmth of the sun. The pack of young wolves bounced and bounded beside her, licking her feet like it was a game. It tickled and she giggled at their antics. The familiar setting became suddenly strange, surreal from questions she never thought to ask before. How did a cave in the mountainside have a man-made door? Had it always been there? Had she just never noticed or was this the fiction of dreams interspersed with the reality of childhood memories? Ylva ran her hands over the carvings in the wood which told the story of Lys. They were the same drawings as on Håkon's scrolls. Her brain must be playing tricks on her.

The wolf pups barked in front of her. Ylva giggled as they nipped at each other's tails and her ankles. The pups were ready to play and explore. Ylva was ready for the same. The winter kept her cooped indoors. She needed to stretch and run and breathe again.

"Let's go," she said to the pups before taking off into the forest.

The little wolves followed her. They played "chase" amongst the trees. Ylva laughed as she jumped with them over fallen trunks and ducked under low branches. The pups trotted through the cool water of the babbling stream. Ylva came behind without enough care. Her tiny foot skidded off of a slippery rock. She fell backwards, trying to catch herself with her hands, but the hard ground and her tiny wrist did not make a good pairing. Pain shot through her arm. She cried out. Sitting up, Ylva examined her arm. This made her cry harder. The bone was crooked and looked like it would pop right out of her skin.

The wolf pups gathered around her. They licked her teary cheeks and nuzzled against her side. Ylva knew she couldn't just sit there and wait. She stood up on her shaky feet and tread carefully back through the forest, watching each and every step. She gingerly held her wounded arm against her. "Help!" she called through her pain-filled whimpers as her cave home came into view.

Who was she calling for? Reality again mixed with fantasy and blurred the lines of truth in her dream-state.

"Sweet girl." The same voice from her previous dream bounced around the insides of her mind with its familiar warmth. "What has happened?" A figure stood in front of her...a man. Her eyes couldn't bring him into focus. He was shadowed by the sun shining down from behind him. His hands reached out and took her arm. He held it softly with gentle fingers. "I am afraid it is broken," he said.

Ylva felt fresh tears roll down the sides of her face. "Will it always be broken now?" she asked.

"Oh no, my dear child," the man replied. "It will mend, and if mended properly, will be stronger than ever."

"How long will it take?" Ylva asked.

"It depends on the break," he said while placing his palms around the broken place. "Perhaps I can help speed this one along."

Ylva watched his hands. A light glowed between them, causing her skin to tingle. When he pulled away, her bone was straight once again. The pain disappeared. She moved her wrist, bending it and twisting it. She could move it as though the injury never happened. "Can you do this with all broken things?" she asked.

"Sometimes. But most things must go through the slow process of healing in order for Lys to complete all the work He wishes to be done. The key then is trusting through the pain." Then he leaned forward and kissed the top of her head. She looked up, straining to see his face...but it was like he was being masked by the light.

Ylva woke expecting for the room to be bright but it was dim, lit only by the flicker of the small fire. Vǫrðr and Shura's yellow eyes watched her. She tried to sit up but pain burned in her ribcage. An unwanted whimper escaped her lips. Vǫrðr stood.

"My lady," Erland said, stepping quickly to her side. "You must be careful." He reached out to her.

"I know," she whispered as she took his hand so that he could help her sit. Only then did she realize her armor had all been removed. Her torso was now wrapped tight under her linen shirt. While she knew this was meant to hold her aching bones in place, it didn't do much for helping her breathe. "How long have I been asleep?"

"Several hours," Erland replied. "The sun has long been up, but clouds from a storm have kept the day dark."

"Has the scout returned from the valley?" Ylva asked.

"Yes," Rohan answered her question. He was leaning against the far wall of the small room. He pushed himself off it and walked toward her bedside. Dark circles were forming under the prince's eyes. His face was still covered in the dirt and blood of the previous night's battle. He looked down at her, his brow furrowed. He rubbed a hand over his jaw and around the back of his neck.

"And?" she asked, pushing for more information.

"Askadalen is filled with more of the Bardung, the same monstrous warriors who attacked the Keep," he replied.

"Bardung? That's what we're calling them?" Ylva asked. The name was reserved for the deranged who battle against themselves, against peace. It was fitting. This inhuman army bore no desire for any kind of order...only destruction. "How many?"

"Hundreds, maybe more." Rohan's voice sounded weak, tired...even a little shaky.

"At least we know how to kill them now," Ylva offered in an attempt to bring a bit of solace to the prince's troubled demeanor.

"True, but consider their strength," Rohan said. "Even with the most skilled warriors and most adept archers, they will still take many lives. Last night there were fifty Bardung against a hundred warriors of the Realm; even after your discovery, they slaughtered many of our soldiers."

Ylva pushed her feet over the side of the bed and rubbed her head. This enemy was indeed formidable, for many reasons. "Strength isn't their only asset. These things—the Bardung—are smart...strategic."

"What makes you say that? I thought they rampaged like animals," Rohan replied, no indignation or haughtiness in his question, only curiosity.

"They may have behaved like ferocious beasts, but they weren't just pillaging at random. They were hunting...hunting you." Ylva watched the prince's eyebrows raise at her insinuation. "I watched one come for you like a predator stalking its prey. It looked to no one else and stopped for nothing else. It meant to kill you, Rohan. I think that is why they came to the Keep."

Rohan turned away from her and paced the room. Ylva watched him and waited. She imagined this was much to process at once. She knew what it felt like…someone wanting you dead.

The prince broke the tense silence. "Something is orchestrating their movements and we need to find out what. I doubt those monsters came up with an assassination plot on their own."

"The priestess," Erland said, though it wasn't clear to whom he was speaking or if he even meant to answer the prince's question. But Ylva had been thinking the same thing.

"More legend." Rohan rolled his eyes.

"Come now," Ylva said, "I think we are beyond doubt, prince."

"Perhaps we are, Wolf Queen," Rohan replied with a deep sigh. "Tyr and I will return to Grålås and inform King Vakr. You and Erland should go back to the Northlands, as you need to heal and ready the clans."

"Send a falcon to the clans," Ylva said, standing to her feet. She held a hand to her aching side. "I have wanted nothing but to return home since the moment I left. But I believe Lys called me to this—I will not retreat to the Northlands now. If I go home, the Darkness will still come… in time it will even reach the Ibharüng. I won't wait for it. Instead, I will go to the Darkness and make it regret its plans."

"Ahhh!" Senka seethed. She threw her chalice across the room. It crashed into the stone wall with a loud clank. Her wine splattered and dripped to the floor. Her ravens fluttered and squawked. She looked over her shoulder to the Bardung soldier cowering behind her. "You have failed."

He uttered no sound but bowed his head.

Senka approached him with slow footsteps. "I am so tired of abiding failure," she said as she reached the soldier. She caressed his cheek with her slender fingers then clutched his chin, digging her black nails into his grey skin. "I will abide it no longer." She abruptly released him then crossed the room to the fire.

"It is time to wake, my pet," she cooed over the flames. "We cannot let her discover who she truly is. We must rid the world of her ourselves."

Senka smiled as a soft screech echoed around the ruins.

CHAPTER THIRTEEN

No MATTER how many times Rohan rode through the gates of Grålås, he felt both a sense of peace in being home, and suffocated by reminders of his royal duty. This duality only made him more ashamed. This city was safe while others in Väljalil were not. His future was secure while others had had theirs stripped away. It was time he grew beyond the angst of youth and accepted his place in this world.

"Your father will be glad to have you home," Tyr said.

"I will be glad to see him as well," Rohan responded, "to see how his health fairs."

"Has the king... your father, been unwell?" Ylva asked the prince. He flinched at her words. He always jumped to assumptions—his insecurities on the lookout for slights against his abilities when there were none. Rohan could see that Ylva's now furrowed brow and soft eyes attested to her genuine concern.

"He has been ill recently," Rohan replied.

Ylva nodded. Her horse's footing faltered a bit in a patch of deep mud. She winced at the motion and grabbed her side.

"We should have someone take a look at your injury when we settle at the castle," Rohan said to her.

"Please don't go to any trouble on my account," Ylva said. "I can manage."

"It's no trouble." Rohan halted his horse in front of the castle entry and dismounted before offering Ylva his hand. "Besides, if you insist on being a part of this, you need to be well."

Ylva stared at him for a moment, her lips pursed. Then she nodded and accepted his help down from her mare.

The wall's torches offered just enough light to push the shadows into the corners of the room. Rohan sat at one end of a large wooden table. A feast lay before him; roast pheasant, braised deer with stewed vegetables and bread that was still steaming. The spiced aroma of the seasoned meat made his mouth water. Rohan's stomach growled as a reminder that he had not eaten all day.

He poured wine into his cup. It sloshed a bit over the lip. He ignored the dribble and passed the pitcher to Tyr, who sat at his side. Erland had already taken a spot across from Tyr when steps were heard coming down the hall.

Rohan stood. He thought it would be Ylva but was surprised to see his father hobbling toward them with the help of his attendant.

"Father, I didn't expect you to join us," the prince said.

"We have guests," Vakr replied. "It's not every day we entertain members of the Ibharüng." The king looked at Erland and tipped his head. Erland stood hastily and reciprocated the gesture.

"Are you sure you are well enough to be out of bed?" Rohan whispered, helping his father sit at the opposite end of the table.

"I am well enough to sit in this chair and eat a meal," Vakr answered him.

Rohan returned to his own seat when Ylva's voice caught his attention.

"I'm sorry if I'm late," she said, walking through the doorway with her dogs at her side. Her pants and armor had been replaced with a light green shift under a dark green apron dress. Ylva fidgeted with the metal broaches and beads that fastened it all together.

Rohan cleared his throat and tugged at his own tunic before sitting. "You are not late," he said.

Her lips curved into a slight smile as she took the seat next to Erland who smirked at her. "What?" she muttered to her companion, adjusting the straps of her dress.

"Nothing, my lady," Erland replied with a chuckle.

"They gave me these while they washed blood from my armor." Ylva elbowed Erland in his side. Rohan laughed to himself.

"Ylva, this is my father, King Vakr," Rohan said. "Father, this is Ylva, Leader of clan Ibharüng. She is the Wolf Queen."

Vǫrðr and Shura grunted at the prince.

"It is an honor, Your Highness," Ylva said, bowing her head in respect to the king.

"The honor is all mine, Ylva," Vakr replied. "I have heard much about you."

Rohan watched Ylva's eyes widen but he couldn't be sure if it was shock or anxiety at the king's admission. He was a bit shocked himself. He had never heard his father, who now watched Ylva with a warm smile, mention her before tonight.

Conversation circled the table between bites of the bountiful meal. King Vakr regaled the table with tales from his younger years. For the first time in weeks, life brightened his eyes and colored his cheeks. Rohan didn't think he would ever see it again and it made him happy. He almost hated to dim the mood with talk of the Bardung, but it had to be discussed.

"Father, what say you about this army building in Askadalen?" Rohan asked.

Vakr took a careful sip from his cup before leaning back in

his chair. "There were stories of the war with the Darkness—of those, generations ago, who imprisoned the priestess and her dragon."

"And you believe those? Do you believe the prophecy as well?" Tyr leaned forward, resting his chin in his hands. His curiosity appeared genuine, though Rohan knew his friend did not believe the prophecies—or at least he hadn't. But they couldn't deny what their own eyes had beheld at the East Keep.

"What I believe is not as important as what is or what truly could be coming. You should go to Kunnigstad," Vakr replied. "Speak to the Keepers."

"The Keepers?" Ylva asked.

"The Keepers of Knowledge," Rohan answered. "They reside in the library in the southern city. If there is any truth to this prophecy, or any information about Myrkr's priestess and her dragon, it will be found there." The prince turned toward his father, "but is it wise for me to go when you are—"

"I am fine," Vakr interrupted. "You will be king one day, and a king must know what to delegate and what he must do himself. This is something you must do, my son."

His father was right, though Rohan was uncertain whether or not the king's increased strength would be enough to keep illness from gripping him further. He hoped it was a good sign.

"Tyr, make the necessary arrangements for us to go to Kunnigstad," Rohan said.

"Of course," Tyr replied.

"Well," King Vakr said as he pushed his chair back, "this has been the best evening I've had in quite some time. I hate to see it come to an end, but I'm afraid I must retire for the night."

Rohan stood to help his father.

"Before I go, I do have a question for you, Ylva," the king said. His smile faded just a bit and anxious lines now wrinkled around his eyes.

"Ask anything, Highness," Ylva said.

The king leaned in and whispered to her. Rohan could barely make out his words, something about a gift.

"It is true. And you need not fear death, my king—the Light has won your heart. I have seen it." Ylva reached out and squeezed the king's hand.

Vakr's wide smile returned and his eyes glistened. He patted Ylva's fingers lightly, then proceeded to stand. His attendant was already waiting to lead him to his room. Rohan helped him fully to his feet. "I like her," Vakr whispered in his son's ear.

"She's growing on me," Rohan replied. "Goodnight, father." He handed the king to his attendant.

"I will see to the arrangements for Kunnigstad," Tyr told the prince. He also stood to leave.

"Thank you. Be sure Erland has a room for the night," Rohan responded.

"I prefer sleeping outside Ylva's door," Erland asserted.

"I will be fine, brother," Ylva said to him. "It has been days since you have had a comfortable bed and a warm fire. Let them find you a room. Nothing will happen to me here."

Erland nodded and followed Tyr out of the hall.

"I should probably get some rest myself," Ylva said, about to stand.

"Wait—would you stay for a few moments longer?" Rohan asked. He had questions he could no longer contain. "My father asked you about a gift. I heard what you told him, that you saw his heart…what did you mean?"

Ylva sighed. She looked to her wolves who sat dutifully at her feet. When they didn't rescue her from having to answer Rohan's question, she bit her bottom lip. Vǫrðr nuzzled his nose against the palm of her hand. She nodded to the dog like she was accepting his silent advice. Then she turned to Rohan's waiting gaze.

"There is a legend among my people. They have long believed that a wolf's eyes are like lamps that can see into a man's soul and determine his character. It is their gift from Lys, their creator." Ylva paused, giving her wolves another glance. "Some say they can share that gift with someone they deem worthy, or perhaps I am merely more wolf than woman." She laughed to herself then continued, "But Lys saw fit to bestow that same gift upon me. Like the wolves, I can see into the hearts of men. I can watch how the Light and Darkness have taken hold of them."

Ylva straightened her shoulders like she was bracing for Rohan's reaction. The prince couldn't blame her. A few days ago he would have thought her insane. He would have laughed at her claim. But now...it occurred to him that perhaps his mind was changing about the prophecy—and maybe even the Wolf Queen. She still irritated him with her seeming self-righteousness, and he still found her stubborn. But Ylva was no liar and was careful with her words. She didn't spin stories or embellish the truth. Rohan couldn't pretend to understand these otherworldly gifts any more than he could fathom a dragon being real—but he decided that if Ylva believed it...well, then he believed her. At least he very much wanted to.

"What is it like...the things you see?" Rohan asked her.

Ylva's brow wrinkled and her eyes squinted. She inhaled and exhaled like the action would give her the right words.

"It's like memories and thoughts and desires all come to life and create a mask which covers their faces," she said finally, the words bursting out of her. "Sometimes the mask is bright and full of joy and peace. Sometimes it is dark and looks only like death."

"Is it frightening...the Darkness?" Rohan inquired.

"It's more sad than anything else," she answered. "Mostly because it's too common. Even in good people, there is more

Darkness than they would wager. Except children—they tend to be good through and through, all light on the inside. Any darkness attached to them they wear on the outside. It hasn't had time to sink in yet."

"Have you looked into my heart?" the prince boldly asked.

Ylva nodded her affirmation.

"And what did you see?" As soon as he asked the question, he wanted to take it back.

"You were this beautiful, tragic mix of grey. Not enough to look dead, but too much to look fully alive. It was like you were caught exactly in the middle."

Rohan hadn't expected that. Not that he knew what to expect really. What could he do with that? Was he supposed to do anything at all? He thought about asking her these questions as well but stopped himself. It would be too vulnerable, it felt weak. He already felt so exposed to her. He didn't want to look weak.

"I should let you get rest now," he simply said.

"Of course," Ylva replied. Then she and her wolves left.

Rohan sat at the table alone until the candles burned out. Then he headed to bed, hoping his mind would quiet enough for him to sleep.

He didn't sleep a wink. He tossed, turned and paced his room and thought too much about things he couldn't sort out in one night. Things he hadn't even thought about in a long time, things he didn't want to think about. Things like losing his mother and whether having her around longer would have made a difference in him, in his soul, in what Ylva had seen. It was strange—he never realized how much he missed his mother, but suddenly everything hidden was confronting him. Talk of his gray heart opened locked doors in his mind. It revealed secret worries like trying to fill his father's shoes and wondering if that was possible, or even right, or just an expectation he put on himself. It exposed his doubts and fears about the Darkness and the Light, and if he could lead his people to victory in this coming war. Could he even win the war for his own soul or would it always be the murky mix it is now?

In the middle of his pacing, the fire in his room died but he barely noticed the chill in the air. Sunlight peeked in through his window and returned a bit of warmth. Rohan sighed. He flopped onto his bed hoping he could steal an hour of sleep before the day fully began. His eyes closed...he felt his mind release, giving way to his fatigue.

"Rohan," Tyr said, knocking on his door.

The prince grumbled into his blanket and sat up. "Come in."

"You look horrible," Tyr said.

"I can always count on you to make me feel better after a sleepless night," the prince replied with a roll of his eyes. "Why are you here so early?"

"Sorry, it couldn't be helped." Tyr looked down at the floor for a moment. When he looked back at Rohan tears hung in his eyes. "It seems your father took a turn for the worse during the night. He may only have days remaining."

Rohan stood. He focused on his own breathing long enough to gather his thoughts and calm his emotions. "Then I should make haste to Kunnigstad and back. Stay here and take care of things in my absence," he said.

"I think you should be the one to stay, Rohan. I can go..."

"I will go. It is what father wanted—it is my place." Rohan grabbed his boots and slid one on.

Tyr conceded with a quick nod. "Ylva and Erland are already awake. They will be ready to leave with you shortly."

"The Wolf Queen is injured; it would probably be best if she stayed here as well," Rohan said.

Tyr chuckled. "I certainly won't be the one to tell her so."

"Even if your future king demands it?" Rohan taunted with a raised eyebrow at his friend.

"Apologies, my lord," Tyr's words dripped with sarcasm, "but I think I am more afraid of her wrath than yours." He snickered and exited the room just as Rohan threw his other boot, hitting the closing door instead of Tyr.

CHAPTER FOURTEEN

YLVA, Rohan and Erland left Grålås while most of the city still slept. The prince had requested once again that she go home. Ylva wouldn't give up this quest, fractured rib or not. She had already told the prince once that she would continue on—one night in a dress wasn't going to soften her or her resolve. She had sustained far worse injuries throughout the multitude of battles she had fought in her lifetime. Would Rohan fret so much about this if she were a man?

Ylva shouldn't let her mind go to that place but in her weaker moments she did. As much as she proved her strength and valor, she still felt as though most men saw her as more fragile. In the beginning, even her own clan gave voice to their perceptions, wanting her to keep her distance from the front lines of battle. Ylva did not fault her clansmen. She knew they respected her leadership and gifted her their loyalty. But she was the first shield maiden to lead them and she was petite, even as maidens went. It was easy for them and others to underestimate her. She was careful not to underestimate herself.

She didn't want the prince to underestimate her now. Perhaps he wasn't. Perhaps he was being thoughtful and concerned.

Perhaps it was just her insecurities fighting inside her. Ylva learned long ago to catch those thoughts the moment they took up space in her mind. She learned to drive them out—to fight them—especially with the Darkness gaining strength and preying on weakness. She lifted a silent prayer. *Lys help me.*

"We should find water soon," Erland called back to her.

"I think there is a stream just near those woods." Rohan pointed toward a small cluster of trees in the distance.

"You think?" Ylva questioned.

"I have only been to Kunnigstad once, as a boy, so it's all only vaguely familiar," Rohan responded.

"Are you sure you even know then if we are headed the right direction?" Ylva half teased.

"It is directly south of Grålås. I think I know which way is south," Rohan scoffed. "Besides, your clansman is the one leading—are we sure he is going the right way and not off into vast wilderness?"

"Vast wilderness?" Ylva laughed. "Don't you think that's a wee bit dramatic? Even so, Erland is a human compass. If we were indeed headed into vast wilderness it would most definitely be on purpose."

"And t'would only be to abandon the prince," Erland called over his shoulder with a chuckle.

"I could consider that talk treasonous," Rohan said, though his smirk made it clear he was continuing the jest.

"Do not worry, Highness, I'm sure you'd find your way home...eventually." Erland laughed again—a robust, deep, belly laugh.

Vǫrðr and Shura howled in response to Erland. Both were bouncing alongside the horses, enjoying the jovial mood as much as Ylva. It was nice—the laughter...it kept away the tension of larger matters for the time being. It afforded her a few moments to enjoy her surroundings. The aesthetics inside the stone walls of the Keeps and city didn't impress her...but these wide open spaces were full of vibrant color and sweet aromas. It wasn't the forest smells of home but rather of wildflowers and tall grass. Ylva breathed in deep. She leaned her head back and let the sunlight warm her skin. This was a different beauty than her home in the Northlands but it held a majesty all its own.

They closed in on the grove of trees. Ylva could hear the babbling of water flowing over rocks. The wolves barked and trotted ahead of them to get a drink. At the stream, Ylva dismounted and her mare immediately dipped its nose into the cool water. She squatted down to refill her waterskin. Rohan and Erland did the same.

Ylva took a long drink of the fresh water. She wiped a few drips from her chin as she looked at the scenery. What had first seemed to be just a small grove of trees was really a larger wood. It stretched south, inclining with the buckling of the earth into hills and ridges that seemed to go as far as she could see. The changing terrain meant the rest of their ride would not be as smooth. Ylva rubbed a hand along her stomach. Her leather corset and linen bandages kept a sturdy grip on her ribs, keeping them from shifting. Sudden movement still brought pain but it's intensity was lessening. The healer in Grålås had given her some feverfew to take. She didn't like the bitter taste but it did help ease her aching.

"We have a few more hours of daylight before we should find a safe place to make camp for the night," Rohan said. He splashed water on his face and the back of his neck.

Ylva was about to respond when a bird cawed overhead. She looked up to see three ravens perched on tree branches, watching them. A shiver went down her spine and tingled outward to her fingertips. "I hate those birds," she muttered to herself.

"What?" Erland asked her.

She made eye contact with him, then the prince, before looking back toward the ravens gesturing for them to follow her gaze. One of the black birds squawked at her again—then all three took flight. Their departure would have made her feel better but for the haunting sound that echoed through the trees. It was like nothing Ylva had ever heard before, a screech tangled with a roar. Vǫrðr and Shura growled in reply.

"What was that?" Rohan asked.

The light of the sun dimmed as a large shadow passed over them—the silhouette of an enormous winged creature. The wolves barked.

"I think we are about to find out," Erland said and drew his axe.

Ylva did the same and Rohan drew his sword. The three of them and the wolves gathered close together, facing outward in a small circle. The creature circled back. They watched its shadow block the light once more as it came closer. It screeched again—this time the trees shook. It's flapping wings made the air swirl and bluster around them like a hurricane. The sweet smell of nature that had filled Ylva's senses moments before was now tainted by the stench of brimstone.

The horses whinnied and fidgeted in their places.

"We can't fight that, not with the weapons we have," Rohan said.

"What do you suggest we do then?" Ylva asked. "Try to outrun it?"

The beast flew back around, lower this time, breaking through the trees causing branches to crash down.

"Or hide from it?" Rohan suggested. "Either way, standing here doesn't seem like a good idea."

He was right. They couldn't stay where they were. If they moved now they might be able to stay ahead of it. They mounted their horses and took off, over the stream and through the trees toward the hills. Ylva whistled for her wolves to follow—they obeyed, sprinting around trees and jumping obstacles.

Ylva slid her axe into its keeping and retrieved her bow.

"You really think you can shoot it?" Rohan yelled beside her.

"I can try," Ylva replied. She nocked an arrow and, when the trees cleared enough, turned in her seat so she could take aim. A nudging thought poked at the back of her mind, telling her this beast was what they had feared. When she caught full sight of it she froze. Her belief took a moment to catch up with her eyes as it flew right front of her. Black as night with flaming eyes above its pointed nose. Smoke puffed from its nostrils. Its bat-like wings stretched out from its long body. The dragon had come, dark and terrible.

It screeched again. Ylva's horse bucked, making her lose her seat. She tumbled onto the ground, her side searing with pain as she hit hard earth.

"Ylva!" Erland yelled.

Ylva forced herself onto her feet as quickly as the pain would allow. She began to run forward, looking for cover.

"Ylva!" Rohan called, turning his steed. He circled passed her then galloped toward her with his hand outstretched. She put her bow over her shoulder so that she wouldn't lose it and began jogging in the same direction. He slowed just enough to grab her forearm and she locked her hand around his. The prince pulled her up. She grabbed hold of the saddle with her other hand to gain the leverage needed to toss her leg over and find her seat behind Rohan.

Ylva took an arrow from the quiver on Rohan's saddle. She nocked it and said to the prince, "Keep him steady."

"Are you really going to try this again?" he asked her.

Ylva had to try. The dragon was still charging toward them. Though her body hurt and was quite possibly more broken after that fall but she would survive it. So Ylva turned and took aim. She let her arrow fly. It hit the dragon's neck but seemed to bounce off its hard flesh. She readied another arrow. This time it hit the beast's wing, ripping a hole through the thinner skin.

The dragon released a high-pitched piercing roar and pulled back. Ylva thought it might be enough to scare the thing away. It wasn't. The dragon lengthened its body and pulled its wings into a streamlined dive.

"We're going to need that place to hide very soon!" she exclaimed.

"I think I see something up ahead!" Erland shouted. He pointed ahead of them, just to the right.

Where the trees began to thicken, the ground pushed upward into a huge rock formation. The stone opened like a mouth.

"Erland, you ride toward that cave. See if it is big enough for the horses," Rohan ordered. "We will go in the other direction— under the cover of the trees and try to steer the dragon away. We will circle back to you."

"Aye," Erland agreed. Ylva's mare had followed them—he herded it alongside his own horse toward the cavern.

Rohan and Ylva traveled in the opposite direction, her wolves at their heels. The dragon followed them. They were forced to slow down as the forest grew thicker around them. Ylva could no longer see the dragon—she hoped it couldn't see them either. But she could still hear it growling and breaking trees.

Ylva and Rohan remained silent. The wolves were on edge, the hair on their shoulders raised and ears at attention. They stepped lightly through the brush. The horse's labored breathing grew heavier as they rode on and Ylva could feel the steed's muscles tense and twitch beneath her legs. Soon the sounds of the dragon seemed further away…enough so that they felt it safe to circle back and meet Erland at the cave.

CHAPTER FIFTEEN

THEY DID NOT LIGHT a fire to warm the damp cave for fear it would attract the dragon. For hours after they took refuge inside its rock walls, they could hear echoes of the beast's screeching above them. As night arrived, they still didn't trust the silence—so they agreed to take turns keeping watch until morning. Ylva took the first shift. She was in too much pain to sleep anyway. Every inhale sent a wave of discomfort through her body while each exhale brought only a momentary reprieve.

Ylva took a seat near the mouth of the cave where she could lean against the cold stone. Vǫrðr and Shura stayed by her side—their heads on her lap like a blanket. She tried to stay as still as possible. Movement triggered agony in her bones but stillness made sore muscles ache all the more. Falling off a horse was painful business, for which she didn't see relief in sight. What feverfew she had left wasn't enough to get her through the night. She decided to save it for the next day's ride. Perhaps it would be enough to dull the pain and keep her conscious on the last leg of the journey.

Ylva didn't regret her decision to stay on this expedition. Her body regretted it…but she knew Lys ordained this quest. Ylva had no doubt that this miserable cave was exactly where she should be. It didn't make sense, but something drove her forward. She couldn't turn around now—she wouldn't go back. There was purpose in this, even if she didn't understand it. In the pain and the unknown there was a closeness to the Light that she hadn't felt before. No, perhaps she had felt it some time long ago, closer even and more familiar. It merely got lost somewhere along the way. Its warmth and sound and image had faded but what Ylva felt now was its return. Or maybe she was the one returning to something left behind.

Erland snorted in his sleep and Vǫrðr's head popped up. The wolf grumbled then laid back down, nuzzling his nose under Ylva's hand. She absently scratched between his ears as she looked out the cave's entrance. Stars peaked through the foliage. Ylva focused on their specks of light, an attempt at forgetting the pain in her ribs.

"Ylva," Rohan whispered, startling her just a bit. The prince was crouched beside her. "It's my turn to keep watch. You should get some sleep."

Ylva started to move but a twinge stopped her. It wasn't so bad she couldn't move, but she felt too tired to make the effort. "I'm fine here," she said. "I can sleep like this."

She waited for Rohan to protest, to tell her that he was right and that she shouldn't have come. She expected him to reprimand or chastise her in some way. But he didn't.

"Fine," he responded, "then I'll just sit here beside you…"

Shura sat up to glare at him as he made to sit next to Ylva.

"…if that's okay?" he asked, and Ylva wasn't quite sure if he was asking her permission or the wolf's. When Shura moved to join Vǫrðr, the prince sat and leaned against the wall beside Ylva.

Ylva would have chuckled at it—the Prince of Väljalil seeking permission from a dog, but it would hurt too much to laugh. In a way it was endearing. The wolves were warming to him ...she found she was as well.

"Try to get some sleep, Wolf Queen," Rohan whispered. The prince sat close enough to her that their shoulders touched. "Tomorrow's ride will be a bumpy one."

Ylva yawned. She leaned her head back and closed her eyes.

Ylva scampered through the woods trying to keep up with the pack of wolf pups as she looked for wildflowers and berries. The forest around her home only ever changed with the seasons. The colors were the same, the smells were the same, the sounds were always the same. Birds chirped. Chipmunks rustled in the tree branches. When a storm was near, thunder clapped. The wolves howled at full moons. This dreamy memory felt like every day of her childhood...until it didn't.

She foraged just a little further than was her habit, following a line of berry bushes past her invisible boundary. On the other side of the thick shrubbery and through the dense trees came a new sound. It was similar to her voice but louder, deeper and more fearsome. Ylva peeked through the bush trying to see its source. The wolf pups became very still and shrank back like they were ready to run home. Ylva thought she should do the same. She couldn't though—not before she knew what was there with them.

She waited only a moment before two very tall creatures walked between the tree trunks. They were kind of like her but larger, much larger. The sight of them made her heart beat hard against her chest while goosebumps spread down her arms. It was both exciting and terrifying. They *were* her kind, but... something shook her. These tall beings wore scowls on their faces— even from a distance she could see that their hands and clothes were covered in blood. A part of her wanted to run to them, to touch their skin and see if it felt the same as hers. Her feet seemed rooted to the ground. Another part of her, a bigger part, a louder part, told her to run away.

One of the wolf pups nipped at her heel to get her attention. All the others had already started to retreat. Ylva gave one last look to the large tall creatures like her. Then she turned away to follow the pups.

"You ventured quite far today, little one," a figure called from the doorway of her humble dwelling. He was still blurry around the edges. She couldn't see a smile, but she could hear it in the way he spoke.

"I saw something, in the woods...something that looked like me," Ylva said still catching her breath from the run home.

"Ah." He stepped outside and took a seat on a stump.

Ylva climbed into his lap, still unable to fully see his face. "There are more like me?"

"Humans? Yes, many more," he replied.

"Do they live far away?" Ylva was puzzled as to why she hadn't seen them before. Why hadn't he told her about these *humans* before?

"Some do, but some live quite close by in a village."

"If my own kind is so close, then why do I live here with you and the wolves?" Ylva saw family groups in the woods. Birds, deer, even the ants each lived with their own kind. For the first time in her young life she felt confused and out of place.

"Humans are fickle creatures, little one. They get so caught up in things that have no real matter that they forget that the Light is enough—that Lys is the one thing that can fill the void in their souls." He paused to tap his finger against the tip of her nose. Then he pulled her in closer. "You are special. Lys has a purpose for you, one that requires you to know who you are without the intrusion of other opinions."

"I don't understand," Ylva said.

He hugged her, leaning his cheek against her head. "One day

you will. You will see what this time has meant—what it has all been about."

. "Will I always be separated from them?"

"Little one," he replied, "when the time is right, you will join your kind once again. You will find people to love and people who will love you. When you do it will mean all the more."

Ylva snuggled into his arms. His presence was enough to quiet her questions. She always felt peaceful, safe and the most like herself in his arms, like she was wrapped in the Light itself.

A noise in the cave broke through Ylva's dreams, waking her. The very beginning of a new day offered its soft light outside. Vǫrðr and Shura were both gone—Ylva assumed to seek out their own food and water. She felt afraid to move, wary of the pain that would come. Something heavy pressed on her shoulder. Prince Rohan was leaning against her, sound asleep. She almost jerked away but something about the peace written on his face stopped her. There was a small comfort to it—she didn't want to withdraw from it just yet. She tucked her own head against his and closed her eyes. She felt his fingers against hers. She could hear him breathing beside her.

Ylva felt something stirring. She had never thought of herself as having need of a man, or of love. Even though she barely knew Rohan, she wondered if this was how love began...from a moment of solace drawn from another person.

One of the horses whinnied outside. Rohan jerked awake. The sudden movement brought a nauseating wave of pain over Ylva—the room spun for a moment. When it settled, she saw Erland standing at the cave entrance holding the horses.

"I took the horses for water upon daybreak," he said. "There's no sign of the dragon—we can leave whenever you both are ready." Her friend looked at her with a smirk.

Ylva felt heat flush her cheeks. "I'll be ready in a moment," she said, trying again to stand. Dizziness pushed her back down.

Rohan grabbed her arm for support. "Are you all right?" he asked.

"I'm fine. Or I will be," Ylva replied. "I just need some water."

"I've got it." Erland handed her a waterskin, already full to the brim.

Rohan's eyes didn't leave her as she took a long drink. "Are you sure you are strong enough to continue?"

Ylva nodded. "I'm not, but Lys will make me so. I'm sure of that."

Senka stood on the top of the tower ruins. The stones around her, once a glorious monument to Myrkr, now disintegrated into rubble. Her anger only fueled her mission. Soon she would rebuild all that her master once ruled.

A painful squawk echoed through the air. Her dragon was returning to her. She had seen his efforts and his injury. She waited, ready to tend to his wound.

"Come my pet," the priestess called to her beast.

The dragon landed beside her. Stones cracking and crumbling beneath him.

Senka approached him with an outstretched hand. She touched her blackened fingertips to his snout. "Don't worry. You are still young—still growing and learning. They have not defeated you," she cooed.

The dragon flapped its wings—then issued a long hiss caused from the pain in doing so.

"I will take care of that, my pet," Senka said.

The Priestess of Myrkr turned round. On the ground, at her feet, lay the corpse of one of her soldiers. His skin was gray and his veins black. Inky blood seeped out of a large wound on his chest. Senka reached into it and pulled out his heart. It looked only like darkness—black and shriveled. She lifted it as an offering to the dragon.

The beast took it and ate it. Within moments, the tear in his wing stitched back together. He roared his pleasure.

"There, all better now," Senka said to the beast. "Let us give you more time to grow, then you will have another chance, I will see to it…and soon."

CHAPTER SIXTEEN

YLVA'S BODY ached from the long ride through the mountains to Kunnigstad. The small range made it difficult to see into the distance and easy to doubt a city even existed. Finally, homes and small villages tucked into the hillsides began to reveal themselves. The sun hung low when they seemed to cross over the horizon and follow a declining path through the cliffside. The sea became visible below.

At the base of the mountains stood a city, bright and colorful, lining the rim of the dark blue water. While Ylva had seen the ocean before, this appeared even more grand. It was a place that felt larger than life—like a surprise hidden at the edge of the world.

As they came down the main street—which was parallel to the shoreline—Ylva took in all the ways this city differed from Grålås. It was warm and light. Cleaner. The ocean air blew salty with a hint of fresh fish...but it wasn't unpleasant. Even the people seemed different. Ylva couldn't put her finger on exactly why...but something about them was unlike anything she had known. Maybe it was the colors and fabrics of their clothes that contrasted with the dark furs worn further north. Maybe it was the hum of laughter and conversation accompanied by the music of street performers. The people here seemed more free...the way they spoke, moved and carried themselves. Like they could do or be anything they desired. It was mesmerizing.

Ylva was struck by it all, lost in it long enough to think perhaps these people knew something about life she hadn't yet learned. It would be easy to look at the outward beauty of this place and believe such a thing. But Ylva knew better than to judge outward appearances. The further down the street they strolled, the deeper she looked into their eyes. The colors ultimately turned gray...and Darkness exposed itself in her Sight. Kunnigstad was much like every other place in Väljalil...just with prettier clothes.

"There," Rohan said. "Rullheim, home of the Keepers lies just ahead." He was pointing to a large building at the end of the street. It was made of stone and looked like it had been carved directly into the cliff. It had tall columns inscribed with runes and a large gate made of iron which squeaked when it opened.

Ylva, Rohan and Erland dismounted their horses before entering. The hand who took them tried to stop her wolves from following but had no success controlling the dogs who only snapped at him and stayed at her side.

"Greetings," a pleasant voice echoed off the high ceiling and bounced around the walls of the entryway. The man it belonged to smiled at Ylva as he walked to them. "I have been waiting for you." He took Ylva's hand gingerly in his own and stared at her as if he knew her. "I've been waiting for all of you," he said. He released her hand and seemed to come back to himself. Then he offered a bow to the prince. "I am Elior."

"Are you a Keeper?" Rohan asked.

"Goodness, no, just a servant," Elior replied.

"We are here on a matter of great importance and must see the Keepers at once," Rohan said.

"Of course, Highness," Elior replied. "I can take you to them straight away." He ruffled Vǫrðr's fur as he turned. The wolves followed him with tails wagging, bouncing behind him like they had been reunited with an old friend.

There was something about the man. He didn't seem much older than Ylva. His skin was a deep olive and his black hair hung in loose curls around his face. They accentuated his warm brown eyes that were bright—full of light and joy. He walked like there was nothing in the world that could weigh him down, his bare feet almost skipping down the corridor.

"Here we are," Elior said as he opened a large door at the end of the hall. His smile had grown, if that was even possible. "I hope you find what you're looking for." Then he gave Ylva one last nod before exiting.

Ylva watched the empty space Elior left behind. He gave her a strange sense and she wasn't sure if she was more comfortable in his presence or absence.

Then Rohan interrupted her thoughts. "I am Prince Rohan. I'm here to speak with the Keepers."

Rohan's voice brought Ylva's attention back to their mission and their new location. Rows and rows of shelves lined the room. Each one filled with scrolls, both of parchment and animal skin, as well as carved stones and pieces of wood. They were generations of words stowed in haphazard heaps and covered with a thin layer of dust. The stale air caused Ylva to rub the tip of her itchy nose. Erland sneezed.

"Come this way," a scratchy voice called from further inside the room.

They followed the call through a maze of stacks until they reached a back corner lit by candles. Surrounding a tall table stood three men. They looked old in age with long white hair and beards. Wrinkled skin peaked out of dark brown cloaks. They reminded Ylva of Håkon, except they looked too serious and bothered.

"I am Prince—"

"We know who you are," one of the men interrupted.

"We know why you have come," another added.

"You want the knowledge of the Darkness. Of the dragon," the third finished.

"The dragon is the Darkness," the first man corrected.

"Ah yes, that is true," the third—or was it the second?—replied. Ylva's head spun at the way the three men talked without pause like they were sharing one mind and had forgotten they had guests.

"Yes, the *dragon*," Rohan nearly shouted the word. He must have been just as perturbed by their banter.

The three Keepers all turned their attention to the prince, looking less than amused with him.

"My apologies, but this is important," Rohan said. "What can you tell us about the dragon?"

"The dragon is the Darkness," the Keeper repeated his earlier statement.

"But what does that mean?" Ylva stepped into the conversation.

All three Keepers looked at her like they couldn't decide what she was or why she was there. They gazed at her so intensely that she too now wondered whether or not she belonged there. Vǫrðr and Shura sidled closer to her, always knowing when she needed them.

Finally the three old men turned from her and each went to a different shelf to retrieve a scroll or stone. They moved like they knew exactly what they were looking for and had no doubt it would be in its proper place—though to Ylva, the entire room seemed nothing more than a mess.

The first Keeper opened his scroll and read, "Always has there been Lys. For nearly as long there has been Myrkr."

"They have warred against one another for the hearts of men since the beginning of all things," the second Keeper read.

"We know all this," Rohan interrupted, rubbing the back of his neck.

The third Keeper coughed, then lifted the vellum he held and read, "Myrkr sought to control men, to tempt them and tame them. Thus he created a woman."

"Myrkr *created* the priestess?" Ylva asked. That didn't seem right at all. Lys created *all* things. Myrkr is merely a cheap imitation. He couldn't have that kind of power, could he? She looked to Erland, who had been a silent observer. She knew he believed as she did. His own brow furrowed with confusion. His arms crossed over his chest as if in some sort of protest.

"Created is a poor translation," a Keeper corrected looking between Ylva and Erland. "Myrkr captured a woman's heart and remade her in his image, turning her to complete darkness. He inhabits her mind and body and soul. He has done so for centuries."

"Then how could the priestess live for so long if she is truly just a human turned to the Darkness?" Rohan inquired.

"Myrkr's power keeps her death at bay for as long as she does his bidding," a Keeper responded.

"But I doubt there is anything human still alive in her." another offered "She is more like a shell."

"Can she be stopped?" Ylva asked.

"She was stopped," a Keeper said matter-of-factly.

"Three generations ago," another Keeper began to read again, "the Dark Priestess was entombed in the ruins of the High Mountain, forever buried in the belly of Skämd."

"You might want to check a newer scroll," Rohan said with a smirk, "because whoever wrote that one may have misused the word forever."

"The priestess has returned," Ylva said, trying to quench the frustration she could see rising behind their squinted eyes. "The dragon has risen again."

"Are you certain?" one Keeper asked in alarm, his bushy

eyebrows arched and his lips pursed.

"We have seen it ourselves," Rohan answered. "We need to know what to do about it."

"We can tell you what was done before," the second Keeper told them.

"Pardon me." Ylva was getting frustrated. "But what was done before didn't work. Not truly." They had come all this way looking for answers. Kunnigstad—the City of Knowing, home of the Keepers of all Knowledge. This was the place where they were supposed to find a solution…not just history repeating.

"We know our ancestors entombed the priestess and the dragon, but we need to know how to *kill* them," she said.

The Keepers' faces softened. They rifled through the stacks of parchments and carvings in front of them before looking back to Rohan and Ylva with sad expressions.

"We are sorry," one said, "we have read nothing on the subject. We can only surmise."

"A theory is better than nothing." Rohan shrugged.

"The priestess is the Darkness," one Keeper began.

"And the dragon is also the Darkness, incarnate," another added.

"They are linked. When one slept, then they both slept," the third said.

"It is quite possible," the first spoke again, "if you kill one, they will both die."

Tension loomed over them for a brief moment.

"But you don't know *how* to kill either of them?" Rohan asked, although it felt to Ylva more an admission of defeat rather than a question.

"That's why they didn't kill the dragon or the priestess the first time." Ylva sighed. Their journey had been in vain. She was exhausted and in so much pain that she could barely stand—yet it had all been for nothing—an aching, maddening nothing. They would find no answers here.

CHAPTER SEVENTEEN

YLVA WAS BEGINNING to regret not going home when she had the chance. She had believed Lys led them here, had led her here, but for what purpose? They knew nothing more now than when they had first arrived and it was unlikely they would find anything of much substance. After speaking with the Keepers, she and Rohan had been allowed to look through the scrolls themselves but they barely knew what they were looking for or where it could be found. It would take years to read through every rune in Rullheim and years were not something they had. She wished now she had gone with Erland to check on the horses.

"Have you found anything helpful?" Elior asked, carrying a tray of food with him.

"No," Rohan replied.

"I am sorry," Elior responded. He set the tray down and took two bones off it which he tossed to the wolves who lay at Ylva's feet. "I've brought you refreshments. You need your strength, I'm sure."

"Thank you." Ylva smiled at him. It was awkward, the way he looked at her. She wanted to ask him what he saw, what he knew of her, but thought herself silly. She had never met this man before and there was no reason to think he knew anything of her—that he meant anything other than to offer them hospitality.

"Yes, thank you." Rohan reached between Ylva and Elior to grab a chunk of bread. If Ylva didn't know better she might have thought the prince was a bit jealous.

Actually, she did know better. She was fairly certain he was jealous and she liked it. But why did she like it? Was she beginning to feel something for Rohan? She did find him less annoying the more time they spent together. And he was handsome. And he had this way he would look at her that made her skin warm.

Ylva swallowed. She didn't have time for girlish musings. There was a dragon to slay and they were no closer to discovering how.

"I don't think we will find anything here," Ylva said. "If the Keepers haven't found knowledge of how to kill the dragon or the priestess, what hope do we have?" She picked up the small carved stone she had been studying and went to return it to its shelf. Its weight and the stretch required to lift it worked against her. She felt a stab of pain to her ribcage. Ylva lost her breath for a moment and nearly dropped the tablet.

"Ylva." Rohan was almost immediately at her side. He touched a hand to the small of her back to steady her. "Your injury has worsened. You need rest."

"We need a solution to the Darkness," Ylva snapped, trying her best to ignore the spark of electricity she felt from his touch. "Rest is a luxury that can wait a bit longer."

"It is a luxury we must afford if you are to be well enough to continue." The prince's words were a soft whisper, a breath against her cheek.

Ylva felt that warmth, a tingle that weakened her knees. She rested her hand on the table to keep her balance.

Rohan moved a bit closer, careful that his hand, now on her

hip, didn't hurt her. "We will find a solution," the prince encouraged.

"Of course you will," Elior said. "Solutions are always to be found—just not always in the places we look."

"Perhaps I need rest too," Rohan said, "because I'm not sure if that did or didn't make sense to me." The prince laughed at himself.

Ylva smiled at the sound of Rohan's comment, deep and withholding nothing. It was another true thing he had offered of himself.

"Let me show you all to your rooms," Elior said. "I already have them prepared for you."

"Yes, please," Rohan said, keeping his hand at Ylva's back as they followed Elior out of the room and down the corridors.

When they reached their doors Ylva was reluctant to move away from the prince and from his touch. It comforted her in a way she hadn't expected. "Goodnight," she told him.

"Goodnight." He nodded and went to his own room, shutting the door behind him.

Shura whimpered as the door closed. Vǫrðr stared at it like they were waiting for him to return. Ylva caught herself waiting for the same thing. She shook her head and closed her own door before looking at her lupine guardians. "Since when do you two even like him?"

The dogs grumbled in response, something between a howl and a growl, like they were asking her the same question in return.

"I'm too tired for this," Ylva replied. "Let's just get some sleep." She laid herself slowly down on the small cot by the fire and the dogs curled up on the floor beside her.

"Try again, little one," the voice told Ylva.

She knew he was standing behind her without ever having to look. She could feel his presence near her as easily and completely as she could feel a hug. It usually made her stronger, him being there. Not now. This time she felt small and weak.

Ylva's tiny hands gripped the handle of the axe. It was heavy and pulled at the muscles in her forearms. She had to strain just to lift it but she gave it all she had, pulled it back and then hurled it toward the trunk of a large tree in front of her. Even with all the strength she had to give, the axe fell short of hitting its mark and stuck in the ground.

"I'm never going to get better at this," Ylva cried. "I don't want to do this anymore."

She turned to run away from the makeshift training ground.

Large arms caught her and pulled her close. The man stooped down in front of her. His gentle hands wiped the tears from her chubby cheeks. She could see the edges of him clearly but not his face, though she knew he wasn't frowning. He never frowned at her.

"It's all right, little one," he whispered to her with tenderness. "You must have patience with yourself. Things take time, some more than others, but you mustn't give up."

"But this is too hard." Ylva snuggled into his chest. "I'm not strong enough. I'll never—"

"It will come," he interrupted her muffled whining, hugged her and rubbed her small head. "Keep at it and you will grow stronger in more ways than you realize and when the time is right—it will come."

Ylva sat up in bed. The sudden movement made her side burn. She was getting tired of this. She was tired of the pain. Tired of not having a clear path. Tired of these dreams that only added to her frustration. They weren't normal. They felt orchestrated and familiar yet just outside of her grasp. What were they supposed to mean? Why were they coming to her now?

Ylva rubbed her hand over the back of her neck. She got out of bed and slipped her boots back on. It was far from morning but she needed air and space.

Vǫrðr and Shura went to follow her. "No, stay," she commanded.

Vǫrðr whined.

"I will be fine. I promise." When the dogs conceded and laid back down, Ylva left the room.

She wandered down the dark corridors in search of a way outside. At the end of a long hallway she found a set of twisting stairs. A draft blew down them. Thinking they must lead outdoors, Ylva climbed the spiral until she came to a door. It opened to a small balcony that overlooked the city and the water.

At the ledge stood Elior. His back was to her. His arms were above his head and moving about like he was painting the aurora across the black canvas of night. She didn't want to interrupt so she turned to leave.

"It is so beautiful, isn't it?" Elior's question stopped her.

"It is," Ylva replied. "I didn't mean to intrude on you."

"You are never an intrusion." He turned and smiled at her before looking back at his imaginary masterpiece.

"I take it I'm not the only one who couldn't sleep?" Ylva asked.

"And miss this?" Elior responded. "There is too much beauty in the world that goes unseen."

Ylva stepped closer to the ledge and stared upward. It was enchanting, the darkness of night sliced open with a streak of blue and green light, the bright white of a million blazing stars poking through. She had seen nights like this before but tonight felt different—unique. Had she missed the magic in it all before now?

"You are injured." Elior spoke as though his comments were

clearly connected though the abrupt change caught Ylva off guard.

"Yes," she managed to reply. "I was wounded during an attack on the East Keep."

"I can help with that." Elior reached toward her side.

Ylva backed away just an inch. "A healer has already wrapped it—now it just needs time."

"Maybe its time has come." Elior winked.

Ylva stared at him now, not the outside of him but the inside. She focused her gaze deeper, waiting for her gift to illuminate some aspect of this strange man that would offer insight. There was nothing. No Light. No Darkness. It wasn't like with Rohan who was this perfectly mingled muddle of gray. There was just nothing. It was is if she had no gift at all. She couldn't see anything beyond his surface. It was unsettling.

"Who are you?" Ylva asked.

"Elior, a servant," he replied, his face never losing its warm smile. "And I can help with your injury."

"How?"

"I have a gift, maybe more of a knack, for healing," he responded. "I think I can help you."

Ylva hesitated but, while she couldn't read his motives or nature, she felt Elior trustworthy. "All right," she agreed.

Elior reached out to her again. She stiffened but didn't back away. He touched her bruised and swollen side with the very tips of his calloused fingers and closed his eyes. Ylva waited, watched for some sign that something might be happening. Everything seemed to stand still. Suddenly, no sound could be heard. Then the flames of the torches froze in place. Her eyes and ears must have been playing tricks on her. As quickly as she thought the world had halted in its place it all came spinning back to motion.

"There." Elior pulled away. "How do you feel?"

Ylva almost laughed out loud. He hadn't done anything. Had

he? She inhaled a long, deep breath then blew it back out in a puff of warm vapor. It didn't hurt. She lifted her arm, twisted and bent over, all without so much as a twinge.

Elior patted her shoulder. "When you return to your room, you can remove your wrapping. I am certain you will no longer need it." Then he turned and left.

Ylva watched him go with her mouth agape. She believed in gifts from Lys but this was more than she had imagined. Perhaps it was less. There was no spectacle to it. It was quiet and small and easy to dismiss. Her own gift was not something others could ascertain, but to her it was all-encompassing and impossible to ignore. She felt swept away by it. Elior's gift was nothing like that, at least not from her vantage point. It was strange and pressed the boundaries of her faith, just like Elior himself. He was unlike anyone she had ever met, except somehow…he wasn't.

CHAPTER EIGHTEEN

ROHAN HAD SPENT the better part of the night tossing and turning, trying not to think of Ylva. He didn't like the idea of being
smitten. He didn't like the word smitten. Females were smitten
with him, not the other way around. But...Ylva was very
different from any other woman he had known. Not all in good
ways. Instead of sleeping, he worried about her; whether she was
okay or if she was able to rest. He almost went to check on her
but didn't want to wake her. Who was he becoming? What had
she done to him?

The prince could take a bit of solace in the fact that Tyr
wasn't around to see his downward spiral into a romantic mess.
Is that what he was now? Tyr would think so, and tell him so,
more to get under his skin than anything else. Ylva was already
under his skin. Why? She wasn't the most beautiful woman he
had ever seen. She wasn't the kind of woman he had ever
thought he would want at his side. Yet, in just a short time, she
had become exactly who he needed at his side. She challenged
him. It felt uncomfortable—like he was pushing closer to his true
self. He now saw that between the rebellious rogue and the
future king dwelt the best version of himself and she pulled that

man out into the open. Maybe it wasn't even about romance at all.

Rohan slipped on his boots and strapped his leather bracers to his forearms. He grabbed his leather cuirass and carried it with his sword to gather the horses. He hated going home with no strategy to fight this supernatural enemy, but Rullheim and Kunnigstad offered nothing in the way of answers. It now only made sense to return to Grålås and seek his father's wisdom.

The stable hand and saddled horses met him at the gate in preparation for the long ride home. Rohan strapped his armor to his chest as Ylva and her wolves approached.

"Good morning," Ylva greeted him briefly before attending to her mare.

"Morning," Rohan replied. He latched his sword and sheath to his saddle then glanced at Ylva. "Feeling better this morning?"

A wide smile lit her face. "Yes, actually, much better," she replied. "Thanks to Elior."

"Elior?" Rohan almost choked on the word.

"Yes, it was quite remarkable," Ylva began. "I couldn't sleep last night, and I found Elior. He also has a gift and he healed my injury."

Healed her injury? Rohan wasn't sure if he was still skeptical of such gifts or just of Elior.

"I was happy to do it," Elior interrupted the prince's unspoken questions as he carried full waterskins to them.

"You have a gift? Like Ylva's?" Rohan asked the man.

"Yes, I guess you could say that," Elior replied. "Our gifts are born of the same thing."

His answer seemed cryptic. There was a secret hidden in it, Rohan was sure of it. He didn't like it. He didn't like Elior. In the back of his mind he knew it was all because of Ylva. He didn't like the way this man looked at her...as though he really saw her. He didn't like the familiarity in Elior's gaze. *He* wanted to be the one who saw her, who was familiar to her in a way no one else ever could be. *Shut up, Rohan,* he scolded himself. He was the future king of Väljalil and didn't have time to act like an envious boy.

"I am glad you are well, then," Rohan spoke to Ylva. He offered a smile to cover his frustration but it must have fallen short because her own wilted when she looked at his face. He wanted to say more to her, to reassure her that his lack of joy had nothing to do with her. He chose instead to focus on the business at hand. "I thought we could ride to the South Keep, get a report from the East and send word for the military commanders to meet in Grålås to discuss our options."

Ylva stared at him, like she was trying to read his thoughts. "All right," she replied.

"Actually," Elior cut in with a raised hand, "I might have an idea. Well, it's not an idea so much as a thought that might lead to an idea."

"What is it?" Ylva asked him with a hopeful smile.

"Well, sometimes you need to look at the information you have from a different perspective," Elior stated, "so I started to think—if light is the opposite of darkness and the dragon is the Darkness, then…maybe it can be defeated with light."

"So…what, we throw a candle at it? Or a torch maybe?" The prince laughed at his own joke.

"Rohan," Ylva rebuked him with a sharp whisper.

"I don't think that would work," Elior replied dryly, his face flat, without any sense that he understood Rohan's response was in jest. "But perhaps discovering how it accumulates its strength from the Darkness will show you what kind of weapon to make from the light."

Rohan and Ylva stood staring at the servant. Elior's perspective had promise. It was more insight than the Keepers offered. But it was incomplete.

"How do you suppose we do that?" Rohan asked, all humor disappearing.

"Oh, I don't know that." Elior grinned.

The prince was losing his patience. He wanted to roar in frustration but opted for a bit more control and inhaled a deep breath.

Ylva touched his arm—he released his tense breath and embraced her calm.

"We will figure it out, somehow," she said. "Perhaps someone can be sent to spy on the dragon and the priestess?" Her eyes looked at him earnestly and with compassion.

She was doing it again—pulling the best parts of him to the surface and pushing back the immaturity. "Yes," Rohan replied, "once we arrive at the South keep, we'll find the best scouts to go to Askadalen and report back."

"I shall accompany you," Elior said.

"No, I don't think that is a good idea," Rohan responded.

"Not all the way to Grålås, Highness," Elior corrected, "just to the South Keep and from there I will head to the East. I can help carry word of your request to send more scouts."

"Why?" The prince asked. "Don't the Keepers need you?"

"They care very little for what I do," Elior replied. "They barely know I'm even here most of the time."

"But why do you want to go to the East Keep?" Ylva asked the servant.

"I heard you all speak of what happened there, of those who are hurting and in need," Elior said. "I believe I can be of help to them."

Rohan wanted to protest. He wanted to keep this peculiar man as far away from him and Ylva as he could. But if he had truly healed Ylva, then he could be of use with the refugees at the Keep. Now was not the time to refuse help for selfish reasons.

"I will send a letter with you alerting the commander of my

approval and to welcome you accordingly. Shall we get you a horse?" he asked.

"Thank you, but no, Highness," Elior replied just as the hand came into view leading a donkey. "I have all I need."

Rohan looked Elior up and down once more. His linen clothes didn't seem like they would do much to keep him warm. He still walked in bare feet while his donkey was packed with barely more than a waterskin and bed roll. The harsher weather further north would probably come as a shock to the man's optimism, but Rohan would let him discover that on his own. The commander would take care of him once he arrived anyway so it was no matter to the prince now how the servant chose to travel.

"We should be on our way then," Rohan said. He was about to mount his horse when Erland ran toward them, waving something wildly in his hands.

"Prince!" Erland called out. "A falcon has come from Grålås. It's urgent!"

Rohan took the small scroll from Erland. As he read the runes scribbled across the parchment, he felt as though a boulder had rolled onto his chest, its weight pressing into his lungs and heart.

"What is it?" Ylva asked.

The prince didn't look at her. He didn't dare look at anyone.

"It is word from Tyr," Rohan explained. He couldn't feel the tips of his fingers. His voice didn't sound like his own but he knew he was the one speaking because each word sucked the air from his lungs and made it more difficult to breathe. "King Vakr, my father…he has died." Rohan's vision blurred with warm tears that wanted to spill out with his words but shock wouldn't allow them. He just stood there, staring at the tiny piece of parchment that had flipped his world on end. He knew death was coming for his father but much like any son must, he hoped it would change its mind.

"Rohan." He felt Ylva's hand on his shoulder and placed his

own palm on top of it. His name hadn't been a question—just an assurance...full of grace...that someone was there. He took strength from it.

No one spoke or moved. They waited on him. It occurred to him that the whole kingdom would be waiting on him if he now only stood there...aching.

"Erland," he said and it sounded more fragile than he would have liked.

"Yes, Highness?" Erland responded.

"Take Elior and Ylva to the South Keep. Get reports from the commanders," Rohan ordered. "Tell them what has happened and that we will conference at Grålås in a week's time. I will ride ahead to the city to make preparations."

"Erland can see Elior to the Keep and then come to Grålås," Ylva said as she moved to stand in front of Rohan, requiring him to look at her. "I will come with you."

Rohan expected Erland to protest; however, when he saw the expression on Ylva's face, it was clear that she would not be argued with nor deterred.

Vǫrðr and Shura came to stand on either side of the couple looking up at Rohan as though to further quench any ideas that he had a choice in the matter.

If the choice had been his, Rohan would have chosen for her to come with him anyway.

CHAPTER NINETEEN

ROHAN SAT at the foot of his father's empty bed. He had been sitting there most of the day. Tyr had handled the necessary arrangements before he had even returned from Kunnigstad. Rohan was glad for his help. Unanswerable questions stared him down: how does one bury their father? How does one commemorate their life in a few moments of a single day? It cannot be done. That is what Rohan had decided. This was one day and they would make it a grand ceremony to honor their beloved king, but Rohan would spend every day hereafter honoring his beloved father. At least he would try. He was still unworthy.

The prince fidgeted with his black coat. It felt heavy on his shoulders. It was a chieftain's coat. It was the King's coat, bearing his seal in gold stitching across its back. Rohan had traced over the stallion insignia before putting it on. Now it felt like it burned into his skin.

He wasn't ready to be king. He wasn't ready to lose his father. But this did not in any way influence the circumstances.

"Rohan," Ylva's voice lilted from the door and across the room, hitting his senses like a tender kiss.

The prince looked at her as she stood in the doorway. She was beautiful there. Her long blonde hair was dressed in braids and waves that framed her delicate face. She wore a ceremonial dress and long coat with the same gold brocade against black linen. Its dark fabric made her fair skin appear even lighter. There was something almost ethereal about her in this moment. When did she become beautiful? Had she always been and he overlooked it?

"It's almost time," she said, stepping toward him.

"I know," he replied but didn't move. "I'm not sure I can do this."

Ylva's hand touched the crook of his neck, her fingers warm on his skin. Her eyes filled with sympathy as she looked into his. "You can." Her lips curled upward just a little.

Rohan placed his hand over hers. "Not alone," he said. "Stand at my side."

"Rohan." Ylva pulled her hand away from his shoulder but he kept hold of it. "It is not my place," she said, squeezing his fingers.

"I'd like it to be." The prince stood up, still holding her hand. There was only an inch or so left between them. He stood close enough to smell the lavender in her hair.

"Please, I don't care about protocol or what people will think." It was true—he didn't. He knew what her presence directly beside him would communicate to those onlooking. He knew that minds would swirl and tongues would wag. He wasn't asking for her hand...but he knew he wanted her next to him in this moment. Ylva offered him some sort of strength. He had known it in Kunnigstad and he accepted it now.

His heart was too downcast to argue, even with himself.

"All right," Ylva replied. He could see the seed of doubt in the way she bit her bottom lip. He surmised that in those short seconds she had done her own analysis of what he was asking... of what it would look like...of him. Whatever had gone through her mind had been enough to persuade her to concede. For the briefest moment, he was floating.

"Highness," Tyr interrupted with a word and a knock on the already open door. "I'm sorry to intrude, but it's time."

"Of course," Rohan said. On any other day he was sure his friend would offer a teasing remark or at least a raised eyebrow at the sight of him holding the Wolf Queen's hand. Not today. Tyr only nodded in reply. Rohan and Ylva exited the room in front of him, still hand in hand.

They remained linked until they reached the outer hall. Near the large exterior wooden doors lay king Vakr's body on a wide plank. Rohan released Ylva's hand and approached his father. It took fifteen steps to cross the space. Fifteen agonizing steps where the only sound was Rohan's heart hitting the inside of his chest. With each footfall he inhaled. The air felt thicker—it seemed to hang off him like weights. Each inch sharpened the image of the King's pale cold skin. Fifteen steps and fifteen breaths until the prince reached his father and knelt beside him for the last time.

"May I be half the man you were," Rohan whispered before kissing Vakr's cold forehead.

As soon as the prince stepped back, six of the castle guard, three on each side, lined the body. They hoisted it onto their shoulders and began the processional. To the beat of heavy drums, they marched down the center street of Grålås toward the funerary mounds. A solemn parade of chieftains and dignitaries followed their King one last time while villagers and guests mourned from the sidelines.

They were mostly a blur to Rohan. Occasionally he would catch the clear face of a small child in its mother's arms or an old man standing at attention. He heard the intermittent wail of grief between the banging of the drums. He wanted to add his own tears…but knew that he couldn't. Right now he couldn't be a son mourning his father. Now, he was the future king and needed to summon the strength to allow the people to grieve instead of drawing focus onto himself.

Rohan glanced at Ylva who looked so regal as she walked silently beside him. He was sure people wondered at the Wolf Queen and her guardians, Vǫrðr and Shura, who strode close by her as always. He wondered at her, at how he came to know her, to be graced with her friendship. Were they friends now? There had always been plenty of women who wanted to know him, who would consider it lucky to be close to the Prince of Väljalil. But he knew he was the lucky one to know *her*, the Ibharüng chieftain. The closer they got to the burial grounds, the more he felt certain she was the only thing keeping him standing. He wanted to reach out and take her hand again, but knew it was a line he shouldn't cross here.

They walked for about a half mile outside the city walls towards the small hills that were encircled with stones. These signified the final resting places of all the former sovereigns of Väljalil. As they reached their destination, Rohan came to a halt by the newly built pyre. Tyr stood on one side of him and Ylva on the other. He watched the guard lay his father's body on the furs that covered the heap. They placed Vakr's shield under his head and his sword in his hands. Some bowls of spices and oats, along with his bow, axe and helmet lay in a circle around the dead king. When they finished, Rohan stepped forward.

"You have fought well, father," the prince began his benediction. "You have honored Lys with your life and in your death. Go in peace now. May the light lead you toward the hereafter and the darkness never again touch you." Rohan swallowed down the tears that were threatening to fall—then he nodded toward Erland who, having been given the honor by the prince, held a lit torch nearby.

Erland laid the torch inside the pyre, and the dry wood burst into flame. It burned bright and hot. The smoke spiraled upward like a path into the beyond. Rohan just stared at it as though it held the soul of his father in its billows. Any wish that this was but a nightmare vanished with the heat of the fire. He couldn't hold his tears behind the levee of duty any longer. A few spilled down his cheeks in slow streaks.

A hand touched his. Rohan looked down to see Ylva's small fingers interlacing with his own. The gesture calmed his aching heart just enough to keep him steadfast until the cremation was complete. When the fire had died and the ashes were covered in fresh dirt, Rohan placed the header stone on the grave. The other chieftains and leaders of the realm placed their stones one at a time until only one gap remained. Ylva, the last clan leader, picked up her stone and carried it to its space. She set it down then placed a kiss on her fingertips before giving the stone her last touch. Then she returned to Rohan's side.

Together they led the march back to the castle. This time no drums resounded, just the quiet chatter of the chieftains behind him. The streets lay empty, no one waiting for another glimpse of the soon-to-be king. Rohan preferred it that way.

CHAPTER TWENTY

THE BANQUET in King Vakr's honor still roared with laughter and the regaling of stories until the wee hours of the morning. Rohan took some small pleasure in hearing the other's talk about his father as a young man and a friend—not just as king. Perhaps he would be allowed the same grace to be human...to be himself. Unless that sort of grace is reserved for funeral feasts.

No matter how hard Rohan tried, he could not shake the belief that he would never live up to the large-than-life version of his father that he sculpted in his mind. He sat at the head of a large table in a room full of warriors and leaders and felt like just a little boy amongst them. His outer demeanor may have worn the veil of confidence—his posture and strong voice giving the illusion of comfort in that chair. Inside he flinched at every word and gesture. He wanted to retreat.

"You can excuse yourself," Tyr whispered to the prince as though he had read his mind. "No one expects you to stay the entire time. They know you just lost your father." His friend's face was kind with a bit of concern around the edges.

Rohan wasn't sure if he believed Tyr. He didn't really know what anyone expected of him. He felt like every move should be calculated, perfect. Even if some in the room were understanding, he knew others would think less of him because he retired first. Or was he supposed to leave first to signal that they could do the same? Perhaps they had all spent the night waiting on him and were internally livid at being kept there so late. This all felt like things he should know. Did he know them and just couldn't recollect them at the moment?

Rohan gave up. He was tired in every sense of the word and couldn't play this game anymore tonight, not without losing. "Goodnight then," he said to Tyr. The prince stood and offered a quick word of thanks to his guests who rose from their seats and nodded their heads as he exited the hall.

The rest of the castle became eerily quiet as the echo of revelry faded the closer Rohan drew to his room. His anxiety was no less boisterous, however. The prince needed to calm his thoughts and silence his fears long enough to sleep. He closed his door and crossed the room to unlatch his window. He pushed it open and inhaled a deep breath of the cool night air. All of Grålås was silent and dark, save a few candles or torches in the occasional window.

"Sweet prince, you seem so tired," a silky voice coiled around his thoughts.

Rohan turned around to see a woman standing in the middle of his room. She looked like smoke and fire. Her red hair faded to black then seemed to melt into her dress. Her skin was so pale it was almost like she wasn't alive. A mask of charcoal paint was smeared across her eyes.

"Who are you? How did you get in here?" Rohan asked, his body tensing in wait for her response.

"I'll forgive your ignorance," the woman said as she ran a stained finger across her bottom lip, her eyes surveying Rohan.

"I asked you a question," the prince said, growing uncomfortable in her presence.

"Careful, Rohan, Prince of Väljalil," she replied, "you don't want me to lose my patience so soon in the conversation."

"I am afraid I am already losing mine," he retorted.

The woman's mouth curled into a wicked grin. "Apologies, *Highness.*" She spit the word like it was a joke. "I am Senka, High Priestess of Myrkr. I have come with an offer."

Rohan felt adrenaline pump through his chest as his mind and muscles readied themselves for attack. He placed his hand on the grip of his sword. "There is nothing you have that I want."

"I wouldn't be so sure." She began to slink toward him.

Rohan drew his sword and stepped away from her. The two began to circle slowly.

"You are so full of fear, sweet prince," Senka said. "You doubt yourself."

An argument waited on the tip of his tongue, but the prince couldn't speak it out loud. He couldn't deny the truth even though he didn't want to give this enemy the satisfaction.

"It is nothing to be ashamed of." Her voice sounded breathy as she spoke. It reminded Rohan of a serpent hissing.

"I am not ashamed," the prince responded.

Senka laughed. "Of course not." Her eyes narrowed and for a moment Rohan swore they turned to fire. Then she blinked and it was gone. "Dear boy, we don't have to be enemies. I come to offer an alliance to the future king, one that will bring peace to the realm."

"I will make no alliance with you," Rohan said, repulsed by the very thought.

"Not even if I can make you a greater king than your father?"

Sweat was beginning to bead on Rohan's forehead. His grip loosened and his sword lowered just a bit. He knew it was wrong, that he couldn't, that he shouldn't…but all of his insecurities screamed at him to listen to her.

"I can give you power your father never had. Together we can make your kingdom the greatest that has ever been," Senka said. "They will build monuments in your honor and herald your name through the ages."

"Let me guess—I get all of that and all I have to do is sell you my soul?" Rohan asked, regaining a tighter hold on his blade and his senses.

"I have no need of your soul…"

"But Myrkr does?"

"Myrkr needs for nothing; he merely wants to help you," Senka replied. "Besides, you don't believe in all that anyway, do you?"

"Don't you?" Rohan asked.

"What I believe is of no matter. This is about you, sweet prince, about you reaching your destiny." Senka moved to look out the window. "There is a city out there. Beyond that, four lands make up a kingdom that is to be yours. You can't lead it on your own. You need my help."

"You're right," Rohan said. "I can't lead it on my own." He took slow steps toward her, his sword at the ready. "But I don't need you." The prince raised his weapon and meant to cut down the priestess but he froze, stopped by invisible hands.

Senka turned to face him, one palm raised. "I thought we could be friends, you and I." Rohan watched her fingers constrict together. As they did, his own chest grew tighter and tighter until he could barely breath.

"No," Rohan choked out the word as pain seared inside him.

"Who are you to tell me 'no'?" Senka's eyes blazed again—this time, Rohan was sure of what he saw. "You are not pure. You are not noble. Any light inside you is a dwindling flame. You are nothing but a weak mix of shadow the Darkness is waiting to devour."

You were this beautiful, tragic mix of grey. Not enough to look dead, but too much to look fully alive. It is like you are caught exactly in the middle. Ylva's words leapt from his memory. He hadn't known what to do with them then. Now…

now he knew they weren't to cause worry. They indicated only a choice. That was a power he held. The Darkness could not devour him anymore than the Light could—not without his consent. Rohan was unsure of so many things…of Ylva, of being king, of his own worth. But he was certain he would not yield to Myrkr or his priestess.

The prince fought against the unseen force that held him still. "It will not!" He shook and screamed as he worked with all his strength to break free of her hold. His heart hurt all the more, agony shooting down his arms and legs. He didn't stop, didn't relent.

"No!" A voice screamed from the doorway.

"You," Senka seethed. She twisted her hand and Rohan's pain stopped as everything went black.

CHAPTER TWENTY-ONE

YLVA CHOSE to forego the night's revelry in the great hall. She would have been glad to honor King Vakr but enough of her day had been spent surrounded by too many people. Her weary mind needed a break so she sent Erland in her stead after apologizing to Rohan for her intended absence. The prince looked a bit disappointed, hesitating before offering her his understanding and a simple goodnight that felt anything but simple.

The entire day had been layered with emotions. On the surface, Ylva had grieved her king. What she knew, what she had seen of him suggested an honorable man, one worthy of the noble ceremony. She hadn't spent much, if any, of her life even thinking about the king until recently. Not long ago news of his passing would have meant very little to her day-to-day life. In a matter of one meeting, one interaction, she found that all had changed. Her heart had been marked by his warmth, his sweetness and his light.

Underneath the veil of mourning, Ylva worried over things to come. She knew worry was only the younger sister to fear and offered nothing of substance to the situation. It was difficult to avoid it fully. An army grew in the Valley of Ash and the dragon was in their midst. Ylva knew they would fight, that they would give their last drop of blood to see the Darkness thwarted. The uncertainty came in what would be the best *way* to fight. They could battle with all their might—but without a plan or without some knowledge of their enemy's weakness, could they do more than their ancestors? Ylva didn't want to put the Darkness back to sleep—she wanted to destroy it so that the children who sat by Håkon's fire would never need to fear this threat. She never wanted *her* children to fear it either.

Her own children. It was a strange, unsettling idea. Ylva had never given thought to children of her own. She thought of her clan, of leading the Ibharüng—not of love and family. She was always the girl detached from everyone else, the one raised with the wolves. Maybe she didn't think anyone would see her as someone to have children with so she never let herself dream it.

Things felt different now. Now there was Rohan. Did she see a future with him? The notion sounded a bit foolish to her sensibilities. They had been thrown together in this quest to stop Myrkr. They shared a common goal and had thus built a camaraderie. At moments Ylva thought it could be more, that friendship had sprouted and would blossom into something deeper. She couldn't be certain but wondering had been the undercurrent of her day.

Ylva's thoughts swirled and distracted her so that she didn't even change out of her funeral dress. She flopped onto her bed, her mind too busy and her body too tired to undress. She closed her eyes and breathed deeply. One by one, she mentally pushed aside the things that were working to steal her rest. Sadness, worry, fear, doubt, confusion…she would need to deal with each in time and in the proper way. Ylva would place them on a shelf until she could view them with fresh eyes under the guidance of Lys. In the meantime she would think of grace, strength and things that brought her joy. It was how she kept the Darkness from creeping into her own heart. Slowly, Ylva took her thoughts prisoner and found enough freedom for herself to drift off to sleep.

Vǫrðr's growl broke into Ylva's dreamless slumber.

Ylva opened her eyes. "What is it?" she asked her guardians as she sat up and stretched her back and shoulders.

The dogs seemed preoccupied by something outside her room. Shura was whining and clawing at the door. Vǫrðr's fur stood on end.

Everything was quiet. Ylva thought the dogs heard mice or some other vermin and were antsy for a hunt. "Hush now," she whispered her command.

Both wolves only grew more agitated. Ylva almost gave them a firmer order when she heard a voice cry out in pain. She stood up and grabbed her axe before flinging her door open. Her wolves took off down the hall and she followed. Laughter still echoed from the Great Hall behind her as the deep scream in front of her grew louder.

Vǫrðr and Shura halted just inside Rohan's door. They growled through bared teeth and their bodies stiffened, ready to attack. Ylva slid to a stop just between them and gasped at the scene inside.

Rohan stood with his sword in the air as though he wanted to strike, but his body wouldn't obey. Instead he slowly twisted with pain in his frozen stance. His skin burned red. He shook from the agony and effort of working against what paralyzed him.

"No!" Ylva screamed.

"You," a gravelly voice replied. It was a woman with dark hair and flaming eyes. She stood on the other side of Rohan. She twisted her hand and the prince went silent...then he fell to the ground.

Another scream stuck in Ylva's throat. Tears stung her eyes. Rohan lay so still, his face paled. Was he...? Ylva didn't even want to think the word.

Vǫrðr snarled louder. Shura snapped.

Ylva looked up from Rohan's lifeless body to the woman who was staring at her. "What have you done?" Ylva asked, clenching her fingers around the handle of her axe.

"Isn't it obvious?" Senka replied with a wicked sneer. "*Why* —that is the question you should have asked."

Ylva's terror and anguish turned to rage. She charged at the woman who held her hand up in the same way she had toward the prince—but whatever she attempted must have failed. Her eyes widened in shock as Ylva only drew closer. Ylva slashed her axe through the air. It sliced into the woman's collarbone. Ylva heard the crack. She pulled the axe backward ready for another attack.

The woman screeched as she touched the blood streaming out of her wound. "How?" She stumbled backward. Her mouth was agape in horror and her bottom lip quivered. She blinked. "This is impossible!" She snarled.

Ylva paused, taken aback by the woman's reaction and the sight of the black liquid now oozing over her chest and hands. It resembled the bleeding wounds of the Bardung soldiers they fought at the East Keep. The pieces clicked into place in Ylva's mind.

"You are her, the Priestess of Myrkr," Ylva barely whispered, pointing her axe at the woman. The priestess panted and stared at her own blood like it was the first time she had ever seen it.

"This cannot be," the priestess stammered. "This cannot be true!" She finally looked to Ylva. "I should have killed you myself."

"What?" Ylva asked.

The priestess began to walk toward Ylva with her eyes blazing brighter and wider. Her nostrils flared with each breath. "I should have known Ivar was too weak, that he would fail. I should have found you and your wolves and ripped your heart out with my own hands." Black blood began to spit from her mouth as she spoke.

Ylva's heart thumped. She backed away from the crazed woman. The room began to feel smaller and suffocating. "You are the woman Ivar spoke of. You drove him mad?" Ylva asked in disbelief. Everyone thought her uncle demented when he raved about a woman in his dreams. But what if he had been mad and yet still told the truth. Did it matter now? There was no defense for his choices. The priestess merely took advantage of his greed. But had it all been about *her*...about killing her?

The priestess lunged at Ylva trying to claw at her chest. Ylva deflected the woman's clumsy attack and kicked her backward. The priestess nearly tripped over the stones bordering the fire. Again she held out her arms like she was trying to manipulate some invisible weapon or force toward Ylva. Her hands quaked.

The priestess shrieked. "It is no matter!" she hissed. "You will not stop me. Whatever a prophecy may say. I am Senka, Priestess of Myrkr, and I will see you die."

Vǫrðr and Shura flanked the priestess and waited for Ylva's next move.

Ylva spun her axe in her hand. "Not if I see you first," she said then leapt toward Senka to strike another blow.

The priestess snapped her fingers and her body burst into flame, dissolving into the fire. Drippings of her inky blood on the floor were all that remained of her intrusion. Except Rohan's still body.

Ylva hesitated to approach the prince. Her heart was already throbbing at the thought he might be dead. The wolves seemed equally hesitant. They took small cautious steps toward Rohan, sniffing as they went. Shura reached him first and nudged his arm with her nose. Nothing. Vǫrðr whimpered.

Ylva set her axe on the floor, kneeling beside Rohan. Her hand quivered as she reached to touch his colorless cheek. His skin was cool but not cold—not like the truly dead. Ylva moved her fingers to his lips, barely grazing the skin. She could feel the warmth of his breath. It was weak, shallow, but there. Hope filled her heart as she placed a palm on the prince's chest to feel for his heartbeat. It was also weak, a bit unsteady, but there. Rohan was alive.

"Thank Lys," Ylva whispered. She touched the prince's face again. "Rohan...Rohan," her voice got a bit louder with each repetition. "Rohan please wake up." The prince didn't budge, his eyes didn't so much as flutter. Ylva turned to the wolves, "Get Erland," she commanded and Vǫrðr took off out of the room while Shura lay beside her.

Senka nearly collapsed as her weak limbs regained their form by her fire side. She screamed. Her chest and hands were still covered, her dress soaked in blood. How had this happened? She was immortal, invincible. Humans could not kill her. They had never before so much as laid a hand on her and yet this...this mere *girl* sliced into her like she was nothing.

Others had come before, thinking they were special, trying to enact a forgotten piece of the prophecy that they were never meant to be a part of. Senka had made them all regret their pride. She had broken them, bone by bone and watched them writhe in agony. Ylva, however—this Wolf Queen, she was not to be trifled with. Senka's mistake had been in thinking Ylva was the same as the others. But Senka realized that Ylva did not yet understand her uniqueness. This would be Senka's way to victory. The girl did not know who she was, not truly, and Senka could destroy her before she found out.

"Come!" The priestess called for one of her servants.

One of the Bardung, a young man she had turned while

invading his village, entered the room. "Yes, Priestess." His voice was rough, having lost the softness of his humanity.

"Come closer to me," Senka said. As the boy approached, she forced herself to stand taller. She rubbed a hand through his hair. He had probably been someone the girls once thought handsome. Now he was just a cracked shell that leaked death and fear. "I need your help."

"Of course," he responded.

Senka smiled at him. Then she gripped his neck with one hand while her other pressed against his chest. Her fingers dug into the tattered fabric of his shirt and pierced the gray skin around his blackened heart. The boy balked against the pain. Senka watched the darkness ooze from his chest and slither along her arm, outlining her veins and dissolving beneath her skin. The boy jerked and seized as the power departed him. When it had all been exchanged, Senka let go and the boy's body fell to the floor. She stretched her shoulder back and her bone popped. Then the sinews and skin of her collar stitched back together until her wound disappeared.

CHAPTER TWENTY-TWO

"Y<small>LVA</small>!" She could hear Erland calling her name from down the corridor.

"I'm here!" Ylva called back. "In the prince's quarters."

"What happened?"

Ylva barely looked up from the prince to see Erland enter with Tyr. She felt afraid if she looked away too long or even moved her hands away from him, that she would find her hope was a false one and the breath imagined.

Erland crouched beside her and placed a hand on her shoulder. "Ylva, what happened?" he repeated softly.

"The Priestess of Myrkr." Ylva's mouth tasted of sand and salt as she replied. "She was here…she did something to Rohan. He is still alive, but barely."

"I'll call for the guards to go after her, she couldn't have gotten far," Tyr said.

"Don't bother." Ylva stopped him. "She didn't come and go through the door. Whatever magic brought her here has probably already returned her to Skämd."

"I'll call for the physician then and post guards at the door in case," Tyr said and then Ylva heard his footsteps exit.

"Are you all right?" Erland asked her.

"I am fine, brother," Ylva responded as though it were the complete truth. She wasn't injured but she wasn't fine. Anger and fear shook beneath the surface of her calm facade. "She is not human, Erland," Ylva said. "Senka, the Priestess—she is full of darkness. What she did to Rohan...she didn't even touch him."

"She is a new kind of enemy, that is all," Erland responded.

"Aye, and she is powerful but she is not invincible. I injured her."

"Good."

The day's light cast a soft glow through the window. The king's physician had come to see Rohan but there wasn't much he could do. Tyr had posted guards at the door. No one else knew what had happened to the prince. Ylva had agreed with Tyr that that would be best for the time being. Let them all think the prince suffered from fatigue and grief. They could buy themselves a few hours, possibly a day, before anyone would ask questions.

Ylva sat by Rohan's side the entire time, whispering prayers to Lys for him to wake. Her wolves lay at her feet sleeping. She was beginning to feel her own exhaustion calling her to slumber. She leaned forward and laid her head on the edge of the prince's bed to rest her eyes.

Ylva ran through the woods, her bare feet barely touching the damp ground. Her heart beat so hard inside her chest that it hurt. Her lungs burned. Tears stung her eyes the moment the door to her home came into view. The wolves who had been laying about in the spring sun jumped up when she drew close.

Ylva bolted past them and through the door, wanting to hide.

"Little one, what is the matter?" The voice spoke as two strong hands took hold of her shoulders stopping her in her tracks. Warm arms wrapped around her, pulling her close.

Ylva closed her eyes tight and snuggled into his chest. In his arms she felt her heart quiet and her breath steady. "I saw something," she whimpered.

"What could you have seen that would make you so upset?"

"It was a man in the woods," Ylva replied. "A hunter."

"You've seen those before," the man said. He rested his cheek against the top of her small head and rubbed her hair.

"Not like this!" Ylva pulled away as her mind replayed the image she had witnessed and the fear began to return. "He was different. His face looked gray and cracked like he was dead, his eyes were so dark. When I looked at him, I felt so much pain and fear. He was a monster!"

The man tucked a piece of Ylva's hair behind her ear and gently wiped the tears from her cheeks like he had done so many times before. He pulled her onto his lap and smiled.

She could see his smile, the curve of his mouth and the brightness of his eyes. His identity was right there—so close she could grab it...yet when her mind made the reach it would blur again.

"He was no monster," the man said. "Just a man."

"But he didn't look like a man!" Ylva contested.

"Men are more than what they appear on the outside, little one. Some are good and bright—some are twisted by darkness. It seems to me, the man you saw was someone who let too much of that darkness in."

"But if that was what was inside, how could I see it?" Ylva asked. She had never experienced such a thing before. She didn't want to ever again.

"You have a gift, little one," he replied. "You are like the wolves—you can see into the hearts of men. It is a blessing from Lys."

"I don't want it," Ylva said. It didn't feel like a blessing. What she had witnessed made her stomach churn and her insides tumble. "It's too scary."

"Oh, now, don't be afraid. I know this is a big gift for such a young girl. I know you are ready. You need not fear it. Fear is what the Darkness wants."

Ylva leaned on his shoulder. "It's hard not to be afraid."

"It is," he said and wrapped his arms around her again. "You must remember that fear will always come, Myrkr will always use it against you...but you get to choose. You can always defeat it. When it tries to take your power, you must take its instead."

"How do I do that?"

"With truth and love and light. Fear can't stand those things. So you pick them up and wield them like your axe."

"I'm not good at wielding my axe," Ylva answered.

The man laughed. It was a deep sound that rung with utter happiness. "You will get better at both with practice."

Ylva felt better. When the man spoke, she always felt better. Not because she always understood or even liked what he had to say—but because she trusted him. He always only did what was best for her. Right now she wasn't sure she could do what he described—but she knew he would always help her. It was a deep knowing...in her marrow and bones.

Ylva sat up as another question popped into her mind. "Why did Lys give me this gift? Does everyone have it?"

"No, not everyone can see what you can. You are special, little one...very special."

Ylva felt something brush against the back of her hand. She yawned and blinked as she slowly sat up. When sleep cleared from her eyes she saw Rohan's hand on hers.

"I didn't mean to wake you." The prince's whisper sounded scratchy and weak.

Ylva wrapped his fingers in hers. "I'm glad you did. I'm glad to see you awake." Ylva could hear the relief in her own voice. She could feel it, like a cleansing breath through her whole body.

"Was the Wolf Queen worried about me?" Rohan's chapped lips curled into a smirk.

"Only a little," she returned the jest.

Rohan's face turned more grim. "It was Myrkr's priestess," he said.

"I know," Ylva replied. "The wolves knew…they tried to tell me, but I…if I had come sooner…"

"You came, that was enough." Rohan squeezed her hand. "I'm just glad you didn't get hurt as well."

"I'm not sure how I didn't," Ylva said.

"What do you mean?"

"Whatever she did to you she tried to do to me—at least I think she did. I don't really understand how she was able to…" Ylva couldn't wrap her mind around the power Senka held.

"I know, she was strong. Whatever sorcery she is capable of is formidable," Rohan said as he attempted to sit up. "She wanted me to form an alliance with her."

"I take it you declined," Ylva managed to reply dryly, working to prevent the upward curling of her lips from reaching a full-blown smile.

"She didn't like being told no." The prince chuckled and rubbed a hand over his chest. "My heart felt the brunt of her dislike."

"If it's any consolation, I took an axe to her collarbone."

"That does help a little," Rohan said, laughing again followed by a wince.

Ylva wanted to stay in this space. It felt light here. They weren't saying everything they feared. "It should have killed her." Ylva's words betrayed her desires. "That blow, the amount of blood she lost…it should have been enough for her to at least lose consciousness."

"We knew she wouldn't be so easy to kill," Rohan answered.

He was right. Ylva knew it was the truth but knowing it and seeing it firsthand differed vastly. When it was kept at a distance, she could pretend things weren't so dire.

Rohan turned Ylva's face toward his with his thumb on her chin. "She's not easy to kill, just like her dragon," he said, "but that doesn't mean she can't be killed. There must be a way."

A fierceness underscored his gaze. Ylva could swear it was solely for her, to offer her strength and courage where her's waned. "When it tries to take your power, you must take its instead," Ylva muttered the words under her breath.

"What?" Rohan asked.

"Just something from a dream…or memory." Ylva was still confused.

"You were dreaming when I woke," Rohan said. "I could tell."

"I've been dreaming a lot lately, strange dreams."

"Strange? How?"

Ylva wasn't sure she wanted to talk about this. Would he think *her* even more strange? Was she willing to risk it? She came with so much peculiarity already.

"I promise I only want to help, to listen," Rohan replied. Could he read her mind or had her face offered the questions her mouth dared not ask?

Ylva took a deep breath then exhaled, trying to pull her thoughts together. "It began at the same time as when we first heard word of the dragon. I have these dreams but they aren't normal—they feel different. It feels as though my mind is trying to remember something…someone…but it's never clear."

"Memories of what?"

"When I was a child...living with the wolves," Ylva answered. "I remember my time as a young girl. I remember the wolves and the cave and the forest, but...it's like there are holes in my memory. Now these dreams are trying to fill them."

Ylva waited for Rohan to speak. She waited for him to tell her she was crazy—that she was just dreaming and it all meant nothing. She watched him contemplate her words. The silence was excruciating.

"I'm sorry," Ylva blurted out. "I shouldn't have said anything. I know it sounds ridiculous—"

"It doesn't," Rohan interrupted. "It doesn't sound ridiculous at all."

"How can you say that?" Ylva inquired.

"First of all, you are the least ridiculous person I have ever met," the prince said as he smiled. "Second, I don't think anything happening right now is coincidence. If you're having these dreams now, then they must mean something."

"But what?" Ylva responded. "It feels like they are lessons I've already learned...but are now coming back to me but from a different place than I remember."

"Perhaps the purpose of these dreams is to direct your mind's attention, trying to remind you of things that now need your focus. Or maybe..." Rohan paused for a moment. "Maybe they are memories that weren't important until now. Maybe now the holes need to be filled."

Ylva could sense it, the same feeling from her dreams, the one that held her perched at the precipice of revelation...but she just hadn't fully arrived there yet. She would gladly take a leap of faith and believe that her visions held meaning—that there was something to it all—but she didn't know into which direction to jump. She still couldn't see a small, yet vital missing piece. When she found it, she believed everything would fall into place—the picture would clear and Ylva would understand in due time.

"Thank you," was all that Ylva whispered to the prince in spite of her abundant thoughts.

Rohan picked her hand up and brought her knuckles to his lips. "I am the one who is grateful to you," he whispered.

CHAPTER TWENTY-THREE

IT HAD BEEN two days since King Vakr's burial—two days since
the priestess invaded the palace. Rohan worked not to let her
invade his mind with worry. She tried. Her words knocked at his
mind's door, whispering of his fear and weakness. It was a near
constant battle to keep them outside. But he had spent enough
time thinking of how unworthy he was to follow in his father's
footsteps. It was all no longer speculation but a blaring reality.
For a brief moment as Rohan sat in the Great Hall listening to
the clan leaders and delegates debate his capacity, he thought it
would be a relief if they refused him as their ruler. He was the
only one with birth rights to the kingship but according to law he
must still be accepted by the free men in the Taking. If they saw
in him what he saw in himself, then they would surely deny him
the crown.

Rohan leaned back in his chair listening to the clamor of
voices; clan leaders from the Northlands, delegates and ship
merchants from Kunnigstad and land owners from Ostlund. They
all were weighing and measuring him—he could do nothing but
listen and wait.

"Rohan is a fine young man, but he is young," one man said.

"Perhaps too young," another added. "What does he know of the world?"

"He has never even seen battle," someone called from the back of the hall.

"That isn't true," one of the military commanders retorted. "I saw him fight the Bardung at the East Keep. He was valiant and strong."

Muttering circled the room as the occupants exchanged details, affirmations and questions. Rohan twitched in his seat. He wasn't sure if he wanted to concede to their doubts or defend himself. He could do neither. The rules of order meant that he could not speak on his own behalf. He could only listen and wait. It was excruciating, particularly since all the while Senka's voice knocked.

"Whether or not the prince can fight is secondary to whether he can lead," one of the clan leaders shouted. This caused the room to quiet. "The dragon has returned, we have all heard news of the army in the valley. We need a king who is wise, who can secure victory."

The hall erupted again. For every voice that affirmed Rohan, there was another who presented valid concerns. There was so much noise—both inside and outside of his own head— that he couldn't decipher the truth. He was realizing that had always been the case. He was never able to find the right thread to hold onto. He was just pulling at strings, trying to look the part for everyone else. He wanted to run. Rohan himself felt ill-equipped for the war they were facing. He longed for nothing more than to ask his father what to do. Vakr would have known.

"May I speak?" Ylva's voice broke free from the chaos. Rohan looked up to see her standing in the center of the assembly. Her wolves lay at her feet, a constant reminder that she was no ordinary woman.

The noise in the room dulled to a whisper.

"It was not long ago that I myself would have doubted the prince," she said. "I had never given much thought to a king but he didn't seem like one, to be sure. I have also seen the army in Askadalen in all its terror. So I know what you are thinking and feeling. But I have seen Rohan face the Bardung and fight the dragon. I have watched him place the responsibility of this war on his shoulders and he has carried it with honor. None of us can know the future, what Lys has in store or how we will defeat our enemy. None of us can say that we are more capable than the prince. The kingship of Väljalil is Rohan's by birthright and I for one see no reason to refuse it. I have faith in the prince."

She mesmerized Rohan as she stood confidently surrounded by men. The delegates and merchants, who knew nothing of her, watched her with doubt or contempt. The clan leaders, who had faced her in battle, looked at her with respect.

One of them, Ull, stood. "I agree with the Wolf Queen," he said with a nod to her and to the prince.

"As do I," Dagr of the Fell concurred.

Others followed suit until nearly the entire room stood to its feet. Rohan still felt unworthy, not of their approval, but of Ylva's. Before, when they had first met, he would have envied her influence and the esteem they gave her—a jealousy founded in fear and ignorance. But now he knew her. He knew her intentions were pure. Any power she wielded in the Northlands was not of her asking. Leadership was born of her character. If *this* woman saw something in him worthy of faith, then certainly he too could find a little faith in himself. Couldn't he?

"We have talked enough," Ull said. "Let us proceed to the Taking and settle the matter once and for all."

"Aye," the gathering echoed.

. . .

The Taking was a sacred matter. The courtyard had been prepared according to the tradition of their ancestors. The great stone seat had been placed at the center. All the leaders from the assembly entered in a straight line. Each held a torch—one by one, they walked to the fire until it blazed. Then they formed a circle, surrounding the stone seat. No one spoke. No one looked around. The dancing torch flames cast shadows about. The stars flickered overhead while the new moon bore witness. When the circle closed, Rohan took his place in front of the seat.

Håkon, the eldest of the holy men stood before him. "Who accepts Rohan as King of Väljalil?"

One by one, the free men stepped forward, raised their torch and spoke. "I accept Rohan." The phrase went on repeatedly, like an audible wave rippling around the courtyard.

With each pronouncement, Rohan expected his insecurity to lessen. In a way it did, but he was also coming to realize that standing amongst these men, it was not their approval he needed. He looked at each of them and knew their voices could never be enough. Then he saw Ylva.

Just like with the stones at Vakr's funeral, she was last to give her vote of affirmation. Her eyes made contact with Rohan's. She didn't falter as she stepped forward, raised her torch and said, "I accept Rohan."

His heart seemed to grow, thumping harder against his chest. He stood a bit taller. Everything and everyone around him became a blur except for Ylva. Still looking only at her, Rohan felt like he could do anything...even be king. She raised her fist to her chest. The others did the same and the gesture made a noise like a solitary drum beat. The rest of the world came back into focus.

Håkon placed a fur cloak around Rohan's shoulders. The elder then handed him his father's sword. Rohan studied it for a moment. He rarely saw his father without it. As a boy he had snuck into his father's room while the king was sleeping...just to hold it. It had felt so heavy then. It still felt heavy but for different reasons.

"Take your seat," Håkon said.

The great stone chair had been carved generations ago, covered in runes that read of honor and sacrifice. It was weathered now, but when Rohan sat upon it he felt its power all the same. It wrapped around him from the inside out.

"Rohan, son of Vakr," Håkon said as he lifted a golden helmet in the air, "swear to rule with humility, to enact justice, to be merciful to your people as Lys is merciful to you."

Rohan took a deep breath. "I swear."

Håkon placed the helmet on his head then turned toward the audience. "I give you Rohan, King of Väljalil!"

The free men roared with cheer.

Rohan didn't feel very different. Was he supposed to? The fear still hovered there, cawing like ravens in the distance. *Wait,* he realized, *those are actual ravens.*

Rohan looked up. A flock of the black birds circled above. As soon as he saw them, one swooped down toward his head. He looked at Ylva wondering if she had seen them too. She had, as had Vǫrðr and Shura who stood beside her—their hair on end as they growled at the night sky.

"Well, well, well..." a seductive voice thundered. The free men looked around, afraid and confused because no body accompanied the voice. "Was I not invited? Am I not one of the leaders of the realm? Do I not rule the High Mountain?"

"You are not welcome here, Priestess," Rohan shouted at the sky as he stood to his feet. His sword held at the ready but the memory of his last encounter with Senka made his hand shake.

"It is no matter. I do not accept you, Rohan." Her voice boomed louder and the ravens squawked.

Ylva stepped beside Rohan, her shoulder brushing against his. Her wolves stood on either side with their teeth bared and bodies ready to lunge.

"I accept no ruler but Myrkr. He will meet this king, Rohan of Väljalil, and his army in the Valley of Ash to take his throne." At Senka's last word, the fire along with all of the torch flames blazed higher and hotter.

In an instant, the fires died back down. The ravens disappeared. All fell silent.

CHAPTER TWENTY-FOUR

YLVA'S WOLVES fidgeted at her feet. They could sense the fear carried around in the murmurs of her countrymen. For the third time in less days, they were all gathered in the Great Hall of Castle Grålås. It should have been a celebration of the coronation —instead, it had turned into a war council. Occasionally someone would shout a call to arms—a call to raid the ruins. Another voice would argue the absurdity in that.

"We should all go home," a clan leader from the Northlands said. "The Darkness is in the valley. We should let it alone."

"It is not just in the valley," Dagr retorted. "The Darkness has already come to the Northlands."

"And to Ostlund," one of the farmers added.

"It is moving slow, biding its time," Dagr continued, "but the dragon has risen now. It will not be long before it comes for us all. It will not stop!"

"He's right." Rohan stood at the front of the room. He still wore the fur cloak of his father. The king's sword was in one hand and the golden helmet in the other. It occurred to Ylva that he somehow now looked taller. "We cannot wait until the priestess and her army are at full strength. They have already attacked outlying villages and the East Keep. They are formidable enough as they are. To wait would be to our detriment."

"How do we fight them, Your Highness?" One of the military commanders asked. "I was at the East Keep. The Bardung are nearly unkillable."

"Nearly," Rohan replied, "but they can be killed. A sword through the heart takes them down." He glanced in Ylva's direction.

"What about the dragon?"

Rohan paused. He looked like he was counting his words, playing them through his head before speaking. Ylva knew he had no real answer to that question. While they hadn't come close enough to the dragon to be sure of anything, they could still recognize the unthinkable strength of the beast. Killing it would not come easily.

"I have seen the dragon," Rohan said. "Ylva and I encountered it on the way to Kunnigstad. We were able to wound it. If it can be wounded, then it can be killed."

"But you don't know how?" Ylva couldn't keep track of who was asking the questions. It didn't matter—everyone wanted to know.

"No, I don't." As soon as the words left Rohan's mouth, the crowd returned to its anxious whispers.

"Quiet now," Tyr said as he stood beside Rohan. "Panic is not the way to proceed."

"Tyr is right," Rohan said. "I know you are afraid. Senka is powerful. The dragon is fearsome. But we must not lose hope."

"Hope? In what?" A delegate shouted.

"In Lys," Ull said, stamping his walking stick on the floor. "Lys will not abandon us to fight Myrkr alone."

One of the merchants laughed. "Come now old man, where was Lys the last time the priestess rose?"

Håkon, who had been seated next to Ylva, stood to his feet

and replied, "I know there are many among you who do not believe in the old ways, no matter—you don't have to believe in order for them to be true. I don't know why our ancestors were unable to destroy the priestess before. But their failure doesn't have to be ours. We must fight the Bardung. We must try or we will all fail—and this time there will be no walking away for any of us."

"He is right," Rohan said. "The Darkness means to cover the whole of Väljalil. Senka will not rest until we are all destroyed or turned. If we wait, we are sealing our own dark fate. We cannot let fear control us or stop us—that is what the Darkness wants. We must fight it and we must do it together."

Ylva watched Rohan stand before the gathering just as he had on the night at the North Keep, the first night they had met. But this was not the same man. This was not the anxious prince trying to win their approval. This was no boy trying to play the part. She knew he was afraid, as they all were. She could see the insecurities pricking at his mind each time his jaw clenched. He fended them off with a strength that had been hiding away in his heart. Ylva could see it now.

When emotions ran high, it became hard for her to stifle her gift. Without trying, the reality of men's hearts would flash to the surface of her mind's eye. Looking around, she saw the deeper places where emotion and experience mixed with faith and skepticism. A picture was being painted of this moment in these men's souls. In a room full of the murky grey of trepidation, Rohan's heart shone as a bright light. She could still see the Darkness trying to bleed its way in from the outskirts...but with each beat, Rohan pushed it back.

No, this was no longer, the boy-prince. Standing before her now, she saw the king. Ylva only wished he could see himself the way she could. Perhaps if he could see the grace and strength within himself, he would not have to fight so hard against the self-doubt that plagued him.

"We will meet on the edge of Askadalen in a fortnight," Rohan commanded. "Bring every able-bodied warrior. We will bring war to the Bardung and to their priestess!"

Fists pounded on the tables and against leather breastplates, echoing the deep grunts of affirmation from men who gained hope from their king. Men who found the confidence to do what must be done.

"Who's with me?" Rohan raised his sword into the air as he exuberantly shouted the question.

Everyone in the room stood. "We are with you!" The words resounded like thunder which rolled into the roar of a battle cry, one that had often been uttered though its truth usually forgotten. One that they needed to believe now more than ever.

"May the light lead us," Rohan shouted.

The assembly replied in one unified cry, "and the Darkness fear us!"

The clouds of a coming storm masked the dawning sun. The mood at Grålås hadn't much changed. Ylva could see it in every countenance she passed on her way down the corridors toward the castle doors. Hope was a fickle thing. It could flood in and yet just as quickly, flee like waves running from the shore. It remained present but its strength ebbed and flowed with the pull of the unknown and uncertain.

Yet the resolves within Väljalil had not waned. The clan leaders and ranking free men all headed home to ready for war. Determination and a bit of faith peeked through the gray like thin rays of sunshine. Ylva could feel a sort of energy crackling beneath the haze of concern. There was a fight in the people of Väljalil, one on the verge of emerging in force.

"Will you not come with us?" Dagr asked as he met Ylva in the already bustling courtyard.

"She has been called on a different path," Håkon answered for her. He smiled wide and it made his long beard move.

"I have missed you," Ylva said as she turned to her old friend. She took hold of his arm and kissed his leathery cheek.

"And I you," he replied. "But do not worry about the Ibharüng. We will gather the warriors and shield maidens and meet you in the valley." He patted her hand and they walked together to his horse.

Ylva felt torn. She missed her home and her people. She was their leader and should be the one to explain everything while offering them comfort and inspiration. "Perhaps it is better if I come home with you, I am—"

"You are right where you should be," Håkon interrupted her. "Lys has a plan for you and you must follow his leading. You cannot go backwards...only forward, my dear. Home will be there when you finish with this quest."

"I know I am to go on to the East Keep and then Askadalen now...but I don't fully understand why," Ylva said. When she had left Kunnigstad there was no thought of returning home to the Northlands—only to see this through. Everything felt different now. Vakr had died. Rohan was king. She was worried that if she didn't return today, then she may never see home again.

Ylva didn't like the taste of that fear—bitter on the back of her tongue. She wanted to spit it out but swallowed it down instead. To return with Håkon wasn't a bad thing—yet it would only delay and distract her. Her elder was right. She needed to keep moving forward if she was to be of any real help in defeating Senka.

"Answers to why are not always necessary, my dear," Håkon said. "If it is what you feel you *must* do, then do it. The full reason will come in due time. You are special. I have always said so. You were the one who discovered the weakness of the Bardung and perhaps your insight will be needed to decipher how to slay the dragon. In any case, I can assure you…you are more valuable here then you would be at home."

"I'm not sure if that makes me feel better or worse." Ylva chuckled. She helped Håkon onto his horse.

"A good leader is equal parts invaluable and expendable." He smiled down at her. "You have taught your people how to do what needs to be done. You go and do what you need now."

"I will," Ylva said. There was the smallest crack in her voice as emotion splashed over the top of the dam she had been using to keep the homesickness tucked safely inside.

"Take care of her, Erland," Håkon ordered.

"I always do," her faithful companion replied over her shoulder.

Vǫrðr and Shura yipped beside her as though offering their goodbyes. Ylva reached down and ruffled her hand through the fur on top of their heads. "Come, we should prepare for our own departure," she said.

"Already done," Rohan replied as he walked to meet them, leading their horses behind him. A bright smile lit his face. The dark circles and pale skin that had been in evidence since his encounter with the priestess were now gone.

"You look well, Your Highness," Erland said as he took his horse's reins from the king.

"It is a new day," Rohan responded.

"That it is," Ylva said moving closer to Rohan. "Are you sure you should go with us?" She asked in a hushed tone so that only he could hear her question. "I am sure you have responsibilities here now."

"My greatest responsibility is to guard this realm," the king answered. "Tyr can handle the incidentals in the meantime."

"You could wait a few days, meet us in the valley with the others." Ylva wondered if he needed a bit more time after the whirlwind of the past week and the loss of his father.

"I remember someone once saying we shouldn't wait for the

Darkness. Instead, we should go to it and make it regret its plans." Rohan winked at her and then mounted his horse.

"Yes, I remember that too," Ylva replied getting on her mare. "She was very smart."

"She has her moments," the king replied.

The three of them trotted out of Grålås toward the East Keep with the wolves not far behind.

CHAPTER TWENTY-FIVE

A LIGHT RAIN misted overhead as they reached the East Keep. Ylva was grateful they had been able to avoid stronger storms. The heavy clouds that loomed over them the entire ride suggested they wouldn't have such luck. She would have fully ignored their ominous tone but riding through the massive gate of the Keep's tower, it seemed as though the darkness was not just about the weather.

Ylva's last visit to the East Keep lacked much joy but it was worse this time. Street vendors had all but disappeared, substituted with the displaced who sat clumped around small fires— their meager belongings laying in the mud. The atmosphere was more solemn with the abundance of glassy eyes and downturned mouths.

"Is it possible it is worse here than before?" Rohan asked.

An old woman coughed as they rode past her. Her face covered by dirt and she looked weak, as though she hadn't eaten in days. "I didn't think it could get worse but…" Ylva said. Then she blinked: the woman's peachy flesh began to turn. Using her Sight, Ylva could see the grey of death creeping up her neck, shrouding her last remnants of life.

"...this isn't natural," Ylva said shaking her head, as though she was emerging from a daydream.

"What do you see?" Rohan gazed hard at his subjects, squinting his eyes like he was trying to look past reality into what Ylva could see.

"This isn't natural," Ylva repeated. "It's not like anything I've seen before. It's like a disease...an infection that is spreading."

"I don't like the sound of that." Rohan adjusted his seat as he turned toward the barracks. The Keep's commander was already coming out to meet them before they dismounted.

"What news do you have?" The king asked him.

"I only just returned myself," the commander answered. "There has been no news from the spies sent to the High Mountain, but my men said more and more refugees have been flooding in."

"As we can see," Rohan said.

"Some are sick. We don't have enough shelter for them, which is why they are camped in the streets. We are lacking the food and supplies necessary for this many people," the commander reported. "What we had on hand is now severely depleted."

"Send a falcon to Grålås," Rohan told him. "Tell Tyr I am requesting more supplies to be sent immediately. As much as is possible and quickly."

"Yes, Highness." The commander nodded. "Right away. The inn is full so I have made arrangements for you three here in the barracks."

"Thank you," Rohan responded. "I'd like to be notified as soon as the spies return."

The commander nodded again and then left to do as he had been told.

"I will go see if there is anything I can do to help," Erland said.

"Go," Ylva replied, and Erland followed after the commander. "Perhaps we should do the same," Ylva said to Rohan.

The king agreed and the two began to walk back down the street. The king helped to stoke dying fires. Ylva gathered water to distribute. It didn't seem like enough. These people needed food.

A woman, probably about Ylva's age, sat with a baby in her arms. The tiny being squirmed and fussed. The woman whispered and cooed to the child, trying to ease its distress. A little boy sat next to her. His hair matted and his face was dirty. His eyes widened with delight at the sight of Vǫrðr and Shura.

"You can pet them," Ylva whispered, "but carefully."

He smiled and reached out to the black wolf. Vǫrðr bent his head down and under the boy's hand. Shura joined in with a lick to the child's face. The boy squealed with delight. For a moment, his mother smiled. This caused the grey creeping over her to shrink back.

"They don't just need food for their bodies, but for their souls," a kind voice said.

Ylva turned around. Elior stood behind her with a basket of bread and root vegetables. He still wore only his linen tunic and pants. His feet were caked in mud. But his smile was large. "You look well," Ylva said. He did. In the midst of the sadness and pain, he was this spark of joy that spread out to those around him like firelight in a dark room.

Elior directed his smile toward her. "I enjoy serving others," he said as he began to hand out small amounts of the food he had carried. He touched the faces of those in need and called them by name like he had known them their whole lives. He asked about their day. He encouraged them that tomorrow would be better. He took out a damp cloth and wiped foreheads and cheeks as he whispered prayers to Lys on their behalf.

"Elior." Rohan joined them. His back straightened and his shoulders tensed.

"Highness." Elior dipped his head in a slight bow. "I am sorry about your father." The way the servant looked at Rohan made Ylva wonder what he was really thinking. It wasn't that his words seemed untrue—it seemed there was more to be deciphered in the breaths between them.

"It appears you've had quite a lot of work here," Rohan said.

"Ah, yes." Elior went back to his tending. "That is certain. More come, several each day, and more in each group suffering with sickness."

"What do you think is infecting them?" The king asked.

"It is hard to say. Hunger and cold make breeding grounds for all kinds of nasty ailments," Elior replied. "Some seem to be more heart-sick than anything else."

"Heart-sick?" Ylva questioned.

"I don't mean love lorn if that is what you are thinking." Elior chuckled. "But despair can be as infectious and deadly as anything else."

"That is *all* you think it is? Despair?" Ylva asked.

"Is that all *you* think it is?" Elior asked her.

"No," Ylva's reply wasn't much more than a mutter.

Elior didn't respond but his smile changed. His eyes narrowed and he looked at her as though he thought she knew something. Could he sense what her Gift allowed her to see? Was he more aware of the supernatural than most?

"What can be done?" Ylva asked him.

"Nothing...everything," Elior answered.

"That's helpful." Rohan rolled his eyes.

Ylva gave the king a quick glance in an effort to quiet his growing impatience. She turned back to Elior, crouching down beside him. "Can't you just heal them, like you healed me?"

The servant paused in his work, wiping a feverish sweat from an old man's brow. "I have for some, those I could," he replied. "Healing isn't easily replicated for the masses. Some sickness is not really sickness at all, which complicates things further. In those cases, healing has as much to do with their will as my own."

Elior returned his attention back to the elderly man. Ylva watched him intently. She didn't understand all that he meant. But he seemed to care so deeply for these people that she was sure he wasn't intentionally withholding something from them.

"Let me help," Ylva said. She knelt beside Elior and the elderly patient. She drew a ladle full of water from the bucket she had with her and held it to the old man's lips for him to drink.

"Thank you," Elior said, his hand resting on Ylva's shoulder.

Rohan cleared his throat. Ylva looked at him over her shoulder. His cheeks were flushed.

"Are you feeling all right?" Ylva asked him.

"Fine." Rohan's answer was sharp. "I should confer with the commander." He walked away before Ylva could say anything else.

"The king does not seem himself," Elior said. "Is something the matter?"

"I don't know," Ylva replied.

"He has a lot on his mind, I am sure."

"Yes…of course." Ylva knew the past several days had been a burden on Rohan. He could hardly focus on the grief of losing his father before immediately undertaking the mantle of a king on the brink of war. She would like to think his sudden mood was unlike him, but she reminded herself she really didn't know him well enough to say. Did she? Was there something else, something she still wasn't sure she wanted to suspect? If she didn't know better, she would think Rohan was once again acting jealous. Of Elior? She laughed to herself in an effort to ignore the flutter in her stomach.

Ylva focused her mind on helping Elior amongst the refugees until long after the sun set. Walking back to the barracks, she couldn't distract her thoughts from meandering toward Rohan. "I wonder where he is?" Ylva muttered.

Shura yipped and lifted her head and ears.

"That's not a challenge," Ylva told the dogs who replied with a grumble. "Fine," she told them, "help me find the king."

Both dogs tilted their noses upward and sniffed at the air. Vǫrðr then bent down to smell the ground. It only took a few seconds before the wolves caught a scent. They trotted down a corridor and up a set of back stairs to the top of a tower. Ylva followed not far behind.

Rohan was leaning against the stone wall, staring across the darkened landscape toward the valley. He only averted his gaze from it long enough to glance at Vǫrðr and Shura who laid down at his feet. "Since when do they like me?" he asked.

He hadn't looked for Ylva but he must have known she was there. "Since the dragon, I think," she replied. Almost on cue, a faint shriek echoed from the mountain. Ylva shivered.

"If the spies do not return…"

"They will." Ylva stood beside the king, placing a hand on his forearm. She wanted to offer him some comfort, some assurance.

"I hope you are right, and I hope they come with information we can use." Rohan stood up straight and ran his hands through his hair and over his neck, stretching his back.

"You are worried."

"Shouldn't I be?" Rohan finally looked at her. Dark circles formed under his eyes and his brow creased. "The armies of Väljalil are gathering at the edge of Askadalen in two weeks. I have no strategy to offer them except to charge headlong to their deaths."

"Those armies would rather give their lives in battle, sword in hand and faces splattered with the blood of their enemies, than to sit and wait for death to steal them away," Ylva said. "And just because you don't have a plan now doesn't mean you won't have one when the time comes. There *is* still time."

"Not enough, I fear." The king grew quiet. His gaze looked far off again. It seemed to Ylva as though his thoughts had followed.

The silence between them felt charged. She wanted to say something, to break it, to bring back the ease that had grown between them. Her mind was so full of the faces of the sick, Senka and the dragon—but she didn't want to talk about those things. She didn't want to give anymore voice to the crisis they faced...not now. For now she wanted a few moments of life without war and worry, but couldn't find a piece of it solid enough to offer it to the king. Instead, she just stood beside him and stared out into the night.

Rohan's voice split the stillness. "Why are you here?"

Ylva wasn't quite sure what he meant. The hint of desperation in his tone made her nerves stand on end.

"Why did you come with me?" His eyes moved back and forth over her's, like they were searching for her answer before she could speak it.

"Because Lys pushed me onward," Ylva replied. Rohan looked away from her and she could tell he didn't like her answer.

"So it was only for Lys?" He muttered the question more toward his feet than to Ylva.

"Few things in life are so linear, so simple," Ylva replied. She reached and pulled his face to look at hers. "You asked me to come with you, that first night in the North Keep—so here I am. I will be with you until we have seen this through." She stroked his jaw with her thumb. "Not *just* for Lys."

"I don't know why I wanted you to come back then," Rohan admitted. "I think I was trying to prove something to you or myself, or everyone else."

"And now?"

"I still don't quite know but I am grateful you are here," he replied. It was another complete truth ringing in Ylva's ears. Rohan stepped forward, closing the already small gap between the two of them. He rested his calloused hand against Ylva's cheek. "I'd like to kiss you," he whispered. Ylva could feel his warm breath against her lips.

Ylva smiled at his question. "Is the king asking for permission?"

"No." His voice was suddenly rougher. "Rohan is."

"In that case..." She leaned into him, waiting for that moment of gentle contact. The whole world slowed down. To move just an inch had become a painstaking voyage over uncharted waters. Ylva had never kissed a man before. The tingle on her skin brought a wash of nerves and anticipation.

"Highness." With the single word everything sped back up.

Ylva swallowed down the rush of the moment and pulled away from Rohan to see Erland standing at the top of the stairway. Heat flushed her cheeks.

Rohan coughed. "Yes, Erland. What is it?"

"Sorry to intrude," he replied, "but the spies have returned from Skämd."

CHAPTER TWENTY-SIX

YLVA FOLLOWED Rohan as he jogged down the steps, eager to see what the spies had learned of their enemy. She ignored Erland's raised eyebrow and cheeky smirk as she passed him. Her skin still held the residue of anxious expectation, its prickle only just beginning to fade.

Her mind changed paths from imaginings of the coming kiss to intrigue of the spies' news. She hoped they would have something to offer that would be of encouragement to the king.

Upon entering the commander's quarters, her hope splintered. There was no hum of information being passed, no bits of excitement to stoke the fires of passion for their cause. The commander looked aggrieved and the only stranger there, Ylva assumed him to be the awaited spy, could barely stand. Elior stood close by helping bear the man's weight so he would not fall.

"What news? Where are the others? Did you not send three men to the High Mountain?" Rohan asked his questions in rapid succession.

"There were three," the commander replied. "This man is the only one to return."

Rohan stared at the commander for a moment. His steely gaze softened before he turned to the spy. "What is your name," the king asked him.

"It is Leif, Highness." The spy's voice was weak and scratchy. Elior offered him some water. He sipped it.

"Tell me what happened," Rohan said. Ylva noted the gentleness in his voice. She knew the king had been waiting for this moment and needed something of substance to move forward with. If her hope had cracked, Rohan's looked to have shattered. Yet, with this frail man, Rohan offered a calm and tender expression.

"We made it to Skämd...all three of us," Leif responded. "We climbed the ruins and followed a path into the mountain, through corridors beneath the surface." He paused to take another sip of water. "There were many Bardung soldiers about, they were terrifying to look at, but we stayed hidden."

"You did well, then," Rohan said and smiled.

Leif looked down at his dirty fingers. "We knew we were getting close when we heard it." He shivered then continued, "The dragon. It was in a large cavern with the priestess. She spoke to it like it was her child or pet. It looked weak. She was hurt."

Rohan turned to look directly at Ylva, both recognizing the timing.

"Go on," Rohan told Leif.

"She called in one of the Bardung." Leif's voice cracked and tears glazed his eyes. "She killed him. Clawed right into his chest like she was going to pull out his heart." The spy's pitch changed and he spoke faster like he was reliving the fear and panic. "Her veins turned black—her wound began to heal. All the while the dragon looked to grow stronger. I swear that is what it looked like."

Leif began to cry. His lip quivering beneath the salty drips. It was not like a warrior of the realm to show such emotion in the presence of their commander and their king. Ylva knew the display meant the man's ordeal had been a horrible one. He needed comfort.

She stepped forward and took his hand and looked into his sad eyes. "You are safe now," she assured him.

Leif nodded. He sat himself up straighter and wiped his face with the back of his hand, smearing the dirt over his pale skin. Ylva noticed his extremely pale skin. She used her Sight to see the Darkness gripping his heart like a fist. It would squeeze tighter with every beat, pulsing like ink into his veins and dimming the colors of life to the gray that was becoming too common. Her stomach soured.

"What happened to you...and the others?" Ylva asked the spy.

He swallowed hard. "It was so shocking," he said, turning to Rohan. "Highness, we tried to stay calm, to remain strong, but...but..."

"I understand, Leif," Rohan replied. "You did nothing wrong. Tell us what happened next."

"Ander made a noise. He was trying to back away, he was so scared that he forgot where he was. He almost fell. It caused a small sound, but still, the dragon heard it and shrieked." Leif was speaking fast again. Ylva could see his heart beat faster and the Darkness grow with each anxious word. "We tried to get away but she saw us. She screamed—it didn't sound natural. We started to run. She barely moved—I swear she just lifted her hand and Ander stopped. Then he came up off the ground and crashed into the stone wall."

Ylva's Sight discerned a gray color now creeping up Leif's neck and down his fingers. She wanted to silence him...but it would do no good. It wasn't his words that harmed him.

"She did the same to Den. I wanted to help them—"

"You couldn't have," Ylva interrupted him. "You escaped so that you could complete your mission. That is honorable."

"Yes," Rohan agreed. He turned away and paced the room.

"I think she did something to me," Leif whispered to Ylva.

"What do you mean?" Ylva asked.

"When I was running away, she yelled something to me." His hand began to shake. Ylva squeezed it. "She said I would be hers, then I felt something—it was like claws dug into my back and my chest felt tight. For a minute I could barely breathe. Now I feel sick."

"Sick?" Rohan turned back round to Leif, but his eyes were set on Ylva.

With a grave glance toward him, she confirmed for Rohan all he needed to know. Whatever infected Leif was the same thing she saw in the refugees lining the streets. Senka had been in their villages. Those she couldn't grip tight and take with her, she still tried to sway from the inside out. Not all, but enough.

"It is with the Darkness, is it not?" Elior asked. Ylva guessed he already knew the answer.

"It will grow in him, pulling him back to her unless he can be rid of it," she agreed.

"Heal him," Rohan ordered.

"This, this I cannot," Elior replied to the king. Ylva found it peculiar that joy never fully left his eyes even amid a somber expression.

"What do you mean? Is it you can't or you won't?" Rohan's voice raised a hair. His tone grew angrier though Ylva could see him making the effort not to lose his temper.

"I told you before, Highness, this kind of sickness is as much about one's will as it is about the body. This isn't a disease. It's not an illness that cripples the flesh or the mind. This is an infection of the soul. It is Lys and Myrkr at war. In the battle between Light and Darkness, man's greatest weakness and weapon is his ability to choose."

"I am not choosing to feel this way," Leif argued. He tried to stand on his own but swayed a bit. Elior stabilized him with an arm around his back and a shoulder to lean on.

"I know, son," Elior told him, "but you are not choosing to release it either. The Darkness is gripping all of your memories tightly—the moments of your pain and bitterness. It's using them to keep hold of you. It will do so for as long as you allow it."

"Then how do I release it?" Leif trembled as he asked.

"I can help you," Elior answered. "You are already doing an admirable job of pushing against the Darkness and preventing its complete hold. Now you must find the thoughts you can hope in and focus on them."

"This is nonsense," Rohan growled. He pounded his fist on the table.

Vǫrðr and Shura barked.

"Rohan!" Ylva reprimanded. She knew he had been walking close to the line of frustration but anger would do no good.

"I can't say nothing!" Rohan countered. "This man is dying, others are dying! What kind of healer are you if you can't help them," he asked Elior. "You say you have a gift—use it!"

"I will do all I can," Elior promised. He helped Leif to his feet and the two left the room.

"Rohan." Ylva made an effort to soften her voice. "None of this is Elior's fault. He is not to blame."

"I don't blame him for what is happening. I blame him for justifying his own shortcomings with talk of Light and Darkness. He offers a meaningless hope."

"Hope is never meaningless." Ylva's pulse hastened as she spoke. She began to sweat…she might even cry. She bit her lip to quell unwanted tears and heightened emotions.

"I don't like him, Ylva. I know you do, but I don't." The color of Rohan's face returned to its earlier shade of red. "He speaks in riddles. It's tiresome. If he can't be of any real help, then he should return to the Keeper's and leave us be."

"He is helping," Ylva argued, "just because it isn't in the way you want—just because it isn't so cut, dry or easy—it doesn't mean that he isn't needed."

"We have different definitions of need," Rohan scoffed. "We *need* to defeat a dragon. Ylva, how can we do that if we can't stop the priestess's effect on one man? If we can't save him, Leif, can we save anyone at all?"

Something wasn't right. This was more than stress and concern. This reaction was darker though Ylva wasn't sure why. Perhaps he was such a mottled mix of Light and Dark that he was easily pushed from one side to the other. But Ylva saw it happening right in front of her eyes. She wanted to look away, to pretend that the brightness that had begun to take hold wasn't fading back to murky gray again. "You are a fickle thing, King Rohan," she said. "One moment you are all hope and light and the next you are clouded with doubt again. Lys—"

"Don't speak to me about Lys," Rohan cut in. "I do not see him anywhere."

Ylva tightened her hands into fists, her nails dug into the skin of her palms. Her chest rose and fell with hard angry breaths. "Look harder," she seethed, then brushed past Rohan and out the door with her wolves at her heels.

Ylva paced her small room arguing with herself about whether or not to go back. There were still things to discuss and plans to be made. She wasn't ready to face him again. Her mind and heart were a jumble of antithetical ramblings. Could you want to run to and away from someone at the same time? Had she been too hard on him given the circumstance? Had she started to give her heart away too quickly? Would his lack of faith always be at war with her unwavering convictions? Would it be impossible for them to move beyond?

Ylva wanted to scream. She didn't for fear of causing unwarranted alarm in the barracks. She hated not knowing what to do when it came to her personal, inward conflicts. She fought so hard to yield only to the Light and not allow confusion, loneliness or other hungry things to pull her off course. She needed Rohan to do the same. Ylva did not fear doubts, but she could not be the only one to fight them. For the sake of Väljalil, and her heart, she needed Rohan to see beyond them for himself.

Ylva plopped down on her cot. Vǫrðr laid his head in her lap and she scratched his ears. Shura licked her free hand and then nuzzled her head into Ylva's leg. Her wolves always brought her comfort. They were always faithful.

Ylva felt her energy wane. She yawned. "Maybe some much needed sleep will help us see things more clearly," Ylva told the dogs. She laid down, closed her eyes and whispered into the ether, "Help him to see you."

"Why do I have to go? Why can't I stay here?" Ylva whined.

"Because it is time," the man said as he tucked her stray hairs behind her ears. "You are ready. Your heart is ready."

She placed a small hand on his, holding his fingers tight. "You will come with me though."

"No, little one, not in the way you want me to." He snapped his fingers and two wolf pups, one black and one light grey, trotted to his feet. "The wolves will go with you."

"I don't want to be without *you*." She began to cry.

He hugged her like he always did. "You will never be without me. I will always be close."

Ylva huffed through her nose trying to calm herself enough to speak her shaky words. She could smell the sweetness of him. "Will I see you again then?"

"You will always be able to see me...if you look hard enough."

CHAPTER TWENTY-SEVEN

YLVA COULD SMELL something familiar while she dwelt in this world of visions. It was so strong it woke her from her dream and carried her back to reality. She opened her eyes and inhaled the sweet scent. What was it? It smelled like spice and flower mixed together into something new... something uncommon. It tricked her senses, drawing her backward into memory. Just as purple heather painted her imagination with visions of the mother she never knew, this scent sketched a picture of someone she thought she must have known once before.

Then the man's blurry face suddenly flashed bright in her mind. He made her feel safe. That was the only thing solid enough for her to hold. All the other details slipped and slid around. She couldn't grasp them long enough to make sense of any of it. She searched that past for clarity.

The cavern home where she lived as a child was real. She could visualize it and smell the mustiness of it. The wolves were real. She played with them. She snuggled against them for warmth. She ran through the forest with the wolf pups nipping at her heels. She was sure of all these things—certain that those same wolves had marched her back to the Ibharüng village.

She could picture it so clearly. Night was falling outside. The moon was full. The pack led her into the village, howling as they went. She thought the place strange and the people even stranger. They stood in their doorways and stared at her, entranced by fear or shock. It didn't occur to her then that she was the peculiar sight…a little girl with dirt on her face, surrounded by wild dogs.

The wolves led her to a man…a man named Ivar. He was tall and his beard was red. The closer she walked to him, the more his outward form faded away to reveal the Darkness within him. It was frightening to look at—so much anger and fear twisting through him like wild vines. They were thick and thorny and hid all the light as they crept from deep inside the chambers of his heart outward along the path of his veins. They got darker the closer she came toward him.

"Who are you?" he asked her. His body trembled and twitched with each word he spoke and each step she took. It struck her as odd—this large, ferocious man, quaking at the presence of a little girl.

"I am Ylva, daughter of Magnus," she replied to him.

She remembered saying the words with such boldness. Where had the confidence come from? She never even knew Magnus, her father, but she somehow knew those were the perfect words to speak in that moment.

If the ground had shook like Håkon tells it, Ylva didn't feel it. Something happened, however, because as she stared at Ivar, the Darkness within him shrieked. It shrank back like a pained animal. She felt nothing else, saw nothing else, but…but she smelled the spice and flowers like in her dream.

She hadn't remembered that before. Was it the man from her dreams? Was he there, had he been there all along? Suddenly a flurry of new faces and new voices had crashed into her life. Had they pushed him out? Could there have been someone with her all along and she merely lost sight of him? A piece had always been missing in her story, something between her and the wolves. Something or someone that had taught her, loved her, but she had ignored the defect in her recollection for so long. Could it now be calling out, begging her to remember? Why? Was this a ploy from Myrkr to distract her or a gift from Lys to strengthen her?

Ylva growled and turned over in bed, burying her face in the fur coverings. Trying to recall these buried memories exhausted her. She had told Rohan to look harder—but then she didn't want to herself. She didn't want to waste time with all this. Was it a waste of time? There were too many questions that she didn't have answers to.

Your heart is nearly ready.

Ylva sat up. She heard a voice as if someone was in the room with her. *Heart*...the sound, weight and depth of the word set a realization ablaze in her. Her spirit quickened. Something previously lost now flickered in her mind. It was no scheme of Darkness, of that she was sure.

CHAPTER TWENTY-EIGHT

"You are a fickle thing, King Rohan," Ylva said. "One moment you are all hope and light and the next you are clouded with doubt again. Lys—"

Rohan couldn't pretend he had faith. He wished he did—that he could be so sure as Ylva. He had tried and now felt too tired and fearful of what was coming to keep aimlessly proceeding. His patience with the Light...his hope in it now dwindled. "Don't speak to me about Lys," Rohan interrupted her. "I do not see him anywhere."

Ylva's eyes widened for a moment before squinting into a hard glare. "Look harder," she said through her clenched jaw before brushing past Rohan.

The king pounded his fist on the table again. He hit the wood so hard that his knuckles ached. His anger flared at Ylva, at her unwavering faith that made him feel unworthy. He was also angry at himself for losing his temper. He was mostly angry that she was right. Elior wasn't the problem—not for the reasons Rohan had scolded him anyway.

The commander cleared his throat. "What are your orders, Highness?"

Rohan stood straighter and adjusted his tunic and bracers before turning around to look at the two men still in the room. "We will ride out in the morning; we will travel the length of the Valley for a final reconnaissance of our enemy. Supplies should arrive from Grålås soon. See to it that they are distributed as needed. Then gather whatever soldiers the Keep can spare. Ready them for battle. You'll leave for the north side of the Valley in a week's time. We will meet you there."

"Aye." The commander bowed his head before exiting.

Only Erland stood with the king now. Rohan was hesitant to look at the man. Ylva called him brother—he would surely take her side. Rohan didn't want to argue further but sensed more was coming. The large Ibharüng warrior stared at him, his arms crossed over his chest with an eyebrow raised. "Say it," Rohan told him. "Scold me like your Wolf Queen."

"I'm not your nursemaid," Erland responded.

"But there is something you want to say?" Rohan asked.

Erland looked him up and down with only the slightest tilt of his head. "She sees something in you, though I can't imagine what it could be."

Erland stopped for a moment. Rohan wasn't sure if he was trying to visualize or just counting his words. The king shifted under the man's stare. He couldn't himself imagine what Ylva might value in him. There couldn't be much there to choose from.

"She has faith in you," Erland continued. "Highness, I don't pretend to be a man of wisdom, but I've learned that being a man requires faith. If you can't have it in yourself...if you can't have it in Lys, at least have it in her."

"Would that be enough for her?"

"No. I also doubt it'll be enough for you in the end, but I wager it'll be enough for now." Erland turned to leave.

"Why do you care?" Rohan asked, stopping him at the doorway. "I thought you didn't like me."

"I don't." Erland glanced back. "But I like her... and if the wolves have decided to stop trying to eat you, then I figure I can abide you a while longer too." He left. Rohan chuckled to himself at the sentiment.

Rohan felt the sudden emptiness of the room. The loneliness crept into the hollow and embraced him like an old friend. He had felt alone most of his life, even in crowds. It had become a state of being for him. People saw the prince, now the king—but they didn't see him. He hadn't realized that specter had retreated from him in recent days until its haunting presence returned.

But Ylva had seen him—the real him. Her company fought off his ghosts but they were not destroyed. Would he ever truly be rid of them?

He needed air. He needed to stand under the wide open space of the dark sky where he didn't feel the stale breath of his internal apparitions pressing on his lungs.

Outside, the streets were mostly quiet. Fires crackled. There was an occasional cough or rustle of an uncomfortable dreamer trying to hold onto sleep. But mostly it was quiet, peaceful. Rohan leaned against the outer wall of the barracks and closed his eyes, wanting to remain in that calm space. His mind clanked with doubts and fears. The ghosts of his insecurities didn't want to leave him alone...now he realized loneliness wasn't the only thing tormenting him. With it came phantoms wearing the faces of his father and mother.

His mother...she had been beautiful and bright and warm. She would sit by his bed and tell him stories of the Light. She would sing him songs about the Light. Her voice resounded like light itself—its melody pushed away all his fears. Then she fell sick and couldn't sing to him anymore. The Light didn't heal her. Then she was gone...the light went with her. Rohan had been so young, but old enough to feel betrayed by her faith.

"It's funny how memories work. The way things we forgot tend to slip in at the most peculiar times."

Rohan opened his eyes to find Elior standing in front of him. He was smiling. He was always smiling—somehow even when he wasn't smiling—and it was annoying. How could someone be so happy all the time?

"Excuse me?" Rohan straightened himself. The servant's words finally registered with the king. He spoke of memories like he knew Rohan's thoughts. He couldn't, could he?

Elior leaned against the wall beside Rohan. "Grief is a wily fox. You don't even realize the damage it has done until you are becoming undone."

"What are you talking about?" Rohan asked, his pulse was surging as if his heart was trying to keep up with his brain.

"Your mother...you were thinking about her just now." Elior spoke as though there was nothing to be shocked about in his words.

"How did you...?" Now Rohan's lungs were fighting to take in enough air to keep both his heart and brain from imploding under the strain.

"People say I am very intuitive," Elior replied.

Rohan looked away from the man. He wondered if he looked as unraveled on the outside as he was feeling on the inside.

"You have doubts, Highness." Elior's voice softened a touch, adding more care to his speech. "There is no alarm in doubt. But in my experience, no one holds so tightly to their doubts, when they have seen the things you have, without cause. Loss is as good of a cause as any—with the death of your father still so near, I bet that fox of grief has grown larger as he plays around in your mind."

Rohan stared at him but didn't speak. What would he say? How could a servant from Kunnigstad know such things? Who was this man to make him feel like this, as though his heart burned inside him?

"You don't trust me?" Elior asked.

"No, I don't."

"It's okay." Elior shrugged off the king's response.

"That doesn't bother you?"

Elior tried to hide his smile. "Oh, it stings," he answered. "I wish that you would trust me because I only want to help…but trust is difficult. I can't force it on you, just as you can't force it on me."

"You don't trust me?" Rohan scoffed.

"Should I?"

A defense hesitated on the tip of Rohan's tongue just waiting to be spouted off. It retreated when he looked into Elior's eyes. There was no jest, no offense hiding in them. In the pause, Rohan began to see the man's point. *Should* anyone trust him?

"Highness." Elior leaned in as he spoke, as if he had a secret. "It occurs to me that, if you want others to trust you, then you must first trust yourself."

Rohan didn't respond. Elior added, "Intuitive, remember?"

"Yes," Rohan answered—but it was a shaky admission at best. When it came to all things Elior, Rohan continued to feel a bevy of confusion.

"Pardon me, Highness, I should get back to Leif." Elior stood up and offered a bow to the king before leaving Rohan to aloneness once more.

Slowly the king's ghosts began to again circle his thoughts the way vultures hovered over a dying animal. He didn't know how to be rid of them. He wished he could simply swat them away. He thought of Elior's admonition to trust and Erland's to find some faith. He thought of Ylva and how someone so strong and good could come to stand at his side. He wished she was standing there now with him. The squabble which threatened to create a rift between them… he needed to mend it before it grew.

The fading echo of the dragon's shriek pierced through the quiet, reverberating in Rohan's ears as though the beast was suddenly upon him. His heart constricted, the pain nearly sending the king to his knees. He clutched his chest with one hand—he used the other to hold the wall and keep his balance. The ache felt the same as when Senka nearly killed him. He examined the dark streets expecting to see the priestess saunter towards him with a smirk. She did not appear. No one did.

As swiftly as the pain came, it departed just as quickly. Rohan inhaled, allowing his lungs to expand as far as they could. He wiped a teary residue from the corner of his eye. A voice— still and small in the back of his mind—whispered concerns of the pain that had just crippled him. *Tell someone.* Who would he tell? What could anyone do? It was probably nothing of consequence, just his ghosts toying with him. *Tell Ylva.* No, she could already discern his weaknesses. He couldn't give her more reason to doubt him.

He had spent too much time in his own thoughts this evening. He just needed sleep. Sleep...and everything would be brighter in the morning.

CHAPTER TWENTY-NINE

THE FIRELIGHT DANCED across the stone walls of Senka's lair in tandem with the shadowy silhouettes it created. The priestess stood, staring into the white-hot flames.

"The army is nearly ready," she spoke into the blaze.

The fire flared upward in a sinister response only Senka could decipher.

"More will come as the Darkness draws them," the priestess reassured.

This time the flames surged and popped, the intensity making Senka step just slightly backward. "I'm not worried about the king and his armies, my liege," she said. "They will never make it through the valley. They will never make it to the tower ruins or the High Mountain."

The fire blazed hotter and higher. Senka's cheek felt like it had been licked by the flames. She brought her hand to the sting. "I swear it." She focused on making her voice sound strong and sure. She wasn't worried about Rohan or some clansmen from the Northlands. She couldn't say the same for Ylva.

Senka rubbed her black fingers over her collarbone, tracing the path of previous injury. Her bones ached at the memory. The

Wolf Queen gave her pause. There was still time to break her, to find her weakness and exploit it. Senka already had plans in motion. Myrkr was at work behind the scenes and the priestess only needed enough time.

A high-pitched purr interrupted her scheming as the dragon awoke from its slumber. It uncurled from its dark corner, stretching its back like a cat, then slinking toward its master.

"Hello, my pet." Senka reached out. She stroked the beast's nose. "Are you hungry?"

The creature emitted a soft short growl in response.

"I thought you would be." Senka smiled. She stepped round the fire toward her decayed stone throne and retrieved a small wooden chest. Returning to the dragon, she opened the box's lid. Inside she found a cold heart. It was shriveled and black. The tiniest bit of inky blood oozed from it as the priestess picked it up and offered it to her dragon. The creature took it gently from her open palm and nearly swallowed it whole. It was amazing how such a tiny thing could satiate the hunger of such a large beast, but it more than satisfied.

"We only grow stronger while our enemy grows weaker," Senka said as much to herself as to her reptilian companion.

The dragon straightened its neck all the way to the top of the high ceiling of the cavern. It stretched its wings in the dark expanse. Smoke blew from its nostrils and the light from the fire reflected off its obsidian scales. The animal screeched.

"Don't worry, my pet," Senka cooed, "very soon you will fly free again. This time they will not be so lucky as to escape you." The priestess raised a hand in the air—a raven came from the shadows to sit on her stained finger. "Go. Bring me news of the Wolf Queen and the king." She hissed the names, mocking their authority. The bird squawked before taking flight down the corridor. It was joined by two more of its kind—together they flew out of the dark cave and into the dawning day.

CHAPTER THIRTY

Ylva spent the twilight hours, the last moments before the sun broke through the dark night, trying to complete the puzzle of her memory visions. Or was she actually solving the mystery of herself? She worked to accept her fragmented past because it was the only way to move forward and not drown in the pain of it. But perhaps forgetting the pain meant that she had also lost some of the beauty as well.

For too many years Ylva's confidence had been faulty because it relied on only half a foundation. She played the part so well but was never fully convinced of her own strength. She constantly waited for the collapse. It's why she found it difficult when others had such faith in her. She couldn't see why they would trust *her* or follow *her*. Her visions filled in the gaps—now she finally saw the full picture of herself.

She was the orphaned daughter of a dead chieftain and murdered mother. She was a fairytale told to the children. She was a leader but never certain as to why. Hiding behind her boldness crept the shadow of insecurity created by the history she did not fully understand about herself. Now light finally shone upon it.

She heard a knock. "Are you ready? It's about time to leave." Erland's voice came through the closed door of her room.

"Aye," Ylva replied. "I'm coming." She stood up, stretched the last bit of fatigue from her muscles. She pulled her leather armor over her tunic then reached for her axe. Most of the chieftains carried swords as a sign of their position. Håkon had told her that her father never wanted a sword, for he had preferred an axe. It's why she had chosen to do the same. Or so she thought. She wanted some small connection to him, something that made her feel more like Magnus' daughter. But it had also been more comfortable to her. It was curiously familiar and now she knew why. The companion from her dreams knew this would be the weapon she would wield so he prepared her to use it.

There had been times when she thought she should change to a blade. She had wondered if it would help ensure her own status among the clans—yet she could never bring herself to do it. Swords never felt right in her hand, whereas her axe felt like an extension of her body. The clearer her image became, the more she realized she was just as she was supposed to be.

Ylva slid her axe into its keeping. She stepped outside. Vǫrðr and Shura followed at first, but jogged ahead to drink water from the trough. She watched them stretch and sniff. Vǫrðr suddenly raised his nose in the air. The wolf looked around with his ears perked. He yipped when he found the object of his search— Rohan. The black wolf bounced toward the king. Rohan reached down a hand to pet him. Ylva noticed the crooked smile on the king's face as the dog nuzzled against his chest. Then Vǫrðr pulled back sharply with a whimper, his nose tilted up like he smelled something new, something less desirous.

Rohan pulled away from the dog. His smile replaced with a grimace. It deepened when his gaze met Ylva's. She wasn't sure if he was just disappointed in the wolf's change of mood or in seeing her standing there. She had almost forgotten about their argument— her dreams and thoughts having carried her mind elsewhere. Rohan, however, continued to avert his eyes as he walked to his horse.

A new voice entered her ears. "Good morning, Ylva," Elior greeted her. He led his donkey having well-saddled it with supplies.

"You are coming with us?" she asked.

"Ah, yes," Elior replied. His smile so innocent.

"Your horse." Erland approached her holding out the reins to her mare.

She took them and mounted the horse. Erland and Elior followed suit. Rohan already waited at the gates.

"Come, wolves," Ylva called to her dogs. They followed her as she trotted to meet up with Rohan. "Are you sure about Elior joining us? Wouldn't it be better if he came with the others? Should he come at all?" she asked the king.

"It's fine," Rohan replied. He turned his head but not enough to actually look at her.

Ylva waited for more of an answer. After everything the king had said about Elior, she thought he would at least give a reason for his change of heart. She hadn't wanted him to simply concede his stance. Was that even what he was doing—giving in to her?

"In truth, I wondered if *you* would still ride with me this morning," Rohan interrupted her questions.

Ylva wanted him to look at her. She wanted to see his eyes, to read his expression and gain some insight into his frame of mind. Did he or did he not want her there? "I committed to see this through. That hasn't changed," she answered, trying not to involve her emotions. Last night her memories distracted her, but now the preceding anger returned to her. With it came worry that something had been undone between them. The thought grieved her.

"Has something else changed?" This time the king looked at her and didn't look away.

"I don't know," she replied. She hated the way those words tasted. She hated that they were true. She hated the look he gave her, the pained expression like she had bruised his heart. She hated that he looked away without another word.

They rode on for hours with barely a word spoken among the four of them. Even Vǫrðr and Shura trotted silently on the trek toward Askadalen. It wasn't just the tension of what had transpired between Ylva and Rohan. There was something ominous about the entire journey that stole any waiting words. The East Keep had been a dreary place but the closer the Valley of Ash became, the more dismal the Realm seemed to become. The sky itself grew darker by the mile, like a storm was brewing. Yet no rain came. There wasn't even a breeze to break the stillness. Ylva searched the landscape for some sign of life, but there was only their company and the ravens overhead.

"Are those birds following us?" Elior inquired. He was looking up at the small black flock with one eyebrow cocked. "I don't think that is normal."

"It isn't," Erland told him.

"Look." Rohan uttered his first word in hours.

A thin line of light smoke rose upward just ahead of them. It was barely visible against the grey clouded sky. Squinting her eyes, Ylva could see the silhouette of small houses. Some burned and blackened. Other structures had collapsed into not much more than piles of smoldering debris. A trail of blood stained the dying grass as it lined the path into the heart of the village.

"There is blood…but there are no bodies," Erland said.

He was right. Ylva hated to consider it—but the damage, the red that painted the ground—it was evidence of a horrendous battle. Ylva expected to see buzzards picking over corpses.

The sound of a creaking door made Ylva jerk her head toward its estimated origin.

"Someone is here," Rohan whispered.

Ylva nodded in reply. They needed to be cautious, not knowing what might be lurking in the rubble.

"Is someone there? We are here to help," Elior called out. He was already getting off his donkey.

Rohan grumbled and dismounted his steed, ready to protect the servant if needed. Erland and Ylva did the same. She gestured to the wolves—they trotted off like good soldiers, following their orders to check the perimeter.

"I am Elior," he called out again. He inched his way toward one of the homes. There were holes burned into the roof but the walls remained intact. "I am here with Rohan, King of Väljalil and Ylva, leader of the Ibharüng—"

"Can you stop talking please," Rohan scolded him through gritted teeth. "We don't know who or what is there. I'd rather, whatever it is, not know more about us than we know about it."

"Ah, yes, that is wise," Elior replied.

The door creaked again. This time they saw two small hands pull it open. Then a dirt-streaked face appeared out of the shadows.

"It's just a child," Ylva said.

"You are safe." Rohan squatted down and reached out a hand. Another face came into view behind the child—a boy— this one older. Rohan pulled his hand back and slowly stood up. "What happened here?" he asked the young man.

Both of them stepped outside on shaky legs. The young man kept one hand on the boy's shoulder, for both protection and support. When he was in full view, Ylva could see the blood that had dried on his right thigh and that it surrounded a nasty wound. "The priestess came," the man answered.

"Are there other survivors?" Ylva asked.

The man shook his head. "A few that stayed to bury the dead."

His response signaled the others in waiting. Two more men

and three women crawled out of their hiding places. They all looked hungry and tired at the minimum.

"I can help with your injuries," Elior said, his face creased by his ceaseless smile.

"What is your name?" Rohan asked. "Do you have food? Water?"

"I am Hugi," he replied. "We have some, but not enough."

"Why didn't you go to the Keep?" The king looked at each face. Ylva thought the same question. These people were dying and help was less than a day's journey from here.

"This is our home," one of the women replied. "We lost so much...we didn't want to lose our homes too."

Ylva would have thought the same. She would fight for her home until her last breath. Letting go would seem like an unbearable task in these circumstances. She would want to hold on to whatever she could as well—just like the woman.

"There is more," Hugi said. The others all looked at him with wide eyes, afraid of what he was about to disclose. "There is one more of our people who is alive...but he is unwell."

"Perhaps we can help him," Elior offered.

"His illness is not like anything we have seen..." Hugi looked to the ground, wringing his hands. "It is something *she* did to him."

"The priestess?" Ylva asked. She knew the answer. They all did. They knew what this was. They knew they had little chance of helping stop it.

"Let us see him," Elior said.

Hugi hesitated, looking to the others for silent counsel before nodding in agreement. He led Elior inside his dilapidated home. Ylva and Rohan followed while Erland kept watch at the door.

Inside it was dark—a single candle lighting the room. "I had a fire going...but it seemed to make him worse so we put it out," Hugi said, gesturing toward a still body lying on a cot by the back wall.

Elior took no time to approach. "What is his name?" he asked.

"Ozur," Hugi replied.

Elior began his examination of Ozur. It didn't take a close inspection to diagnose what was wrong. It didn't require Ylva's Gift either. The man's skin was gray and his veins were black. When Elior lifted the man's closed eyelids, even his irises looked murky. It was the same thing that afflicted Leif. The Darkness infected him.

"Relight the fire," Elior ordered in that soft way he always had about him.

"But…" Hugi started to argue but Elior lifted a hand to halt him.

"I know the danger that worries you," Elior said, "but Light is needed to fight the Darkness. Even if it is painful."

Hugi nodded and went to work.

Light is needed to fight the Darkness. Elior's words struck something deep in Ylva. It reverberated outward from her. It was a ripple of truth echoing through the pieces of mystery and prophecy in her mind.

"If I can see the black in his veins and grey of his eyes," Rohan leaned close, whispering to her, "then what is it that you see?"

"I see the same," Ylva began. The outer shell of the man proved painful enough to look at—it made her hesitate to gaze deeper into Ozur's soul. "If I use my Gift, then it will be all the darker. I will see Myrkr's hold entangling everything good in the man and choking the Light out of him."

When Rohan didn't respond, she turned to look at him. His eyes seemed sad. She wanted to reach out, to take his hand. She almost did. She was just about to, but in the time it took to win the argument with herself, Rohan had stepped backward.

"You stay and help Elior. Erland and I will see what can be done for the others before making camp for the night."

"Of course," Ylva replied then watched him leave.

Time drifted slowly as the sun set. Ylva sat on a wobbly stool, watching Elior tend to Ozur. The servant cared for this stranger with such tenderness. He washed his face and hands with a damp cloth, paying careful attention to the wound on the man's forehead. He dripped water into his mouth while whispering encouraging words. There would be moments when it seemed like hope was glimmering through the shadow of death. Elior would smile bright and tell Ozur he was doing well, that he needed to keep fighting.

Ylva felt useless. She kept the fire stoked but there was little else for her to do but wait and watch. She declined food when Erland offered it at one point. Vǫrðr and Shura came and went several times before curling up at her feet to wait with her. Elior didn't speak to her unless she asked him a question. He focused only on his patient. Ylva understood, remaining quietly in the background for support.

Vǫrðr sat up, his ears perked to a noise from outside. Then he yawned and laid back down. Ylva echoed with a yawn of her own. She was tempted to find a place to curl herself up and fall into a sweet sleep. Maybe Elior would call for her if he needed anything. She was suddenly aware of her body aching for rest.

Just as Ylva was about to consent to her own fatigue, Elior jolted to his feet, dropping his bowl of water to the ground. Ozur was thrashing on the bed. Ylva darted to Elior's side—the two tried to hold the seizing man still. He wasn't large but he was strong—stronger than would be suspected. He pushed and pulled until one of his arms broke free. He made contact with Elior's face, knocking him down. The wolves barked and growled.

"Get help!" Ylva ordered the dogs.

Both looked to her before Shura obediently ran outside.

Vǫrðr didn't move. His stance was low and his fur raised, ready to lunge. His eyes never left Ozur.

"Elior, are you all right?" Ylva asked as the servant regained his balance and returned to her side.

"Yes," he replied. "I am afraid we cannot stop this now."

Ylva struggled to keep a hold on Ozur. His activity was more violent. A growl had begun to emanate from his throat. One sharp movement and she was pushed backward. Ozur's eyes opened...but he no longer looked human. A monstrous roar bellowed out of his mouth. He jerked upward, his body stiff and twitching. He tossed the cot over, breaking it as he dove for Elior.

Ylva stepped in front of the servant to make herself a shield for him. She reached for her axe only to remember its place across the room. It now leaned against the wall near where she had been sitting. Her dagger would have to do for now because she couldn't risk the newly woken Bardung attacking Elior. Vǫrðr stood beside her, teeth bared, snapping at the inhuman.

Ozur swatted at the wolf. Vǫrðr dodged and then lunged, biting down on the Bardung's arm. Ylva took advantage of the distraction and sliced her dagger across Ozur's chest. Black blood seeped through his shirt. He roared at her as he kicked Vǫrðr. The wolf landed on the floor with a yelp.

Ylva lunged at the inhuman, trying to pierce his heart. He blocked her with an upheld arm into which she plunged her dagger. She elbowed his jaw before kicking forward to make contact with his abdomen. This forced him to stumble a half step backward, freeing her blade. Ylva didn't hesitate to attack again. She knew she had to be quick on her feet. This Bardung wasn't just strong—he was wilder than the others she had faced. It was as if his new view of the world had him panicked—no clarity existed now in his unfamiliar state of being.

Ozur was quicker. He grabbed her forearm, forcing her to drop the knife as his other hand gripped her neck. His hands felt like stone against her skin, crushing the last bits of air from her throat. She couldn't inhale to refill her lungs. She kicked wildly at him and pulled his wrists, trying to break free.

Elior yelled her name and charged from behind. He used the stool to hit the Bardung over the head. The blow was enough to draw more inky blood...but it didn't stop him.

"My axe." Ylva fought for the words as they scratched their way out of her collapsing airway.

Elior nodded. He made a move toward the weapon.

Everything began to blur and fade. Ylva's arms and legs were getting weaker. She strained to stay conscious, to suck in enough breath to keep fighting a moment longer.

Vǫrðr barked. Another bark followed. It was Shura. Ylva would recognize her guardians even in the darkness. She could hear them growling. She knew they were ready to strike at this enemy again. Their company gave her strength. She pulled upward, using the Bardung's arms for leverage. Then she took what power she could gather and kicked both feet forward into his chest. It proved enough to jar her opponent. He released her. She fell to the ground, immediately turning to find Elior holding out her axe. Vǫrðr and Shura snapped and lunged at Ozur. This gave her a brief reprieve to take hold of her weapon.

Just as Ylva's fingers reached the wooden handle, she heard the door open and crash against the wall. Her vision was still blurry, but she could make out Rohan's boots rushing across the dirt floor. He yelled as he lunged at the Bardung. Ylva held her axe in her hands. With Elior's help, she stood onto precarious legs, prepared to support Rohan. She found her bearings—just in time to see the king's sword plunge into the Bardung's heart. Rohan pulled his sword out of the beast, black liquid dripping from its end. Ozur fell to the floor, still and silent.

The whole ordeal had only taken minutes. Ylva's body and brain only now caught up with each other. Her chest hurt as she took deep breaths.

Rohan rushed to her side. "Are you all right?"

"Yes," Ylva answered. She would be sore but it was nothing some rest couldn't cure.

Rohan turned his attention back to Ozur's lifeless body. It seemed to bother him.

Ylva touched his arm. "It was what had to be done," she told the king. "He would not be saved."

"I know," Rohan responded. He made an effort to smile but it was faint at best, not going deeper than half-curved lips.

"Where is Erland?" Ylva asked. It wasn't like her other guardian to sit back and let someone else fight in his stead.

"When your wolf found us, I wasn't sure what we were dealing with so I told him I would come and that he should stay to protect the other villagers," Rohan said.

"I'm sure he was happy about that." Ylva hoped her subtle musing would lessen a bit of the strain in her words.

Rohan's second effort at a smile was weaker. "I should go back to let him know all is well," the king said. "Then we will return to help bury Ozur as is the custom in Ostlund."

"There will be no need," Elior broke into the conversation. He knelt beside Ozur. He had his cloth in his hand again and was wiping some of the blood from his head and face. He placed the man's hands criss-crossed over his chest. He then used a single hand to close his eyes. "It is as I told the commander back at the Keep—I worry this Darkness is a tricky thing and think it would be better to burn the body."

"Aye," Rohan agreed. "I will tell the others so they can mourn their friend."

"Yes, that would be good," Elior said. He stared back at the corpse. It barely resembled anything human but the servant touched its hand as though it belonged to an old friend. He smiled but without the warm joy that typically lit his countenance. It looked more like a release…the smile at the end of a sigh. A single tear dripped down his cheek and off his chin, hitting Ozur's forehead. Then he did something peculiar. Elior leaned forward, touching his head to Ozur's like he was sharing a final secret with the fallen man.

When he sat back up, his face glistened with more tears. He sobbed softly. The wolves howled beside him, a strange trio of mourners weeping for the heart of a stranger.

CHAPTER THIRTY-ONE

THEY HAD LIT the entire structure around the Bardung, burning it to the ground to become Ozur's final resting place. Rohan watched the flames fade to embers long after the others retreated back to their makeshift camp to find solace in sleep. He also needed rest but knew there would be no peace in it. Would he ever have peace again?

As soon as the question breeched the surface of his thoughts, agony surged through his heart. It felt so intense that he lost his breath. Rohan pulled back the collar of his cloak and shirt. The dying firelight exposed the darkness of his veins as they stretched further across his chest. It had grown deeper and wider since he first noticed the pain at the East Keep—he knew there was nothing he could do to stop it. It was only a matter of time before the King of Väljalil became just another minion of Myrkr.

"Help me," Rohan whispered, looking upward. A small break in the dark clouds allowed a handful of stars to peek through. He focused on the light from those stars. "Please, I know I am not worthy, but help me." Rohan could hear the desperation in the tremble of his own voice.

There was no response. Rohan wasn't sure what he expected. Would Lys answer him in lightning or thunder? Would he hear a voice? Would he feel different? Did his wondering matter when there was really no answer at all? A month ago, he would say there was nothing because there was no Lys. Now, with everything he had seen, and despite his argument to Ylva, he was coming to believe Lys was in fact real...as real as the Darkness at war with him. Perhaps there was no reply to his plea because Lys didn't care for him. Why would he—especially in this present state?

Rohan wiped tears from his eyes before they could fall, a misguided attempt at strength before he joined the others in slumber.

"Why would he help you?" The question slithered through the air.

Rohan sat up. No one else moved or made a sound. The world looked like it had been repainted in shades of gray. He was the only bit of color.

"Why would he help you?" The question hissed over his head again.

"Who's there?" Rohan asked as he stood to his feet with his sword in hand.

The nearby fire popped and crackled to life. A figure seemed to form from the smoke. Her red hair gave a stark contrast to the dark background.

"Senka," Rohan said. Her name left a bitter taste in his mouth.

"Hello, sweet prince," she replied.

"I am king now."

"Are you?" She raised one eyebrow then cackled as she

sauntered closer to Rohan. "A ceremony and a new title doesn't change the weak boy you are inside." She poked a blackened finger against his chest. The touch caused his heart to ache.

He swatted her hand away and raised his sword enough to force some space between them. "I know what you are trying to do."

"I'm not doing anything," Senka replied. "I don't need to do anything when you are doing it all to yourself. The loathing, the doubt…it's a thing of beauty." She circled around him, tracing a hand over his shoulders. Her fingers grazed the side of his neck. She leaned close as she smelled his skin. "I can smell the bitter-sweet stench of the Darkness."

"It doesn't matter," Rohan argued. "I can fight it. I've already held it off longer than most. It won't overtake me. Lys will—"

"Will what?" The priestess interrupted him. "The Light doesn't care for you. You aren't worthy of his care. We both know it."

"You know nothing of me." Rohan moved further away from Senka.

She smiled, a wicked grin that made Rohan squirm under his skin. "I know that the Light could never use someone like you, someone so clouded and unsure. I know that you pretend to be more, to have gained some confidence, but you haven't. And I know Ylva will ultimately see who you really are. She will want nothing to do with you when she does."

"Liar!"

The priestess laughed. "No lie, just a painful truth. The Wolf Queen has already begun to see it. She is losing her faith in you. Though I can't understand why she ever had any in the first place."

"No," Rohan started to protest…but he found no rebuttal. He knew he had disappointed Ylva. He feared all he could ever offer her, or the Four Realms, was more disappointment. He was not his father.

Senka had drawn closer to him again. She was just inches in front of him reaching her hand out, her stained fingers moving slowly toward him. She touched his chest and it felt like she had driven a dagger into his heart. Pain pulsed outward in waves that overtook Rohan and he fell to his knees.

Senka bent down and whispered in his ear, "You will never be enough."

"I...I..." Rohan tried to speak, to offer even the smallest argument in his own defense but he had not the strength or the sense. The only thought he could hold on to was that this was his end.

"Shoo! Shoo!" A loud voice interrupted Rohan's nightmare and startled him awake. "Shoo! Take your murder elsewhere, ravens!" Elior was standing over the king, flailing his arms at the birds. "Sorry to have woken you up, Highness, but those pesky creatures looked bothersome. I don't know how they didn't wake you."

"Thank you, Elior." Rohan wiped his face and stretched his sore back.

"You are most welcome. I am here to help after all," Elior replied.

Rohan still didn't know how to handle this strange servant. He never seemed agitated or uncertain. He always looked to be at peace with whatever was happening around him. Though watching him drive the ravens away did allow for a comical moment.

"If I might." Elior's tone softened. "You seemed distressed in your sleep. Is everything all right?"

Immediately Rohan's mind warred with itself. Was this a genuine show of concern or an opportunity for Elior to point out the king's shortcomings? One side of him wanted to trust in the servant's good nature and even confide in him. The other was too afraid of the man's motives...or perhaps of the truth. "Maybe it was a bad dream. Or maybe it was the ravens. But either way, I am fine. No need to concern yourself with me," Rohan decidedly answered.

"Need or not, care is there, Highness...whenever *you* might need it," Elior responded, "and even when you don't." He winked and then walked away as though something more pressing had come to his attention elsewhere.

Rohan stretched again. He rubbed a cold hand over his face, scratching the stubble on his jaw. The sky still looked dim, only now awaking. Rohan wished *he* wasn't yet awake. His body and mind still dragged with fatigue. More rest would give a welcome blessing but he could already hear the others stirring. He knew they needed to continue on their journey without further delay. He pushed aside wary thoughts and pushed down the pain, and prepared for the day's ride.

Morning had fully dawned by the time the village's survivors began to make their way to the East Keep under the king's orders. Rohan expected more of a protest from them. It turned out that need outweighed desire...so they had agreed. As they headed west, Rohan, along with his original companions, headed further east, closer to Askadalen and Skämd.

The air blew colder than it had the day before. The cloudy sky forever a dismal gray, but instead of misting rain, snow sprinkled like ashes from a fire. It's how the valley earned its name. There were almost always flurries, but they never accumulated more than a layer of dust on the ground.

The despair of the realm continued to increase in evidence as the group rode further past where villages dared to be built. Askadalen was a barren place. No birds chirped from the branches of the dead trees. It was like the land itself was sick and the disease continued to spread. The infection edged outward into the last bits of greenery in Ostlund. Rohan could feel it spreading under his own skin, crawling down his arms. He dared not look to confirm his suspicions. He didn't need to look. He knew.

CHAPTER THIRTY-TWO

YLVA BRUSHED the ashen snow off of her horse's mane for probably the hundredth time. The ride through Askadalen felt endless. The dreary valley, with its forlorn scenery, pressed down on her like a millstone on her back. The heaviness in this place made hours feel like days and days feel like weeks. Even her faithful wolves had lost the desire to frolic and play. They stalked over the dusty ground with heads and tails low.

When it seemed like the landscape was merely one dead tree after another, they came upon the stone ruins of an ancient castle. Mostly it was piles of rubble—but the occasional cracked pillar seemed to grow out of the ground. They stood as remnants sharing a glimpse of its former glory. They were haunting. Ylva shivered as they rode through them and up onto the ridge that lay just ahead.

From the ledge, they could see down into the valley. Skämd, the High Mountain, loomed large. It cast a shadow over the terrain far below. A hundred fires dotted the landscape with their red flames. A thousand or more Bardung soldiers mingled around them.

"How could she have raised this vast of an army in such little time?" Rohan said as he stared at their enemy.

Elior halted his donkey beside the king's stallion. "Oh, the Darkness has been building its army for much longer than we realize. It has been planting seeds, so many tiny seeds, that the priestess merely had to reap the harvest."

Ylva felt his words in her gut. How often had she seen the bits of Myrkr sprout roots in a man's heart and said nothing...done nothing? Nothing that seemed of much consequence now. She had been too content to stay safe in the sacred mountains and care only for her clan that she had not stretched out her hands to nurture seeds of the Light beyond her own borders. Could she have saved some?

Ylva decided to steer her focus back to the present. Whatever could have been done in the past did not change what needed to be done now. Whether it was the fruit of her own complacency or not, they were facing a battle *today*. Guilt would not fight it—it would only feed their fear, so Ylva pushed aside condemning self-talk.

Ylva turned her attention to the column of smoke rising from Skämd. It grew like a billowing beast from the center of the broken-down tower. "Should we ride to the High Mountain? Find the priestess?" Ylva asked Rohan.

"No." The king did not hesitate in his reply. His response came so quick it startled Ylva.

Ylva offered the beginnings of an idea. "Perhaps if we could surprise her—"

Rohan cut her off. "No," he said with barely a glance at her. "From what the spies discovered, there are too many Bardung within the caverns. Even if we could somehow sneak past them, we would still face her dragon. It is better to wait until our army is in place. Pull her attention to battle first."

As if on cue, the dragon emerged from somewhere below the earth. It screeched as it took flight. Ravens cawed from nearby perches behind Ylva. Another screech came from the winged beast.

"That isn't good, is it?" Erland asked.

The dragon had circled the tower and was moving toward them.

"No, it isn't," Rohan replied. "We should ride back to the ruins and take cover for the night."

"It won't do much good with those birds hovering about." Elior pointed at the ravens now circling above them. "They are connected to it—to her."

Of course they were. It made sense—so much so Ylva was ashamed to have not realized it sooner. "We can take care of them." She took her bow in hand and removed an arrow from the quiver attached to her saddle. She fired an arrow that pierced a raven, knocking it out of the sky. As it fell to the ground, another arrow whizzed upward. She looked to see Erland with his bow in hand. The second raven fell. The third made a sound like a scream as it pulled back, holding momentarily in place before retreating. Ylva loosed another arrow but it missed, just nicking the edge of a wing, merely freeing a couple of black feathers.

"Will she send more?" Erland asked.

"Hopefully it won't matter," Rohan answered. "We need only stay hidden long enough for the dragon to give up."

"And if it doesn't?" Ylva didn't intend her question as argumentative—it's just that they had no answer.

Rohan bowed his head for a brief moment. He looked worn. Ylva could sense the effects of this place—how it drained one's will. She could feel her own hopes shrinking, the shadows working to devour them.

"We must pray that it does." Rohan sounded hoarse as he turned his steed. He tapped his heels against its sides and the stallion jolted onward. Ylva and the others followed. Their horses treaded cautiously but quickly back down the ridge and into the ruins.

As they rode back amongst the piles of disintegrated stone from a century's old war, they split up, each looking for the best place to hide. Even Vǫrðr and Shura sniffed about. Ylva couldn't see much that would offer any real shelter from the cold coming night, much less the dragon. She exhaled a silent prayer for help.

Shura barked.

Ylva immediately changed her direction to ride off toward the wolves. She found them both digging amongst the debris near a cracked half-fallen wall. She dismounted and squatted next to Vǫrðr, trying to see what had caught their attention. Moving aside some heavy rocks, Ylva uncovered a thick wooden door. It was bolted with a rusty chain. Ylva took one of the rocks and smashed the metal, breaking its links. Creaking the door open revealed a set of stairs.

"Over here!" she called to the others.

Rohan, Erland and Elior all gathered, peering down into the dark passageway.

"We should be careful," Rohan warned as he took the first step.

Elior stopped him. "We shouldn't descend into the darkness without at least a bit of light to guide us." The servant ran back to his donkey and returned with a torch and flint. As he set the torch ablaze, a clearer view of the passage—and Elior's ever-present grin—could be seen. "There... that is better," he said.

Then the dragon's screech echoed closer. One of the horses whinnied.

"The stairs look wide and shallow enough to lead the horses down with us," Rohan suggested. "We can't afford to leave them up here, unprotected." He took his stallion's reins and the torch before beginning the downward climb.

Vǫrðr trotted in front of the king while the others followed. Shura stuck close to Ylva. They all took their time. Even a mule path like this was frightening for the large animals. As the path spiraled into a soft curve, Ylva's mare halted. Ylva could hear its heavy breath. She slid a hand along the horse's neck, feeling twitching muscles before whispering soothing words in her ear. The animal calmed enough to take another trusting step. Then another...and another...until they reached the bottom of the decline.

"Thank Lys," Elior murmured.

"Indeed," Rohan concurred, although his demeanor didn't signal much in the way of relief.

Ylva was glad for the shelter—even if their surroundings matched the above ghostly ruins. Flickering torchlight revealed tombs carved into the stone walls, some of which were home to piles of disconnected bones. A draft blew in—the wind whistled around them like whispers from the dead.

"We should settle the horses and start a fire," Erland said.

"Aye," Rohan agreed.

"And we should eat and rest." Elior searched through the packs on his donkey's back. "I am sure I have food enough to sustain us for the night."

Vǫrðr and Shura grumbled.

"For you too," Elior replied to the wolves.

Sitting around a campfire usually provided a place to share tales and reprieve from the day's striving. The mood around this small fire was too sullen for stories. Ylva missed Håkon. He would always ensure a good story for every campfire. Her companions looked to need a good dose of the old man's hope—save for the ever-jubilant Elior—who would charismatically weave his anecdotes and allegories throughout his tales.

Ylva watched as Elior happily tossed bits of bread to the wolves. She wondered at his joy. Her own wavered more than she would like. Not that it was completely absent now...but it was small. She very much felt the need to stretch it somehow— to pull at its corners and make it grow until she found strength in it. The longer she observed Elior and the wolves, the more she felt her own joy expand within her. It yielded a moment of peace in the midst of their struggle.

"We should all get some rest," Rohan said, stoking the small fire. "Hopefully by dawn the dragon will be gone and we can be on our way to rendezvous with the army."

"Rest would be good. Knowing how to kill the dragon would be better," Erland replied. He took another bite of the oat biscuit in his hand. "We know how to kill the Bardung footmen. We can battle them with confidence...but the dragon?"

"I was thinking I'd just delegate the dragon-slaying to you, Erland. You're the tallest," the king replied, chuckling to himself. Ylva was glad to see him laugh. It had been so long since he even broke a real smile. Ylva didn't realize how much she had missed it until now—when the curl of his lip made her insides take flight.

"Oh, I'm certain I could do a fine job," Erland countered. "The creature must have a soft spot my axe can hack through." Her friend's own laugh was deep. It bounced off the cavernous walls.

"That it must," Rohan replied. As he said the words, his merriment faded. "Truly...the beast must have a weakness. There must be a way." The way he muttered the last words, Ylva wasn't sure if Rohan spoke to them or himself. "The Keepers said the priestess and the dragon are connected. To kill one means to kill the other," he said.

"Maybe the priestess will be easier to kill," Erland offered.

"I doubt that," Ylva said. She had been a formidable opponent that night in Grålås.

"What if we go for her heart like the other Bardung?" Erland asked.

It was a logical enough suggestion. But so much of what was happening in their world defied logic. It couldn't be that easy.

"I don't think the priestess has a heart," Elior said, not nearly as shocked by the supposition as the others looked to be. The servant took his time coming to the defense of the notion, only offering further explanation when he realized their waiting faces would remain silent until he did. "The Bardung are infected with the Darkness like a disease that eats from the inside out...until no light remains in them. But the priestess—for her, it is not some blight. She uses it as though it is an extension of her body."

"She is the Darkness." Ylva was as surprised by the words that left her lips as Rohan and Erland who stared open-mouthed at her.

"Yes, in a form," Elior agreed with a smile and a wink.

"So we can't kill her?" Erland asked.

"But you wounded her," Rohan looked to Ylva.

"Yes, I hurt her, but she looked surprised. It was as though even she didn't think it possible," Ylva said.

"Priestess or dragon—either opponent will be formidable." Rohan commented as he poked at the fire.

Ylva's mind and heart began to stir with a prospect. "I wish we knew more from the first time..." she said, "some detail that would offer confirmation."

"They failed," Elior responded. "They could have stopped it but the sacrifice proved too great. Thus they opted for a lesser evil. But lesser evil is still evil, and though it slept it did not surrender."

Sacrifice. The word caused a bell to ring in Ylva's soul.

"Sacrifice?" Rohan asked. "What was the sacrifice?"

"The Keepers pages did not say," Elior answered. He glanced at Ylva and she caught a glint in his eye. Something he knew but wouldn't say. Something she thought he was trying to tell her. Something perhaps he thought she already knew.

"Whatever it is, we will figure it out," Rohan interrupted her internal conversation. "This time, no matter the sacrifice, we must be willing to end this for good."

"I pray you have the strength," Elior said the words like they were directed at Rohan but his eyes never left Ylva. Then he interrupted his intense gaze with a pronounced yawn. "We should get that sleep now."

"I'll keep first watch," Ylva offered.

"No, I should…" Rohan began to protest.

Ylva touched a hand to his. "You look like you need the sleep. I don't mind."

"I am fine," the king argued.

"You need to be more than fine." Ylva kept her voice soft. She didn't want him to think she doubted him.

Rohan didn't respond. He didn't look at her face, just her hand on top of his.

"Are you okay?" Ylva was tempted to use her Sight and gaze under his surface, but it felt like it would be an invasion in that moment. Really she didn't want to find out on her own about the inter-workings of his heart…she wanted him to tell her. She knew a chasm had formed between them back at the Keep—was that to be their end? She didn't want it to be. She wanted him to trust her with whatever he was thinking, whatever was causing his brow to stay furrowed and his jaw clenched. He looked like he was in pain. She wanted to help him, to soothe it away if she could.

"You shouldn't worry about me," Rohan whispered as he squeezed her fingers. He moved her hand away from his. He laid down, turned his back to her. "I just need sleep."

Ylva resisted the urge to grab him, to pull him back up and force him to look her in the eye. Was he still angry with her? Had she hurt him so deeply with her doubt? Had his lack of faith in Lys really been enough to warrant those doubts?

Erland began to snore softly. The fire crackled and one of the horses snorted. Despite the momentary peaceful setting, Ylva still felt like she was suffocating. It wasn't the dark catacomb so much as her heart aching. She needed a breath.

With footsteps as light as she could muster, Ylva climbed the spiral path. She was careful to look for ravens and the dragon before fully emerging from the earth. Vǫrðr and Shura had followed her, sniffing the air for the same dangers. When they scampered out to stretch their legs, she knew it was safe.

Ylva filled her lungs with the cool, fresh, night air. "Help us find the way," she whispered. *Help me find a way.* The way to put all of the pieces together from her visions and memories. The way to see how her group fit into this quest...to find an answer to the question of achieving victory over the Darkness. She also prayed for a way for Rohan to break free from the worry or fear smothering his spirit.

Ylva exhaled a puff of smokey breath and leaned her head back. There was the smallest of breaks in the clouds over Askadalen. A string of stars strained to be seen...a half moon peeked through. She smiled. *Light will always find a way to breech the heart of darkness.*

Darkness.

Light.

Heart.

Heart. Her soul stirred again. This time, something came into focus in her mind. A notion turned into a hypothesis...that might be a remedy. Ylva's chest squeezed and tears clung to the edges of her eyes. She wrapped her right hand around her left wrist, rubbing her thumb over the leather bracer. *Sacrifice.*

CHAPTER THIRTY-THREE

THEY RODE north along the outskirts of Askadalen until the mountains in the Northlands came into glorious view. Ylva had been anticipating a glimpse of home to strengthen her resolve. The forests at the feet of the Helig peaks were not as she had left them. Even here on the opposite side of the range from her village, there should have been the same evergreens and wild-flower fields on display in vibrant color. But the hues faded with the sickness that leaked in from the valley. The tall trees showed bare trunks with peeling bark...the fields were dry and brown. All of the Four Realms of Väljalil had been touched by the Dark-ness now. The time to conquer it was coming short. How long before even her home, even at its spot on the far side of the map, became devoid of light-filled life?

Ylva wouldn't allow it to happen. They were so close to the end of this war, of finishing what the generations before them had begun. Already their tents were set and their campfires burned as the warriors of the Four Realms gathered into one army.

"Highness!"

"Commander," Rohan replied as the warden of the East Keep

stepped into their path. A hand was already there to take their horses when they dismounted. Rohan swayed a bit when his feet hit the ground. Ylva wasn't sure anyone else would even have noticed—except Vǫrðr whined and stepped away from her and toward the king. Rohan waved the dog away with some muttering of reassurance. "What are our numbers?" The king asked the commander.

"Come inside where we can discuss the details." The commander pulled back the flap of his tent so they could step inside.

The tent allowed enough space to accommodate sleep and strategizing in privacy but not enough for their full company. "Wolves, stay," Ylva commanded her guardians who both sat down just outside the door as she stepped in.

"I'll go find word of the Ibharüng," Erland told Ylva at the doorway.

"All right, brother," she replied. He marched off into the ranks looking for their clansmen.

The commander closed the tent flap. He stepped around Ylva to the table which was covered by a map of the realm. "We are at just over seven hundred here now—most others are only a couple days ride out."

"They are early," Rohan said.

"They are ready for war," the commander replied.

"That is good because the Bardung will most likely outnumber us." Rohan swayed again, bracing himself with his hands on the table.

Ylva stepped beside him, close enough for her arm to brush against his. "Are you unwell?" she discreetly asked.

Rohan didn't look at her, a now common occurrence between them. Instead, he placed a cold and sweaty hand on hers. "I am fine. I probably just need to eat."

"I can have food brought in," the commander interjected.

"Thank you, that would be agreeable," Rohan replied.

While the commander stepped out to make the order, Rohan stared at the map. Ylva stared at him. Inside the tent was dim, but even with just the single small fire casting a warm glow on his face, the king looked pale. His eyes appeared without spark. She could have sworn she saw him tremble. She considered pressing the matter further but the commander returned quickly. She knew Rohan wouldn't want to have the discussion in front of his subordinate. She would wait until they were alone.

"Even if we come close to matching the Bardung in number, they will outmatch us in strength," Rohan kept his focus on the map and the commander as he spoke. "The Darkness makes them gravely more dangerous."

"Yes," the commander replied. "Thankfully we know how to kill them. My men have been spreading the word through camp that when battle comes, go straight for their hearts."

"Good…" Rohan struggled to speak the word, the sound becoming more of a cough. He clutched a hand to his chest. Ylva touched his arm. The king just shook his head and removed her hand.

Ylva fought to hold back her growing concerns. Something was wrong. She looked to Elior who had been sitting silent behind them but now had stood up. He also watched Rohan.

"We must be sure our men know not to hesitate…" Rohan struggled to breathe in between his words. "The casualties will be too great otherwise…" The king began to choke. He dropped to his knees before falling backwards onto the floor.

"Rohan!" Ylva knelt beside him. She pulled his face toward her in time to see his eyes roll back into his head.

"Get water," Elior told the commander as he knelt on the other side of Rohan.

"What is wrong with him?" Ylva exclaimed in desperation.

Elior went straight to work examining the king. He laid his head against Rohan's chest. "He is struggling to breathe, we need to remove his armor."

Ylva nodded. She tried to appear calm in spite of the fear now surging wildly within her. Her hands quivered as she helped Elior. When they removed the breastplate, Elior pulled at the king's shirt, revealing his secret.

Ylva gasped. A black web of veins had spread across his chest and down his arms—they now crept up his neck. "How did I...?"

"He hid it well," Elior replied.

"No one has ever been able to hide from my Gift." Ylva's tears dripped onto Rohan's skin. She traced her fingers along a single inky line around Rohan's heart.

"No, but we can't see what we choose not to look for." Elior stopped her hand with his own. "Look at me, Ylva."

She hesitated but obeyed. The servant's eyes gleamed with so much grace that she almost couldn't bare to look at him...but she couldn't look away either.

"He did not hide from your Gift, he..."

"He hid from me." Ylva felt her insides shake. "I wanted him to trust me and he didn't. Why?"

"I don't think he trusted himself," Elior replied.

"I failed him." Ylva hated the taste of those words in her mouth as much as any she had despaired to speak over their journey.

"You haven't," Elior wiped her wet cheek with his calloused thumb. "He is not done for. You can help him now."

"How? The Darkness has a hold of him." She saw what had become of Ozur, of Leif— the thought shrouded her hope.

"Yes," Elior replied, "but we can still look for the spaces where light is working to break through. This will loosen Myrkr's hold," with this, Elior then suddenly gripped both of Ylva's hands. He looked at her with unwavering intensity. "Use your Sight now," he said solemnly.

Her Sight? How could it help? What she could see had already made its way to the surface. She typically used her Gift to look beyond the surface of a person and their masks. This allowed her to find the truth—not just about who a person was, but also who they were becoming. But maybe her Sight could see to depths she had not before tested. Could she go deeper than she had ever dared?

Ylva looked back down into Rohan's still features. It appeared as though he was wearing a veil of death. It terrified her. She had been angry with him—had doubted that he could ever become the man she needed. Was she realizing too late that it was no matter—that he had already become the man she wanted? It wasn't supposed to end like this…it couldn't. Whatever had been happening between them needed more time to unfold. Rohan deserved more time. If she stared hard enough, could Ylva will the Darkness to retreat? Or had she already missed the chance to save him? "I'm not sure I can," she told Elior.

The servant squeezed her hand. His eyes were earnest. He looked at her the way Håkon did, when he could see something in her she couldn't see in herself. "Try."

Over and over again, from the time they moved Rohan off the floor and onto a cot, until the sun rose on a new day, Ylva sat by his bedside and searched the depths of his mind and heart. She had allowed her Gift to take her swirling through his thoughts, fears and memories. At times she hesitated, unsure if she should look further. She had shivered at the places already wrapped tightly in Myrkr's grip. She had wept at the sadness and grief that had ripped Rohan's heart wide open. For hours she traveled the path the Darkness had already trod on its way to the king's soul. In the moments where she could bear it no longer, she retreated back to physical reality…but it was no brighter.

Rohan's skin had paled to a sickening gray. A cloudy film covered his eyes. The black in his veins had not spread further but had not dissipated either. Elior would wipe the king's head with a damp cloth and smile while urging him to keep fighting. The servant had tried again and again to push the Darkness back with his own healing touch. It would appear to shrink, to shrivel a bit—for Rohan would sigh in relief. But as soon as Elior removed his fingers, the Darkness would immediately flood back in. The king would seize and release an ungodly roar.

"Help me." Rohan's voice croaked, like it was desperately scratching its way from his throat. A tear spilled from the corner of his eye.

Ylva couldn't stop her own tears from escaping. She wrapped both of her hands around one of his, pulled it to her lips and kissed it softly. "I have tried. I'm afraid I don't know how..." she admitted in a broken whisper. Now sobbing, she slid off the stool where she had been sitting. She knelt on the ground and laid her head against his shoulder. "Lys, please...please." There were a million things she ought to have said, pretty words that she wanted to pray, but this was all she could form in the midst of weeping. She was so tired. Her body felt weak, as did her spirit. She was afraid she had nothing left to give and that Rohan would be lost.

"Any change?" the commander asked from somewhere behind her.

"I'm afraid not," Elior answered.

"Should I send word to Grålås?" The commander's voice resounded louder. Or, maybe he had stepped closer—Ylva did not look up to find out.

"If you must," the servant replied, "but let us not give up hope just yet."

Ylva assumed the commander had left. She wouldn't look anywhere but to Rohan. Elior's words triggered something in her. If she had any hope left, it was small—but small was better than nothing. "I know there is still a small hope inside you too," she whispered into Rohan's ear. "Find it. Hold on to it. Let it lead you out." She kissed his cool scruffy cheek. "*I love you,*" she whispered even more quietly.

Elior went back to wiping the king's brow and dripping water onto his lips. He hummed a familiar lullaby while he worked. Ylva recognized it. It wasn't one often sung by the mothers in her village. It was an older song—one from her own childhood. She realized now that she had heard it in one of her recent visions. Hearing it now brought her comfort. She let herself soak in its warmth. Then she laid her head back near Rohan and feebly sang the lyrics. As she did so, she felt strength imbue her weakness

Quiet, quiet, little one.
Rest your weary eyes.
For all the world is sleeping.
In wait for new sunrise.
So quiet, quiet, little one.
Do not the Darkness fear.
The Light is always stronger.
And Lys is ever near.

CHAPTER THIRTY-FOUR

ROHAN COULDN'T MOVE. He felt weightless but at the same time restrained. And it was dark. He squinted and struggled to see something, anything, but he could only make out what looked like a kind of black water—as though he were in a dark womb. He tried and tried to rage against its invisible walls—to kick and clamor for a way out. Yet no force could be summoned. Attempting to fight only left him tired.

Occasionally a glimmer of light would flicker past his eyes. It was mostly fleeting. He wanted to reach for it and chase after it. Could he reach it? He couldn't tell if he even tried to reach it —or if it was only his imagination playing tricks on him. Then the Darkness would devour the flicker...and he would lose another piece of himself.

It all hurt. His chest, his arms, his legs, his head...it all hurt. Every muscle, every fiber burned and ached. And it was cold. Sometimes he would feel something like a warm hand on his skin and the pain would stop. He could breathe again. No sooner had his lungs exhaled relief than the pain would flood back over him and he would scream. Did sound even come out of his mouth?

Rohan was dying. Not his body—his soul. He could feel it relinquishing bit by bleeding bit. It was the Darkness. He was not strong enough to fight it. He should have known. Not enough Light dwelled in him. What had Ylva said? How had she described him? *You are a beautiful, yet tragic mix of gray. Not enough to be dead, but too much to be fully alive.* Had he waited too long to begin to let the Light in? Had he let it in at all?

He pulled and fought and breathed and ached and screamed. He was so tired. It was so dark. Then the Light flickered again. It looked like a torch moving clumsily along the path toward what was left of him. *Who is holding the torch?* he wondered. He couldn't see. But then he could hear something.

"Keep fighting. You are doing well."

Was he fighting? He couldn't tell? He was weary, but nothing was changing so he wasn't sure the battle was real. Surely he was not doing well. He didn't feel well. He inhaled and screamed again.

"Help me." Did he say the words or just think them? Was anyone there to hear him if he had uttered any words?

Then he felt a tickle on his hand like a kiss. "I have tried... I'm afraid I don't know how."

Ylva! He raged against unseen bindings again. He pulled and stretched and reached for her. *Don't give up on me...please.*

"Lys, please...please."

Yes, please, Lys, please. Help me. If my heart is not worthy enough, let her's be. Let me have the chance to do better—to be better. Or if I cannot, then let me die. Please do not let the Darkness twist me into a monster. Please.

Rohan was mumbling, begging, the same words over and over. Maybe it was just one word...please.

"I know there is still a small hope inside you too. Find it. Hold on to it. Let it lead you out," he heard a voice say.

Hope. Was there any hope left? Yes, there had to be, otherwise why was he praying? Why would he beg unless there was reason to believe that someone was listening, that someone had the power to pull him out of this abyss? Please...please... please...the word turned over and over in his mind. Or was he physically saying the word? It felt loud to him—a primal roar growing louder and louder.

A hum... quiet at first, so quiet he almost missed it. Something made him pause his silent shouting long enough for it to latch onto his senses. It grew louder. The humming...it was a familiar lullaby. He recognized it.

Quiet, quiet, little one.
Rest your weary eyes.
For all the world is sleeping.
In wait for new sunrise.

Rohan's mother used to sing it to him when he was a boy. He would lay in her lap...she would twist one of his blonde curls around her finger while she sang, and he would drift off to sleep.

So quiet, quiet, little one.
Do not the Darkness fear.
The Light is always stronger.
And Lys is ever near.

His mother had such faith in Lys. She would tell him often that Lys was watching, Lys was near, Lys was full of grace, Lys loved him. He did not have Ylva's Gift but if he had he was sure his mother's countenance would have been full of bright, warm light. It would have shimmered like the stars.

There was a flicker—another torch light drawing closer to him. Rohan set his eyes on it like it was his mother's face. He didn't move. He didn't strive. He waited. The light got closer, brighter, filling up more of the dark void around him.

"Come with me."

The pain was leaving. He could breathe again. He reached out like he was taking his mother's hand.

Rohan twitched his fingers. They prickled as the numbness and cold disappeared. He felt a weight on his shoulder and moved his hand to investigate. As soon as his calloused tips touched the soft skin, he knew it was Ylva. He caressed her cheek until she jerked away.

"Rohan." His name was like a gasp. "Rohan." He could feel her fingers on his face. "I was afraid I had lost you."

Rohan blinked. It was still bright. He squeezed his eyes shut tight—then opened them slowly, taking the time to adjust. The room was dimmer than he had realized, but her eyes— staring down at him—glimmered with so much light that he nearly couldn't bear it. "You didn't leave me." His hand found hers and held it tight.

"No," she smiled and he was undone by it. "I am with you, remember?" Ylva leaned in close to him and kissed his forehead. "I love you," she whispered to him. It was music.

He brought her hand to his lips and kissed the bottom of her palm. "Do I deserve it, your love?"

"Love isn't deserved. It is merely given. I have chosen to give it to you everyday from hereafter." She leaned close and kissed his hand. He could feel a tear drip against his skin.

"I will earn it everyday hereafter."

"Don't," Ylva said, "just love me in return. That is enough." Ylva climbed up onto the cot, curling beside him, her head laying on his chest and her fingers brushing against his neck.

"It is already done." Rohan wrapped his arm around her. The two drifted into rest.

Love isn't deserved. It is merely given. I have chosen to give it to you. Rohan heard Ylva's words playing again inside his sleepy mind...but it wasn't her voice speaking them. This voice sounded deeper and stronger. He could swear he had heard it before, long ago, but couldn't place where. The repeated words in his mind, the different voice, the unplaced familiarity…it was enough to rouse him awake.

He didn't know how long they had been asleep. He had some reminiscence of Elior's voice shooing someone away to "let them rest now." He didn't want to wake Ylva and end this moment. As careful as he was not to move her, he felt her stirring next to him anyway. She lifted her chin enough so that he could see her smile. Erland's words—the ones about having faith in her—crashed to the front of his mind.

"I'm sorry," Rohan whispered to Ylva.

"For what?" She sat herself up. "Almost dying? I think I've forgiven you."

"For not telling you sooner, for not having enough faith in you all along when you have kept me alive for more days than you know." Rohan pushed himself up so that he could reach her and touched her cheek.

She placed her hand on his. "It wasn't I alone."

She didn't specify of whom she was referring, but he understood her meaning. She spoke of Lys. Was that the voice he heard echoing her words? He could not deny the existence of the Light any longer. Was that even what he had struggled with all along? Or did he really struggle to accept that Lys could accept…had accepted him? That his mother's words were true and Lys was full of grace and Lys loved him? Perhaps it was time for him to give grace to himself. Time for him to love himself enough to love Ylva; enough to lead the Four Realms. He couldn't afford to do anything less. He no longer could languish in his weaknesses and doubts. The Four Realms of Väljalil couldn't afford it either.

CHAPTER THIRTY-FIVE

"HIGHNESS." The commander stepped just inside the tent. "All the warriors are accounted for and gathering. They await you."

Rohan cupped his hands and dipped them into the water bucket. Lifting them back out, he then splashed water on his face. "I'll be there in a few moments."

The commander nodded before retreating outside.

"Here," Elior said, handing the king a cloth.

"Thank you." Rohan took it to dry his face and hands. He picked up his breastplate.

"Let me help you with that," the servant said, taking hold of the leather armor. He helped to lift it over Rohan's head.

"You do not need to..." Rohan began, but Elior seemed to pay him no attention. He continued to latch the piece in place.

"You look much better, Highness," Elior said, his grin widening as he picked up the king's leather bracers and laced them onto his arms.

"I feel much better," Rohan replied. "Thank you for your part in that."

"I'm just a servant, here to help," Elior responded without looking directly at Rohan's face. He was focused on the task of readying the king for war. When the bracers were tied, Elior picked up the king's helmet and sword. He handed them to Rohan. "You are ready."

Rohan felt the servant's last three words meant something more than just being dressed. For the first time in his life, he felt ready to be king. Ghosts of doubts and fears still haunted the background of his thoughts. However, he found it much less challenging to drive them away when they tried to come forward.

"Things are much easier when you begin to let go of who you thought you needed to be and become who you are," Elior said, now staring directly into the king's eyes.

Rohan felt his heart and lungs pause for a beat. The feeling that Elior could read his mind would never be comfortable—but it was now also in small part comforting. "You *are* intuitive," Rohan told the servant, "and you are right."

"And I am very glad that you were not lost to us."

"As am I," Ylva's voice drew Rohan's attention to her presence. Vǫrðr and Shura stood with her. The black wolf trotted to Rohan's side. "As are they."

Vǫrðr nestled his head against the king's side. Rohan squatted down and scratched the dogs head. Vǫrðr sniffed at his chest, arms and neck, and when satisfied to discover the king's wellness, licked Rohan's face. Rohan laughed. It felt good to laugh—down in the depths of his soul. It felt like this joy had been gone and was now come home.

"They are waiting for you," Ylva said.

Rohan stood and Ylva stepped closer to him. She brought her hands to the sides of his face. "What do you see now?" He asked her.

"I see the man I love, with light in his eyes," she answered. "I needn't look any further to know the Darkness has not won him."

Rohan kissed her forehead. "Let's go then."

Outside the tent, Erland greeted Rohan with a nod of his head and a wry grin. "Highness," was all he said, but with more reverence than the man had before paid to the king.

"Erland," Rohan replied.

Erland took the king by the arm and leaned close. "Careful with her," he whispered.

"I thought the Wolf Queen needs no protection," Rohan replied.

"No, but her heart might," Erland said. "And I would hate to have to kill you just when I'm starting to like you."

"That would be regrettable." Rohan patted Erland's arm. "I promise you—her heart is in good hands."

"Aye," Erland replied.

They mounted their horses and rode to the front of the gathered armies. Their ranks were lit by torchlight as the sun set behind them. Rohan tried to engrain as many faces as he could in his mind as he trotted past them. Men and shield maidens, young and old, all fierce and brave. These were his people—the ones he would proudly fight beside. He halted his horse at the assembly's center. Ylva stopped beside him, her wolves with her.

Rohan looked to her.

"I am with you," she said. Then she looked out over the crowd of warriors. She was regal—beautiful and fearless just like her wolves. Again, she made him feel stronger, as she had at his father's funeral. He hoped to never have to be without her at his side.

It was time to be king. Rohan sat taller in the saddle. He shouted toward the army. "Warriors of the Four Realms of Väljalil! Our enemy sits in Askadalen—waiting to spread its disease throughout our land. It is a mighty opponent—frightening and vast—but not invincible. As it seeks desperately to infect our hearts, we will pierce its heart one monster at a time! Its master will learn that we are not so weak as it once thought!" Rohan paused. Then he glanced toward Ylva. He remembered the words she once told him. Then he continued, "The Darkness may come to devour us, but you are strong and courageous—you will not wait for the Darkness! No, *we* will go to the Darkness and make it regrets its plans."

A cheer, like a roaring wave, began to ripple through the army. They banged swords and axes against their shields. Vǫrðr and Shura howled.

Rohan lifted his hand to quiet them. "Tonight, eat...drink... rest—for tomorrow we wage war on Myrkr!"

Again, the crowd bellowed. Their shouts echoed with power and anticipation. Rohan knew the Bardung, Senka and the dragon were all formidable. He knew that tomorrow's battle would not be easy—though for tonight, he had given his people much needed encouragement. It wasn't his words he knew, but his hope. If a small bit of hope could pull him from the Darkness, then he wagered it could give these warriors the strength to push the Darkness back.

CHAPTER THIRTY-SIX

A RAVEN PERCHED on Senka's hand. The fire light gleamed off its glossy feathers. The same light danced in her coal eyes, a reflection of a reflection that took her sight beyond her cavernous ruins to the torchlights of Väljalil's army.

"The prince is not dead," Senka muttered to herself as her raven squawked. "That girl, she is not to be underestimated." The priestess glared at the image of Rohan and Ylva as it projected from the flames in front of her. The two stood side by side before their pitiful throng. "They think their little love will flourish. They think it will make them stronger, but it will be the very thing that kills them. *I* will have Ylva's heart. I will crush it in my hands. I will watch her die. I will make her prince watch her die, and then I will kill him."

The dragon stirred behind Senka. Its scales slithered against the stone floor. It yawned and growled as it tried to stretch its wings.

"Oh, my pet, the time has almost come for you to vanquish what is left of their hope." Senka touched her free hand to the beast's nose. "Look for yourself into the fire. Tomorrow we will let them come and—" Senka stopped. Something just then in the flames caught her attention.

Standing beside Ylva, Senka saw a man. He was nothing to take note of—thin and unassuming. But Senka saw something within him. He had been the one to shoo her ravens away from the prince. But his familiarity didn't end there. She recognized a look in his eyes from centuries before. It sent a shiver over her arms and down her back. "It cannot be."

As soon as the words left her lips, the man turned his gaze directly at one of the torches. Senka could swear he was looking past the light and into her eyes. The look made her afraid—a rare and loathsome experience for her. The priestess screamed as her anger boiled into hatred. The sudden noise scared the raven and it flew out of the room. Even the dragon jerked its head back at the awful sound of her shriek.

The face in the fire smiled at her. He then looked away.

"You have made a mistake in showing yourself!" Senka raged. "You are flesh and bone—I will peel you apart layer by layer! You will not save them again! You will not even save yourself!" The madness shook her from the inside out.

The dragon crept closer, tucking itself around Senka. She rubbed a quivering hand against its chin. "Tomorrow we will let them come. While they are distracted by those pawns in the valley, you will do something for me, my pet."

The dragon purred.

CHAPTER THIRTY-SEVEN

YLVA HAD a tradition the night before a battle. She would wait for the streets of her village to empty and then go for a walk amongst the quiet homes. She would listen to the last sounds of husbands telling their wives good night and kissing their children. She would strain to hear their prayers for protection. She would smile when she heard laughter or singing. She would offer her own intercession on their behalves.

It was different here. Soldiers slept outside around fading fires. As she walked among them, the noises and last sleepy words sounded closer...louder. They were different too. Loving "goodnights" amid family members had been replaced with final requests from comrades. She did hear the occasional laugh or a bit of snoring. These commonalities made her smile. She also heard quiet prayers offered to Lys. She still offered her own intercession for them—for family left behind, for herself, for Erland and Rohan. Just like at home, she looked to find a quiet spot where she could stare up at the stars and still her own mind.

When she passed the last campfire in hopes of a clear view of the night sky, she discerned a silhouette. "Rohan?"

The king turned round. "Ylva, you should be sleeping."

She walked to his side and slid her hand into his. "I like to take in the quiet and calm first."

"Apparently I do too." He smiled. Even in the dim moonlight, however, she could still see it was feeble.

"This is my first real battle. My first taste of war," he said.

"You did well when the Keep was attacked," Ylva told him. "You will do well tomorrow."

"The Keep came as a surprise," he replied. "I didn't have time to think about it. But I can't stop thinking about tomorrow."

Ylva leaned her head against his shoulder. "You will do well tomorrow. No matter the outcome, there is no fear if the Light has won your heart."

Rohan lifted her hand to his soft lips.

"Besides, you have already won victory over mine." Ylva giggled at her own sentiment. It was strange to her to feel like this about a man.

"No," Rohan replied, causing the butterflies in her stomach to lurch to a frightful halt.

"No?" She pulled away to try and see his face.

"Your heart is not for the winning."

"Then it is for the giving, and I have given it to you."

Rohan brushed his fingers over her cheek before bringing them to rest on her neck. "No," he whispered, his lips curving upward in his charming smirk.

Ylva could feel her cheeks warm. The flutter of the butterflies instantly resumed.

"Your heart is not for the winning, or for the giving, because you gave it away a long time ago. The Light owns your heart. The best I can hope for is that one day our two hearts will entangle as one." He closed the already small gap between them. Ylva could practically feel his heartbeat against her own chest. "I would not wish to take something that isn't mine and would not ask you to give me something that isn't yours."

"And your heart?" Ylva swallowed. The space between them

buzzed, as did her head. This man who had before understood nothing of her or her heart was coming to know her in a way that she hadn't believed to be possible.

"It's still a work in progress." Rohan's lips brushed the tip of her nose.

"It has made more progress than you think." Ylva returned her head to his shoulder. As they gazed at the stars in the quiet, she could almost hear his heartbeat and imagined it coming to match rhythm with her's. Two hearts and two lives becoming one in purpose. That is what she envisioned love to be. Rohan's words then replayed in her mind: *Two hearts entangle as one.*

Heart...the word kept appearing in her recent thoughts. She wished it was solely in regard to love, to Rohan, but images of war crashed against the sublime romance. Standing there in Rohan's embrace, suddenly Ylva wanted to run away from her duty for the first time in her life. The notion frightened her. Though she would never act on it, part of her wanted to hide from what she surmised was to come and pretend that the weight was not their's to carry. Would it all be easier if she had never loved him? Would it all be more worth it because she did love him?

CHAPTER THIRTY-EIGHT

THE ARMIES of Väljalil gathered just as the sun crested the horizon. Clans, farmers and soldiers formed row upon row at the edge of Askadalen. Ylva and the Ibharüng stood at the front lines. Vǫrðr and Shura trotted around her feet.

"Are you certain you wouldn't rather ride?" Rohan asked Ylva.

"No," she replied. "You and the horsemen from Grålås can lead on—we will charge behind you on foot. This is our way…it is what my warriors know, I will fight beside them." Ylva noticed the flinch of Rohan's jaw. She reached out to touch his arm before adding, "and you. I am with you, remember?"

The king smiled. "And I with you."

He was about to mount his horse when Elior approached. "Highness, if I might have a moment, I think it would be proper to anoint the king and his army before battle."

Ylva thought Rohan would hesitate at the suggestion but he didn't. "Do," was his short reply.

"And you as well, Ylva." Elior gestured for her to step beside Rohan. "You have journeyed together this far. I believe it would please the king to include you."

"It would," Rohan responded.

Ylva stepped beside him. He brushed his fingers against hers. The night before and their conversation of hearts becoming one leapt to the front of her mind. She didn't dare linger there too long. She needed to focus on the battle ahead—of what must be done. Still, it was nice to have the fleeting moment of sentiment and dream.

"Good," Elior continued. He held a small bottle of some sort of oil. When he poured it on his hands, Ylva could smell its sweetness. Spice and flowers. The servant touched his oily fingers first to Rohan's forehead and then to her's. She felt a small bit of the oil drip down her nose. "Lys, may your strength go with them and your light flow through them. In turn, may it flow through the warriors they lead." Elior removed his hands from their heads.

Ylva opened her eyes. The sky now looked brighter. The sun still inched its way higher above the gray clouds over the valley —its beams pierced through the smoky cover. It seemed to Ylva as though Lys was lighting the path to their enemy in a brilliant show of favor. Did Rohan see it the same way? She couldn't read his mind but noticed that his eyes followed the sunlight. His face held a solace that made her feel like he understood what she did. She was glad of it.

"You will do well," Ylva whispered to Rohan as she turned to rejoin her clan.

"We," Rohan replied. "We will do well." He smiled. It wasn't charm or a mask to cover fear. It was another true thing—a real smile this time—an honest offering.

As Ylva took her place with Erland and Dagr, in the distance, from the depths of the valley, war drums began to beat. The heavy and steady percussion signaled a waiting opponent. Vǫrðr and Shura growled at the low tones, their hair raising on their shoulders. "Easy, wolves," she whispered to them.

"I don't like that sound," Dagr muttered from her left.

"I don't mind a little rhythm to fight by." Erland chuckled on her right.

"It means they know we are coming," Dagr answered.

Ylva pulled her axe from her belt and lifted her shield off the ground. "Aye, but it doesn't mean they are ready for what we bring."

"Aye to that!" Erland pounded his own axe against his shield.

The king mounted his stallion to ride back and forth in front of his army. "Warriors!" he shouted, halting his steed in place at the center of their throng. At the sound of his deep voice the whole gathering grew still and quiet save for the snorts of the horses. "Today we will vanquish Myrkr's threat! We will take back the whole of the Four Realms! May the Light lead us!"

Without hesitation, a reply of a thousand voices reverberated over the earth, "AND MAY THE DARKNESS FEAR US!" They punctuated the battle cry with a primal roar.

Rohan and the horsemen then sped forward in a near-violent gallop toward the Bardung flanks. They held their swords ready, prepared to shred through the first line of defense and make a path for those on foot.

Ylva, her wolves and her clan, led the rest of the warriors. They ran behind the horses, smashing into the chaos ahead of them. She leapt over the few Bardung the horsemen brought down to clash with the mass left standing. Their inhuman enemy growled and sneered. They showed no fear, only aggression as they charged back at the clansmen. They smelled of death and decay. The stench sickening as it hit Ylva's nose. Black blood dripped from their teeth and corpse-like flesh. There was such a frenzy of mud, men and blood that Ylva kept her focus only on the space within her axe's reach. One by one, she hacked through the never-ending enemy. One by one, she took aim and sliced into their hearts. One by one, she watched them fall at her feet.

Erland, still on her right, and Dagr, still on her left, did the same. Vǫrðr and Shura guarded her back, barking to signal danger at her heels. She spun at their call as they sunk teeth into the inhuman creatures, holding them long enough for her to complete the task of shattering their inky hearts.

Ylva couldn't tell you how long they had been fighting. She hadn't kept track of how many Bardung she had brought down. She couldn't gauge their success or failure by the picture at play around her. She knew most of the blood covering her armor wasn't her's. She knew there were still too many of the undead charging them to mean the end was any closer in sight. She did know the king was safe.

When a few feet of space between opponents gave her a few seconds to catch her breath, she would glance over the battlefield and catch the sunlight glinting off of Rohan's helmet. He had abandoned his horse and was now fighting from the ground—but he was even more fierce than he had been at the Keep. Those few moments of catching sight of him were a balm to her fatigued muscles and afforded her extra strength.

Then a shriek echoed from the High Mountain. It sounded shrill and sent chills down her spine.

"The dragon!" Erland shouted, pointing toward a growing black shadow flying toward them.

"With me!" Rohan yelled in reply.

Ylva, Erland and the wolves rushed to the king's side.

"Do we have any idea how to kill it yet?" Erland screamed.

"Going for the heart has worked so far today," Rohan shouted back.

"The heart it is." Erland smirked and followed the king through the throng to get to a higher vantage point in hopes that they might be able to make an attack on the beast.

Ylva went with them. The monster somehow seemed even larger and stronger. She feared that this meant its skin had also thickened. All of her notions and memories flooded and swirled in a sort of whirlpool in her mind. *The heart... hearts... go for the heart.* There was a way to kill this beast but she feared an arrow or an axe would not do the job.

The trio and extra archers readied their weapons as they reached a ridge on the western side of the fray. Ylva's wolves stood at her side, teeth barred and snarling at the coming beast.

"Aim for the heart—don't miss," Rohan ordered. "We don't want to just make it angry," he added.

The dragon roared.

"I think it's already angry," Erland replied.

They all held steady as the beast approached, barely breathing in wait for the right moment. Almost... almost...almost...*now!*

"FIRE!" Rohan shouted as a signal to release their arrows.

A few arrows clipped the dragon's wings—others merely bounced off his thick scales. One or two found a way to penetrate the creature's skin. Their points didn't go deep enough to hinder the beast...but they caused enough pain for the dragon to hiss and shriek again. It pulled its head up and opened its mouth wide. With an ungodly sound, the mammoth creature inhaled— then exhaled white-hot flames, scorching the ground around them.

"Since when does it breathe fire?" Erland exclaimed as they lifted their shields over their head for shelter.

"It doesn't matter," Rohan responded. "What matters is we stop it, and quickly."

Ylva peered around her shield. The dragon circled again and breathed another spout of fire. It torched warriors of Väljalil and Bardung soldiers alike. The mortals would scream and screech in agony as they burned. The monsters would only fight harder with flaming bodies.

"It's coming back around," Ylva said.

They lowered their shields, ready for another barrage—but the dragon no longer hovered over them, nor was it torching the army. In fact, the beast wasn't attacking at all.

"What's it doing?" Rohan wondered aloud.

Ylva watched the dragon circle overhead. "It's like it's looking for something...or someone."

"Me?" Rohan asked Ylva. "Or you?"

Ylva kept her eyes on the beast as it flew around and around the perimeter of the valley. A sinking pit formed in her stomach as her own eyes searched the crowd. "No," she exhaled catching sight of a friendly face tending the wounded amongst the violence. "Elior."

"Elior! Why would it want him?" Erland asked incredulously.

"Why now?" Rohan added. "Why not just attack our armies? Wouldn't that be a better use of the dragon's ability than killing one man?"

Ylva's eyes seemed to catch sight of the servant the moment the dragon's did. "I don't think Senka means to kill him...not here." Ylva started to run back through the chaos of the battle toward Elior. She screamed his name in an attempt at a warning, but she couldn't outrun the dragon—not with a mass of Bardung still clamoring around her. She sliced and hacked her way through...but she knew she wouldn't make it. "Vǫrðr, go!" She ordered her warden.

The black wolf took off toward the servant. He made better time darting through the melee. He reached Elior just as the dragon did. As the beast's claws gripped the servant, Vǫrðr tried to pull him back, biting and yanking at Elior's cloak. It wasn't enough. The dragon rose higher. Vǫrðr let go. The dragon turned and flew back toward Skämd.

Ylva, her eyes on the dragon, chopped her axe into the chest of another inhuman before turning to follow the creature's flight path.

"Ylva stop!" Rohan's hand grabbed her arm and forced her to halt.

"I must save him!" she protested.

"You cannot face the dragon—you cannot risk everything for one man!" Rohan argued.

"If we cannot risk for one man, then why are we risking at all?" Ylva pulled away from his grip. "We are all just one man worth saving."

Rohan sighed. "Fine, but I am coming with you."

"No, you are king," Ylva responded. "You need to be here."

"I am king and I say if you are intent on going, I am going with you," Rohan countered. "Besides, if Senka wants Elior, then there is a reason and likely not one a good one. Maybe we should find out together."

"Erland." The king turned toward her companion who was busy keeping the Bardung from invading their impromptu conversation. "Find the commander, tell him where we have gone and that I have placed you in charge in my stead."

"Aye!" Erland replied with a nod.

"Let's go, Wolf Queen." Rohan smirked as he jogged past her and her ever vigilant wolves, taking the lead through the fracas toward the ruins on the High Mountain.

"Good." Senka smiled into her fire. "I have been waiting all day for you two to come to me." The priestess smoothed her dress with her slender stained fingers. "I think I should offer you a proper greeting when you arrive." She clapped and one of her undead soldiers entered the dark room. "Gather those left here to guard the ruins. The king and the Wolf Queen will be here shortly. I would very much like to kill them."

CHAPTER THIRTY-NINE

THE ENTIRE LANDSCAPE surrounding the High Mountain was devoid of life—just dry dirt and crumbling stone accented by dead trees. The stench of brimstone and burning ash stung Ylva's nose. Her eyes watered as she and Rohan climbed the cragged steps of the old tower ruins. The rocks of the ancient stairway shook loose beneath her feet. The higher they climbed toward the remnants of the old fortress, the more carefully she tread. Falling would be more than an unwelcome deterrent from their mission...it could be deadly.

Vǫrðr and Shura would jog ahead of them, then double back to Ylva as if they were trying to show her the best route to take.

A raven cawed above them.

"I guess that means she knows we're coming," Rohan said.

"She always knew we were coming," Ylva replied. Since her first meeting with the priestess, she knew they would meet again. Senka didn't strike her as the type to run and hide, licking her wounds in surrender. The two of them facing off against Myrkr's creation was inevitable. The battle with the Bardung in the valley below was merely the introduction. The finale waited at the top of Skämd.

"Then now would be a good time to figure out how to kill her," Rohan said, "…or her dragon."

"Lys will give us the answers in the right time," Ylva replied, "of that I am sure." The inkling of a plan, of an answer had been whispering at the edges of Ylva's thoughts for some time now. Bits and pieces of memories and experiences all working together to form a final solution. She could tell Rohan now. She could give him a moment to prepare himself for what she feared was to come. She still felt unprepared and worried that if she told him now, then he would stop and march her right back down the mountain. She couldn't risk that.

She prayed, a silent monologue of those thoughts and fears, an offering to Lys as they made the trek up Skämd. She hoped upon hope that Lys would give her the strength. She hoped upon hope that her hypothesis would be wrong.

A stone arch stood as the final gate—the last moment of preparation before their enemy would come into view. Ylva inhaled a deep breath and pushed it out to help cleanse her body and mind. She lifted her shield, keeping it just low enough to see over its edge. Her fingers wrapped tighter around the handle of her axe.

She could hear the gruff groans of inhuman soldiers before she could see their gray eyes and pale flesh waiting outside the tower's entry. Vǫrðr and Shura returned their groans for growls as the two wolves stood on either side of Ylva and the king.

The twenty or so Bardung that lined the front of the tower parted their ranks without a word. The priestess stepped out of the shadows, slinking toward Ylva and Rohan. A wicked grin curled her lips. "If it isn't the sweet young lovers," she said, her words resounding like a hiss. "To what do I owe the pleasure of your company?"

"We are here for Elior," Rohan replied. "And we are here to end this."

"I'm afraid I cannot accommodate either of those requests."

Senka ran her black fingers over her collarbone. "But I do believe I owe you something." Her black eyes looked straight at Ylva.

If Senka intended to scare Ylva with this, then she failed. Ylva's axe had wounded the priestess once before—she could do it again. Senka knew it as well. The quiver of her jaw gave her away. "You can try to hide your fear behind a mask of seduction and arrogance," Ylva said, "but I can still see it. You know as well as I that the end has come."

Senka's smirk melted into a sneer. "We will see whose end has come." She lifted her crooked fingers, calling her soldiers to raise their weapons. "Try. Try to get through my warriors. Try to slay my dragon. Try to save your precious Elior. Your own arrogance is showing if you think it can be done."

"We will fight and the end will be determined," Rohan told Senka, "but Elior has no place in this. He is but a servant—you have no use of him but to get us here, so his purpose has been served. Let him go."

The priestess laughed. "Do you really think me to possess any mercy? Even if what you say is true, I would not release him. You would have ended up on my doorstep with or without him because this is where this must end. But I have waited a very, very long time for an audience with Elior—as you call him —and I will not release him."

How could she know of Elior? What did she know of Elior? Memories and notions swirled again in Ylva's mind, merging into a clearer picture. *Could he be? Was it possible?*

"You call him servant," Senka continued, "but he is so much more than that. I thought you two would have figured that out by now, especially you, Wolf Queen."

Senka didn't give them time for rebuttal. She thrust her hand out and the undead at her sides lunged forward to attack.

Ylva and Rohan snapped into action. They stood back-to-back in an effort to offer at least a little protection to one another while fending off the inhumans. Two against twenty was anything but good odds. The wolves offered aide but could only slow down the next opponent for a few seconds before the Bardung broke through to Ylva and Rohan. Nevertheless, Ylva was grateful for every extra moment her companions afforded her.

The skirmish blurred into the blocking Bardung swords, her axe hacking into chests, black blood splattering across her face and her own red blood dripping down her arm. She could see the crimson liquid trickle down her fingers to stain her axe handle. A stinging sensation surged up and down her arm. She couldn't stop to assess the damage but had done enough battle to know it was a wound she would survive.

She couldn't see Rohan. She could hear his sword clank against the metal of their enemies. She could hear him grunt behind her. She could feel his presence there—a shield at her back. She could see the Bardung numbers dwindling. She could hear Senka bellow her disapproval.

Through the last three undead, Ylva saw the priestess coming toward her. Her countenance seemed darker, shrouded with anger —her inky fingers were raised. It looked like she was trying to grab hold of something invisible. She was trying to grab hold of Ylva like she had Rohan that night in Grålås. It wasn't working. Ylva could feel no magic—no unseen force gripping her throat or heart.

"Your dark magic still doesn't work on me, Priestess!" Ylva shouted as she chopped her axe into another black heart.

Senka shrieked again. "Maybe not," she hissed, "but it will work on him!" Senka turned her gaze to Rohan. She clenched her fingers and Ylva heard the king gasp.

"Rohan!" Ylva shouted and kicked back another dying Bardung before turning to see Senka pulling the king across the ground with her hand motions.

Only one inhuman remained between Ylva and Senka. He

charged toward Ylva. Vǫrðr and Shura lunged at him. One grabbed his leg while the other sunk its fangs into his arm. Ylva pulled her axe free from the chest of the dead Bardung at her feet and pivoted, then flung it into the chest of the final combatant.

"Go ahead," Senka yelled. "I will kill your prince."

"I'm...not...a...prince," Rohan choked out as he pushed his feet into the ground. Ylva could see his heels digging in. She watched his veins bulge from strained muscles as he fought the priestess' magic. "I...am...THE...KING!" With the last word Rohan roared, causing the invisible chain binding him to break. The force of his exertion sent them both flying backwards.

Ylva seized this opportunity and rushed toward the priestess. She swung her axe—it sliced across Senka's abdomen. Black blood began to ooze from the wound, soaking her dress.

Senka placed a hand over her stomach and stumbled, trying to back away from Ylva. "These wounds won't kill me," she whispered. "You can't kill me!"

"If I can make you bleed, then I can kill you," came Ylva's unhesitating response, as she raised her axe again.

In a breath, Senka transformed into smoke and vanished.

"I hate when she does that," Ylva muttered to herself. She turned around to find Rohan, to assess his injuries, but the king was already back on his feet and coming to meet her. "Are you all right?" she asked him as she looked over every inch of him for signs of a wound.

"I'm not the one bleeding." His fingers gingerly touched the bloody spot on her upper arm.

"It is fine," Ylva assured him. "We need to get to Elior."

CHAPTER FORTY

YLVA AND ROHAN walked carefully down the cavernous hall-
ways of the ruins. Shura sniffed ahead of them while Vǫrðr's
claws clicked against the stone floors behind them. Shadows—
creations of the torchlights that flickered on the walls—moved
around them in an eerie dance. A breeze caused them to change
beat, but it wasn't a draft. It felt warm and smelled of more
sulfur. Was it the dragon's breath? If so, it meant they were
closer.

Shura stopped, her ears perking.

Ylva squinted into the darkness ahead of them. She could
barely make out two doorways, one on each side of the corridor.
She knelt down and whispered to her wolf. "Which way?"

Shura sniffed again, then crept slowly toward the right. Ylva
followed.

Peering around the corner, Ylva could see a figure chained to
the walls, his arms stretched outward and his head bowed. *Elior.*
"You stay here, keep watch," Ylva whispered to Rohan. "I will
go free him."

Rohan nodded his agreement. Vǫrðr stayed on guard beside
him. Shura joined Ylva— they tiptoed toward the servant, being

careful not to make enough noise to draw unwanted attention to their rescue attempt.

"Elior," Ylva whispered as she reached him.

The servant lifted his head and smiled. How his smile could hold the same amount of warmth in this pit of despair, Ylva would never understand. Still, she felt it warming her soul.

"Ylva, I knew you would come," he said softly

"Of course," she replied. "We must get you out of here."

"You must defeat the dragon," Elior responded.

Ylva took a closer look at the shackles imprisoning Elior. "And we will," she assured him. She went to work fiddling with the locks. If there wasn't a dragon across the way she would have used her axe to break through and set Elior free...but she knew she needed to be more delicate so clamor wouldn't rouse the dragon.

"Have you figured it out yet?" Elior asked. "Have you figured out how to kill the beast?" A glint in his eyes and the tilt of his head revealed he already knew the answer.

Ylva paused in her work. "I think so," she responded. The pieces had been coming together slowly. Light. Darkness. Hearts. Sacrifice. She hadn't said them out loud. She hadn't wanted to believe this was truly the only way. She hoped she was wrong. His expression meant she wasn't. "But you knew all along...didn't you?"

"Yes." Elior smiled. She wouldn't call it a sad smile, but there was a solemnness to it.

"Why didn't you just tell us?"

"You were not ready to know...until now." Ylva wasn't sure if she saw tears that dampened the servant's eyes or if it was just the way the torchlight moved around them. "There was another who bore the same birthmark as you," Elior told her, his voice soft. "An ancestor from the first time war was waged with Myrkr. He would not make the necessary sacrifice. He couldn't bear the cost."

"I am not sure I can," Ylva told Elior. Sorrow threatened to crack her resolve. She could feel it in the dryness of her throat and the tightness in her chest. She glanced over her shoulder to Rohan's silhouette in the doorway. She always believed this kind of love would never find her. Yet, there he stood, just a few feet away. Could she bear to give him up? Could she ask him to do the same? Why would Lys allow these feelings at all if they would not be allowed a life together? Her insides shook as she breathed.

"Loving him…being loved by him," Elior spoke, "knowing a love without fear or agenda—love that puts another first—it was the final lesson to be learned, little one."

He answered a question Ylva hadn't spoken aloud. "How did you…?" Two of his words stopped her inquiry. *Little one.* Her question no longer mattered as much as the truth that was just fully revealed. She wanted to say something…to be given confirmation. "It was you," she exhaled the revelation. "It was you all along…always you."

"Yes, little one." Elior's smile grew even wider. Now she was sure she saw tears crossing the threshold of his long lashes.

"How did I not see it until now?" Ylva asked him, her own tears dripping down her quivering cheeks in warm streams.

"Most must die to themselves before they ever truly see me," Elior answered. "Your surrender has opened your eyes."

"I haven't surrendered anything."

"You have," the servant replied. "You made your choice the moment the idea started to take shape in your heart. You only think otherwise because you don't see the brave girl I do. She has always done what was right, and she will do it now."

Ylva wiped her cheek. She wanted to weep at his words, at the way they made her soul swell and stir, but there was no time for weeping—no time to sit and contemplate this. Maybe that was why the fullness of knowledge didn't come together until these final moments. Maybe it was a mercy given by Lys, one that kept her from agonizing and despairing. More time would have allowed for more temptation to retreat.

"That is why my ancestor failed, isn't it?" Ylva whispered the question to Elior.

"Yes, little one," the servant replied. "He wanted to be brave —but in the end, his own desires betrayed him. He couldn't lay them upon the altar. Just as your axe wounds the priestess, so did his sword. He thought that could be enough—so he abandoned the true path to victory for his own will."

Then Ylva understood. That was why they were here, facing the same enemy a century later—because her ancestor had settled for less than Lys' best plan to save himself. Paying this high price was her inheritance. The cost of selfishness and comfort would be higher—if not for herself, then for her children and grandchildren. Her axe could offer a temporary death to the Darkness. It could put the dragon back to sleep. But it would only force this same responsibility on another—Ylva would not see another carry it. Living with that burden would be far worse than shouldering her current one.

"You could not live knowing this would all come to the Four Realms again," Elior whispered.

Ylva closed her eyes and took three deep breaths to calm her nerves. When she felt like she could proceed she opened her eyes and looked at the servant. "No, I couldn't."

The servant smiled at her again. The knowing smile—the smile that gave her strength and boldness. "There is a key, hanging just over there." Elior pointed a finger toward a spot on the left wall.

Ylva chuckled. "You could have told me that when I first got here."

"Aye, but I think you needed this talk more than I needed to be free of these temporary chains."

CHAPTER FORTY-ONE

"Ahhh!" Senka's voice echoed off the walls. It reverberated in Rohan's ears, a mix of frustration and pain. He tightened his grip on the hilt of his sword.

"Ylva, we must get Elior out now," the king called over his shoulder.

"I have the servant, but we can't leave now," she replied. "We must take the chance we've been given to kill the dragon and stop the Darkness."

"Gladly—but how?" Rohan kept one eye on the corridor as he inquired. He knew Ylva wasn't impetuous—but while they had proximity, they still had no weapon, nor a way to destroy the massive beast.

"Trust me," she whispered, placing her hand on his shoulder.

She stood so close he could smell the sweet floral notes of her skin mingled with the metallic tinges of her drying blood. "All right," he said. He did trust her. With every fiber of his being and with every piece of his heart, Rohan trusted Ylva. He would follow her anywhere. She had proven that she would do the same for him.

"Let's be careful. We don't want to give ourselves away too

soon," Elior spoke as he tiptoed past them and across the corridor to peer into the other room.

Rohan stopped himself from scolding the servant and decided to merely follow close. He did his best to squeeze himself in front of Elior, shielding him from whatever might hide in waiting. Ylva squatted beside him. This cavernous room was much larger than Elior's prison with a high ceiling and carved out walls. The only light came from a single fire burning in the middle of the cavern.

Senka stood by the fire. The light cast an ominous glow across her face. "I need one of my soldiers," she panted. The wound on her stomach continued to ooze blood.

From the dark behind her came a movement. The reflection of flames glinted off the dragon's scales, giving just enough light to create a silhouette of its enormous form. The creature looked as though it could barely fit inside the room. It surely couldn't stretch itself out. Maybe this was the right place to kill it? Or instead, maybe this would be the place of their demise on account of so little room to escape.

"I have no time to send you to the battlefield," Senka muttered to the dragon. She raised her hands like she was pulling something from the fire itself. Smoke billowed out in a cloud that sank to the floor and molded into the shape of three slain Bardung. "If I can't have one good heart, I will have to make do with three broken ones." The priestess knelt down beside the corpses. She reached her slender fingers toward one, digging her claws into its chest and pulling out its heart. They watched as the Darkness drained from it and into her skin and along her veins. She did the same thing to the second and third bodies. Each time her wound would shrink until finally the skin stitched closed. And each time, the dragon would purr behind her.

"Here, my pet." Senka offered the beast what was left of the final heart, now shriveled in her hand.

The dragon took the offering from her. Fire flashed in the beast's eyes as it swallowed it down.

"You see now?" Elior asked Ylva.

"See what?" Rohan inquired as the three retreated back across the dark hallway and into the other room.

"I know how to kill the dragon...how to kill Senka," Ylva replied.

"Kill one and kill the other," Rohan said, remembering their time with the Keepers. "How? Cut off her head, rip out her heart? Because I am fine with either." He was ready and more than willing to raise his sword and bring down this Darkness once and for all. For a moment, he could feel the end of this war at their fingertips, giving him a burst of energy and strength.

"She doesn't have a heart," Elior reminded him. A more solemn answer was written on the servant's face...and Ylva's.

Rohan didn't like the way Ylva stared at him. She wasn't looking into his soul—but it was like she was begging him to see inside of her's. "What aren't you telling me?" he asked.

"It isn't Senka that we must kill; it is the dragon," Ylva replied. Her words came out slowly. Her voice quivered. "Our weapons do no good against it. Even if they did, any harm would be short-lived, just as it is for Senka. The only way to take down this Darkness is from the inside out."

"I don't understand," Rohan said.

Ylva took his hand. "Think about what we just witnessed. If feeding it a dark heart gives it power, gives her power," Ylva paused. She looked to Elior, then down at their intertwined fingers and back to Rohan. "Then we must feed it a pure heart."

"What?" Rohan couldn't possibly have understood her correctly. He hoped he didn't.

Ylva smiled. Rohan watched a single tear as it painted a new line down her dirty cheek. She squeezed his hand tight. "My heart. My heart is pure. The wolves saw it long ago. It's why Lys sent them. It's why they saved me. It's me…I think, somehow…I have always known it."

"No." Rohan felt the word come up out of his throat like a growl. "It cannot be you. How can you be so sure? You are human. Is any man pure? You said yourself, we all wrestle with Darkness."

"Purity of heart is not about perfection," Elior interjected. "Men make mistakes, but they learn from them. They get angry but commit no evil in it. They face fear but do not yield to it." Elior took Ylva's other hand in his. "Your heart is always facing in the direction of the Light. That is the difference." The servant looked to the king. "That has always been Ylva."

"So what? We let the priestess kill you?!" Rohan could not believe the words coming out of his mouth. How was he actually asking that question? His heart thumped so hard that it hurt. Each beat pumping more pain than his body had ever felt before. Water dripped somewhere and it echoed like thunder in his ears. Time seemed frozen but his breathing was so fast his lungs grew sore. His fingers numbed. His vision blurred.

"No," Ylva replied bringing reality back into miserable focus, "the priestess, even if I were to allow her to kill me, won't consume my heart of her own accord. She will not feed it to her dragon. She is too smart for that."

Rohan could feel the answer that was still coming. It rode on a wave of dread. His stomach twisted and he thought he might vomit. He swallowed down the taste of bile and dropped his head down, unable to look into her face and let her see his weakness. He could not bare to see her strength.

"Rohan," Ylva's palms touched his cheeks. Her hands were cold on his skin, a stark contrast to the warm tears he felt falling. "Rohan, it must be you."

He dared to look back into her eyes. He regretted it but couldn't look away. He was desperate to etch every inch of her form into his mind. "I can't kill you, Ylva," he responded, a near whimper, through his tears. "This can't be the way it all ends. Your axe wounded her, perhaps it can wound her dragon—maybe it can pierce his heart? How can we be sure it won't?"

"It won't. It will fail. If not the day, then the future." Her voice had lost its shiver. Was she being strong for him?

"You must do this. It must be you. Our hearts are entangled as one, from the moment we confessed our love they have been so. We must do this together—you and I. We must be strong enough to make the sacrifice no matter what. Remember?"

"I could sacrifice myself...but not you," Rohan whispered, leaning his forehead against hers. "Never you."

"It must be me. And it must be by your hand, because you're the one who loves me. Your action wouldn't be borne of anger or hate or fear...but out of love," Ylva replied. "That love will keep my heart pure."

He did love her. More than he loved even himself. It choked out of him in anguished breaths that burned his insides and hot tears that stung his eyes. He would gladly die in her place—let her cut his heart out of his chest and be the last thing he saw as he drifted into death. Could he do this? Why must he do this? He wanted to curse the Light. She didn't and that is why it had to be her. She, his Wolf Queen, was more than strong and brave. She was faithful even unto death.

He wanted to fight, to rage against the truth. What could he say to convince her to abandon everything she valued? Nothing. He could say nothing. He would say nothing further. Rohan could feel woeful acceptance settling deep in his being, like a great boulder settling down at the bottom of the ocean. He could protest, but he knew he must be faithful unto a life without her.

"I will do this, if it is what must be done," Rohan said. "But I'd like to kiss you first."

Still leaning against each other, Rohan could feel the warm breath of her quiet laugh. "Yes," she replied.

Rohan lifted his chin, his lips meeting hers in a gentle collision. Her hands wrapped around his neck and pulled him forward, deepening their kiss. A lifetime of love and honor unleashed in a singular act of affection. One he would only relinquish for need of breath.

CHAPTER FORTY-TWO

YLVA RELAYED the plan to Rohan. "Elior will distract the priestess so you and I can get close enough to the dragon."

His face was still wet with tears but he nodded.

Ylva's heart might be broken by this, the grief he bore in his eyes. She felt no hesitation in giving herself to end this war and save the Four Realms. She held no regret in the life she lived up until now. But looking into Rohan's face, she mourned the life they would never have. It would not be a sacrifice without love —without a cost. She thought, when the picture of this moment first began to formulate inside her, that it was her life alone she would give up...but now she realized she was wrong. She had no fear in death—that was no loss to her. This, a future with the man she loved, that was what she surrendered for the Ibharüng, the other clans, Erland, Håkon...and even for Rohan himself.

"I am ready," Elior said.

"As am I," Ylva replied.

Rohan looked between Ylva and Elior once or twice before resting his gaze on her. His lips curled up into a sad smile. "I am ready," he managed.

Elior and Rohan exited the chamber.

Ylva waited a moment, gesturing for her wolves to come to her. "Vǫrðr, Shura," she squatted down and rubbed her hand between their ears and under their chins. "Whatever happens, stay with Rohan…he will need you now." Vǫrðr pressed his head into her side and Shura whimpered. "Guard him as you have always guarded me." She kissed each dog's furry head, then stood. She took a deep breath and followed after the others.

"How will we get close to the dragon without it killing us first?" Rohan asked.

There was little in the grand cavern in the way of actual hiding places. But the corners were veiled in shadow.

"Perhaps the darkness itself can be our cover," the king suggested.

"No," Elior replied, "use the light. I will capture Senka's attention. Find a place near the fire. That is what she won't expect."

"Agreed," Ylva responded.

"Then let us get this ending under way." Elior smiled.

Ylva hesitated. Then she said to the servant, "May the Light lead you."

Elior's eyes brightened—his mouth drew up into his usual empowering smile. In this final moment, joy still covered him. It radiated from him in a wave that crashed into Ylva's spirit, dampening her waiting fears. "And may the Darkness fear you," he told her. Then he turned and entered Senka's lair.

"Ylva." Rohan pulled Ylva's attention with a touch to her arm. His blue eyes locked with her's. His stare unflinching. The look shouted a million unspoken words directly into her soul. "I am with you," he said.

"I will always be with you," Ylva replied, then kissed his lips once more. She wanted to live in this moment, to take it all in completely. But if she allowed herself to feel too much, then she would become undone. She couldn't let it linger—as much as she wanted to. Pulling away from him signified the beginning of her offering.

"Priestess," Elior's voice bounced off the stone around them. "You wanted an audience with me."

"I see they have freed you from your chains," Senka answered coolly. From their position by the door, Ylva could see the priestess glance around the room. She was looking for them.

"We both know I stayed in those chains only as long as I wished to," Elior said. "But you…you will never be free of yours."

"Ha!" Senka laughed. "What chains? I am the most powerful being on this earth. Even you cannot defeat me." Senka slithered toward Elior, her back now to the fire.

Ylva and Rohan seized the moment and crept from the corridor to a place behind the high crackling flames in the stone pit.

"You are the weak one now," the priestess hissed at the servant.

"Is that why you wanted me here? To taunt me? To feel superior?" Elior kept baiting her.

"I am superior!" Senka bellowed.

The dragon screeched. It began to slink, uncurling itself and stretching its long neck out.

"We must move quickly," Ylva told Rohan. "We must do this now." She removed her leather breastplate.

"Are you certain there is no other way?" His words tumbled out of his mouth in a state of full-on terror. He grabbed her hand as he desperately pleaded, all of his composure nearly lost.

"I am." Ylva said. She squeezed his hand tightly, trying to imbue him with some of her strength. Or, maybe she hoped to gain from him.

She didn't want this for him. She didn't want it for herself.

But desire and necessity are a familiar balance in the human heart. Serving Lys didn't resolve that tension—it only offered a layer of tranquility, worth and hope in the midst of it. She clung to those things now.

"I have built an army," Senka continued her debate with Elior. "I have seduced your precious mankind and twisted them to Myrkr's pleasure. I have proven my power."

"Does real power need to be proven?" the servant asked her.

Ylva stretched herself up enough to see through the flames. Senka circled Elior like a predator does its prey. Her weakness became more obvious the more she tried to puff herself up. She was rigid with anger. Elior—he remained calm. Without the slightest bit of posturing, his presence filled the room. He made no claims, played no tricks—yet he made the priestess shiver with fear. Ylva could see it in the twitch of the priestess' jaw.

The dragon growled low.

"Rohan," Ylva said. "Do it now, before she unleashes her monster on Elior."

Rohan nodded his concession. His hand shook as he set down his sword and pulled a dagger from his belt. His cheeks grew pale.

Ylva wrapped her hands around his.

"Are we both shaking or is it just me?" he asked.

"Neither," Ylva replied. "It is not we who tremble, but the Darkness." She kissed his knuckles. "I love you."

"I love you," Rohan cried, then lifted the dagger.

She felt the sharp tip of the metal press into her flesh. There was a pinch, a sting, a burning along the nerves under her skin and throughout her body. Ylva kept her hands on her love's for as long as she had the strength.

As the blade pierced her flesh, one last time Ylva opened the door to her Gift. She allowed her eyes to peer past the surface of Rohan's face, his mind, his thoughts, and into his soul. Beyond the sadness cracking his heart, she saw Light. It shone bright and beautiful…it was whole. She wished he could see it for himself. That he could know—in this moment of complete pain and sadness—perfect peace was present and wrapped around them both.

CHAPTER FORTY-THREE

"ROHAN," Ylva said. "Do it now, before she unleashes her monster on Elior."

Rohan nodded his concession. He wanted to appear brave and strong but his body betrayed him. He breathed so fast but it didn't feel like any air reached his lungs. Fresh tears dripped down his cheeks and onto his hands, which he couldn't stop from shaking. He set down his sword and pulled a dagger from his belt.

Ylva's hands found his. He watched her fingers cover his own... her sweet soft fingers hiding his shaky hand and the grip of the knife.

"Are we both shaking or is it just me?" He asked, hoping for some miracle to burst forth and take this burden from him.

"Neither," Ylva replied. "It is not we who tremble, but the Darkness." Her warm lips pressed against his knuckles. "I love you," she whispered.

"I love you," Rohan cried. He prayed for the whole world to slow its spinning, for time to stop and make this an eternal moment.

The dragon growled again—he prayed for the strength to

complete this noble and horrible task, or to be rescued from it. But rescue didn't come.

Rohan lifted the dagger. It felt heavier than normal. He closed his eyes unthinkably tight, unable to look his precious love in the face. He pleaded a final time for his life and for her's. He begged and wept without a single spoken word, all in the span of a few seconds. Then he opened his eyes and pushed his dagger into her flesh.

Rohan felt the blade give as it broke through skin and sinew. He felt her body lurch at the force and the pain. Only then did her hands fall from their place around his own, leaving a cold sensation behind. He pulled her into his arms, then swallowed down a sob and the rising vomit in his throat.

Ylva smiled.

At first Rohan thought he had imagined it, but it didn't falter. As her life faded from her, that smile held fast until the last moment. Her eyes held a steady gaze into his. He knew her, knew she gazed into his soul—she had smiled at the sight. This was his darkest moment, or so he would have thought—and yet that couldn't be what she was seeing.

He wanted to tell her thank you. To let her know that he could divine her vision from her smile. He wanted her to know that it gave him an unexplainable serenity in the midst of his grief.

A final breath broke through her lips in a soft sigh before Ylva's body went limp in his embrace. Rohan leaned close and kissed her forehead. "I will always love you," he whispered through the unending torrent of tears falling down his face. Then he laid her onto the ground.

From somewhere in the shadows of the chamber, Ylva's wolves howled.

"Enough!" The priestess shouted. "I am done with this. You have made a grave mistake showing yourself, coming here. Even your Wolf Queen cannot protect you."

"I need no protection from you," Elior rebutted.

Rohan ran a palm down Ylva's face, closing her eyes, before gently slicing his dagger into her chest once again and gingerly removing her heart. He tried to offer her such care and reverence. His insides lurched at the action—but he knew it was what had to be done; what Ylva had given herself for. Holding her heart in his hands, he realized it didn't look like the others. It wasn't beaten and black like the ones Senka and her dragon had devoured. It was bright red, warm and whole. But then it wasn't just those things. A hint of light peeked from deep within its chambers, a sparkle of hope pushing outward like rays of sun through the clouds.

"In this form I can harm you, I can make you feel pain," the priestess replied to Elior. "I can kill your body. Then I will find her and her wolves and her prince. I will kill them all."

Rohan reached for his sword but beside it, beside Ylva, was her axe. He chose it instead. It felt right. He stood from his place behind the fire, her axe in one hand and her heart in the other.

"Death is no longer a threat," the servant replied. Elior looked toward Rohan and bowed his head.

The dragon inhaled through his smokey nostrils. He turned his head toward the king and shrieked.

Vǫrðr and Shura came running from their hiding places and stood on either side of him. Their teeth bared, their fangs dripping.

"Hungry?" Rohan asked the dragon. He lifted the heart toward the beast.

"No!" Senka howled.

It was too late. The scent of a fresh kill proved too tempting for the beast. It had snatched the heart from Rohan's open hand with a gruff purr.

"You really should have done less talking," the king told Senka.

The priestess raised her arm toward Rohan, her twisted

fingers and hand squeezing the air...but nothing happened. She screamed. She no longer had a hold on him because the Darkness found no place to grip. He had trusted that which was most precious to Lys.

Rohan rushed toward her, raising the axe and swinging it. It came across her jaw, knocking her to the ground.

"You can't kill me!" Senka wheezed.

The dragon screeched. It twitched in place. It pawed the ground and flung its head to and fro. The space was too small—the dragon banged into the top of the cavern, causing the room shake.

"I don't have to kill you," Rohan replied.

The creature's veins began to glow with a bright light. Just a shimmer at first, a flicker dancing under its scales. It grew. It brightened. It spread until it covered the dragon's skin, disintegrating the beast from the inside out.

"A pure heart," Elior whispered to the priestess.

Senka tried to stand but instead doubled over, clutching her stomach. "This will not end things," she coughed, black liquid oozing out of her mouth and running down her chin. "Myrkr will always be." The priestess choked out the words as she vomited more of the tar-like blood.

"Perhaps," Elior responded, "but you won't. And neither will his dragon to ravage this world. And he will never be stronger than Lys. He will always be defeated."

"No...no...I..." The words gurgled and fell flat. With each ragged breath the priestess weakened. Color drained from her hair and skin and eyes. Senka's body shriveled and shrank. She wretched and fell to the floor. She continued to seize and spew the Darkness as Light pushed its way through until neither she nor her dragon were anything more than ash and ooze on the stone floor.

The king wanted to take joy in their victory—while it would be a gift for his people, for now, he could only mourn. In the quiet and the dark of the tower ruins he would grieve his love. Rohan returned to Ylva's resting place by the fire. He sat on the ground and pulled her body back into his arms. Vǫrðr and Shura laid beside him. He wept over her. His shoulders shook with each sob until his throat was dry. At some point, Elior joined him. The servant sat beside him, his own cries joining Rohan's like a tragic duet.

CHAPTER FORTY-FOUR

ROHAN CONTINUED to weep long after his body ran out of tears. Somewhere in the back of his mind, he knew a battle might still be raging outside, a people would need their king to return to them. But he couldn't bring himself to leave Ylva. He couldn't find the strength to stand up and carry her body back down to the Valley. He didn't have the grace left to face her clan, to look Erland in the eyes and tell him what had happened…what he had made happen.

Voices of blame and shame whispered inside his head. They were little remnants of the Darkness scavenging for morsels of regret and self-loathing on which to feed. Ylva wouldn't want him to give into them. He had come so close to the Light, sacrificed too much for Lys, to forsake it all now. It would feel too much like forsaking her. Of all the things he couldn't bear right now—forsaking her topped the list. What life he had left, he would use to make her proud to have ever loved him.

Vǫrðr nudged his head against Rohan's side.

"Your Wolf Queen is gone," he whispered to the dog.

"Do not worry, Highness," Elior said. "She is gone, but she can be returned."

The king balked at the absurdity. He must have misheard the servant's words. Such a thing could not be done and his heart could not bear to entertain the thought. It couldn't bear not to either. "How? You are a healer, I know, but..." Rohan's heart picked up its pace, banging inside his chest, alternating beats of hope and anger.

"I think by now we both know I am a bit more than that," Elior replied. He touched the king's hand. Rohan felt a spark of something. "You said yourself—Ylva gave me her heart long ago. Now I am merely repaying the favor. A heart for a heart. Her heart for mine."

Lys? Rohan couldn't believe what he was hearing. Was that really what the servant meant? The rhythm of hope and anger beat harder and faster.

Rohan fumbled to string together any semblance of words. "If you can do this...if you are more than mere man, why? Why did I have to...why did she have to die at all?" Rohan panted the words, as he could hardly breathe.

"I came to this Realm long ago. I offered man all that is needed to fight the Darkness. I offered myself as I do now. The Light has always been." Elior placed a hand on Rohan's chest. "And the Light will always be...here...with you...fighting that Darkness, holding it back. But this war was wrought by man's choices. So must end with man's choice. Both your greatest weakness and your greatest strength is this gift—choice. It had to be her choice and your's together to yield to the Light...no matter the cost."

"I still don't understand," Rohan replied, shaking his head.

"I am the thing which can and cannot be known," Elior said. "Isn't that what your mother always used to tell you?"

It was. Rohan's mother would speak of the glorious mystery of Lys. She would tell him that the beauty of faith came in the trusting—not in the knowing. The certainty wasn't in the gifts of Lys, but in His goodness.

"Now," Elior said, "let me have some room."

Rohan still couldn't grasp what Elior was suggesting. Confounded, he still obeyed, lifting Ylva's body up so Elior could reach her.

"You have done well, little one," Elior whispered to Ylva, "but you have more to do." The servant closed his eyes and placed a hand on the bloody empty space that before held Ylva's heart.

A light glimmered behind Elior's eyelids. Rohan watched it flicker again and again. Then it grew steady and bright. The glow spread over his face, down his neck and arms until the servant's entire body became illuminated. He grew brighter and brighter, making Rohan's eyes burn. The king squinted to gain relief, but he didn't want to look away from the miracle unfolding before him. He watched the Light pulse and wave beneath Elior's skin and downward toward Ylva's chest. The Light seemed to drip from the servant's fingers and into the chasm of her wound...until even that was filled.

The radiance was more than a glow—it was living and moving and pulling together specks of itself until a shape formed. A new heart molded together from flecks of Light. Then the Light pulled skin and muscle, sewing it all back into place until the only sign of Ylva's injury was the crimson-stained rip of her tunic.

Rohan's heart, the anger in its beat replaced by awe, still pounded hard against his ribcage...like it was trying to reach Ylva's new heart. Something in him could feel her returning.

She gasped and her eyes flung open. They glowed bright with the same light.

"There you are," Elior said and then removed his hand. The Light faded from her eyes and from him.

"Ylva," Rohan said, brushing a strand of her fallen hair behind her ear.

"Did we defeat her?" Ylva asked. Her voice sounded raspy and quiet.

"Yes," Rohan said and laughed, "we defeated her. You defeated her and the dragon."

His Wolf Queen smiled up at him. "You are so bright," she said.

The wells of his tears returned, a fresh batch spilling down his cheeks. Rohan had never cried from joy. He would gladly become accustomed to the feel of it. "I love you," he leaned close and kissed Ylva's head, then cheek, then finally her mouth. He felt her soft fingers graze the line of his jaw.

She pulled away, her breath still warm on his lips. "I love you."

"All is well." Elior's affirmation interrupted the lover's reunion.

"Thank you." Rohan turned to the servant who smiled once more before collapsing to the ground.

Ylva sat up straighter. "What happened to him?"

"He gave his life for you," Rohan told her. "...for us."

Ylva's brow wrinkled and she asked, "How? Why?"

"A heart for a heart," he repeated Elior's words. "You offered your heart to the Light and the Light gave you a new one in return...his own."

Vǫrðr and Shura left their places next to the king and queen to cautiously approach Elior. They sniffed his body and then stepped back, bowing to the servant.

"We must honor him," Rohan said.

"We will," Ylva replied. She took hold of Rohan's hand. "With our lives. We will."

"Aye." Rohan kissed Ylva's head again, then helped her to her feet. Hand in hand they journeyed back down the dark corridors and into the light of day.

From the height of the ruins on the High Mountain, Rohan and

Ylva could see the whole of Askadalen. Above them, the gray clouds dissolved into blue sky. Under their feet, vibrant hues returned like a long-awaited spring. The grass turned a brilliant green. The trees stretched their arms and sprouted emerald leaves. Blooming flowers dotted the landscape. The life that had been held at bay for decades swept back in with a flood of color. Birdsong accented the triumphant roar of their army below as their enemies collapsed around them, the Darkness succumbing to the Light.

CHAPTER FORTY-FIVE

ROHAN HAD THOUGHT they should bury Elior in the king's cemetery in Grålås, but this didn't sit well with Ylva. Elior deserved a majesty far greater. The only place she could think would come close was the foot of the sacred mountains where she had been raised.

A caravan of men, both the leaders and the lowly, traveled across the realm, through the Northlands, and into the forest at the base of the Helig Mountains. When the trees became too thick for wagons and horses, they continued on foot. Ylva, Rohan and their wolves led the procession. Erland, Tyr, Dagr, and three others from the Ibharüng carried the servant.

"Here," Ylva said, stopping in front of a small cave.

"Here?" Rohan asked.

She knew it didn't seem like much. It was no palace, just a modest carving of stone. But it had been her home. It had been her safe place. It had been where Lys had raised her. It felt like the only place worthy of laying Elior to rest. "Yes...this is where our journey began. His and mine, and it is fitting that this is where it will..." She was about to say end, but that didn't seem right. Their journey wasn't ending—it was changing, growing, and morphing into something new. She could feel it transforming into something more full and complete. This was not an ending. "This is where it begins again," she finished.

"Aye, then," Rohan replied. He stepped forward and opened the wooden door. He then stepped aside to make room for Elior's body.

Erland and the others had to bend down to bring him inside. They laid him in the center of the cave. Ylva stood at his feet, the king beside her. She held an axe in her hand. It was much smaller than the one attached to her belt. Its handle carved with the image of a wolf pup. It was the axe she had used as a child— the one Elior had given her. She knelt down beside the servant's body and laid it between his hands. Then she kissed his forehead. "Thank you," she whispered. Then she returned to her place by Rohan.

The king took the golden helmet from his head and placed it just above Elior's.

Erland removed the pendant that he always wore from around his neck. It had been a gift from his mother. Ylva remembered when she had given it to him—it wasn't long before she died. Her bond-brother placed the object beside the servant and stepped outside.

One by one, the clan leaders, farmers, soldiers, shield maidens and parents with their children…each stepped into the small cave and laid down a gift in honor of Elior. Some extravagant in their worldly value. Others took the form of meek offerings but from generous hearts. Each was a sign of reverence and thanks. Soon the gifts filled the space around Elior's body.

When the last person had given their tribute, Rohan and Ylva exited the cave. Joining the assembly was a pack of wolves. They stood silently among the trees. Though it had been quite some time since she had seen them, she had known they were always close, always her pack. Their presence made her smile.

Vǫrðr and Shura stood with her too. The white she-wolf nudged her side. "I know it's time," she whispered to her guardian.

Rohan took her hand.

Håkon stepped in front of them. The elder lifted his hands and offered a prayer of thanks to Lys. It was not the traditional funeral rites or blessings, but then, this was not a laying to rest of a soul so much as an offering of thanks to the Light.

"May the Light always lead us," Håkon concluded.

The crowd replied in a somber uniform utterance, "And the Darkness fear us."

Erland and Rohan laid a stone in front of the doorway to protect the memorial. One carved with runes, telling the story of their sacrifice and of Elior's gift.

The wolves howled.

CHAPTER FORTY-SIX

YLVA STEPPED out of her bath smelling of lavender and roses. The water on her skin mingled with the air, drawing bumps up her arms and legs. Maids and maidens from her clan surrounded her, helping to make the necessary preparations. It felt strange to have them braiding her hair and tying the laces of her cream-colored frock. Suddenly, she felt a pang: she missed her mother.

This day, of all days, should be the one spent in the company of her parents. If they could not be with her in the flesh, she could be comforted knowing they were with her in spirit. She would bear symbols of them. On her head, she wore her mother's bridal crown. It carried an intricate weaving of wood, flowers and feathers. In her hand she held her father's sword. Magnus had preferred an axe in battle, but as a clan leader, he still owned a sword. It was silver and carved with the runes of their family lineage. It had hung on the wall in Håkon's home ever since Ivar's death. Today, according to tradition, she would give it to Rohan.

"It is time," Erland called through the door.

"I am ready," Ylva replied. She took a last deep breath before stepping outside.

Erland looked taken aback. He struggled to speak, his mouth just wordlessly moving. "You look..." He kept stuttering, unable to form another word.

"Thank you, brother," she replied touching his face. "Will you walk with me?"

Erland worked to compose himself. Swallowing, he managed, "It would be my honor to escort you on this day." He then held out his arm. She laced her own around it. "But it will not be I alone."

Vǫrðr and Shura joined the two, one wolf on either side. Together they walked down the center street of the Ibharüng village toward the open countryside. The familiar lane now a hallowed path leading her to her wedding...her future...to Rohan. Her entire clan, bouquets of wildflowers in hand, followed them, creating a joyous train. The gesture made Ylva's heart sing. It was a queen's entourage—it honored her more than they could ever know.

They all journeyed beyond the bounds of their homes, toward the fields covered in purple heather. Snow-capped mountains created a magnificent backdrop to the day's ceremony.

At the center of a circle built of friends and countrymen stood an arbor woven of branches and vines. Under it stood Rohan. He looked down at the sword he held in his hands, the one that had been his father's—the one given to him on the day he became king. As the gathering began to murmur, he suddenly looked up. He smiled when he saw her. Not his usual smile. Not the smirk of the charming prince, though she had come to love that almost as much as the wide deep grin that now brightened his whole face with joy.

Ylva's hands became clammy as she marched toward him. Her heart skipped around, a dance of nerves and gladness. She didn't take her eyes off Rohan. She didn't see exactly when the crowd behind her began to split away to join the rest of the congregation. She didn't even realize when Erland let go of her arm. She barely noticed any of it as she found herself standing face to face, just inches away from the man she was about to marry.

"May Lys bless this union," Håkon spoke from next to the couple. "May he guide your hearts always closer to one another and always toward his Light. May he make you able to protect, strong enough to offer grace, and brave enough to honor one another above all else. From now until this life ends."

"May Lys bless this union," Rohan repeated the elder's vows. "May he guide my heart always closer to yours and always toward his Light."

As he spoke those words of commitment, Ylva grew warmer. It wasn't the sun on her skin so much as the love in her heart for this man. This man who had frustrated and angered her. This man she had come to cherish without realizing when or how. This man who she almost lost and then whom she left. This man to whom she was returned. This man that made her feel safe, seen and known. This man who looked at her with the same exact love blazing in his eyes.

With each word he recited, her heart beat stronger as though it was pushing closer— desperate to reach out and touch his. It kept pulsing in rhythm to her voice as Ylva repeated the same vows to Rohan.

Håkon placed rings on the hilts of each of the swords they held.

"May he make me able to protect," Rohan said, handing Ylva the sword of Vakr.

Ylva spoke in unison with him, "strong enough to offer grace and brave enough to honor you above all else." They carefully traded blades.

Rohan's hand shook a bit as he took Magnus's from her and picked up Ylva's ring before sliding it onto her finger.

She could feel the butterflies taking flight in her stomach as she returned the action. This was it—this was the moment when

two hearts would finally and completely entangle forever as one.
"I am with you," she whispered to him.

"And I with you," he replied.

Vǫrðr and Shura barked happily. The crowd cheered, throwing their flowers into the air. Rohan pulled her, his bride, into his arms and kissed her. This kiss brought to mind the one that she thought would be their last. She was overwhelmed with gratitude for the chance of a million more kisses—a lifetime in his arms. The rest of the world faded around them. Ylva could swear she could hear their two heartbeats match rhythm.

Hours later, the sun was setting, painting the sky orange and purple above the long table arranged for the wedding feast. Torches were being lit around them so that their merriment could continue long into the night. Another horn of honey-mead passed between the bride and groom, now husband and wife. Ylva took a long drink as was tradition.

"Walk with me," Rohan said, holding out his hand.

Ylva took it. He helped her from her seat. She leaned closed to him as they walked through the crowd. People were laughing. Couples were dancing. No Darkness clouded eyes or hearts.

"Are you happy?" Rohan asked Ylva.

She stopped and made his face to turn toward her. "Are you?"

"For the first time in a very long time," he replied, "I truly am." Rohan leaned in and kissed her.

Children laughed nearby. They sounded cheerful in a way that struck a familiar chord inside Ylva. A few boys and girls were dancing and playing. Her wolves bounced around them. Then in their midst, she saw a man, dancing and jumping about to the music. He bore tan skin and dark hair. His wore a simple linen tunic and no shoes. He whirled around—then Ylva caught sight of his face. *Could it be?*

"Elior," she exhaled his name.

"What?" Rohan asked with his eyebrows raised high.

"Look!" she pointed to the man. She tugged Rohan with her as they approached him. Ylva cautioned herself to be sure her eyes weren't deceiving her.

The servant's smile grew wider. He held out his open arms to the couple. "I so hoped to greet you with well-wishes before the evening concluded."

Rohan and Ylva could not bring their eyes into focus. This could not be possible.

"How...are...you...here...?" Rohan managed a string of dazed words.

"With everything you have seen, you still question," Elior replied with a chuckle. He patted the king's cheek. "The Light cannot be defeated—even by death." He touched his hand to Ylva's shoulder. "We are all just a phoenix rising from the ashes of darkness and shadow."

"But you..." Ylva had not said the words aloud. She wasn't sure she had even truly let herself think them at all—that Elior was not just a servant of the Light but rather Lys in human flesh. It wasn't a question of belief. She believed in the possibility. It wasn't a question of her worth. She couldn't deny her value. Perhaps the hint of shame she felt for missing it for so long made it hard to utter the words. "But you are more..." She breathed the words like a confession that ushered in freedom.

"Yes, little one," Elior replied. "I am." He leaned forward and kissed her forehead.

The touch brought with it all the warmth, joy and security she knew from her childhood. But in its familiarity it was also sacred. There was a holiness to it that ignited her soul.

"Will you stay?" Rohan asked the servant.

"Like this? No, not here," Elior responded. "But I will always *be* here." The servant pulled the king and queen into a hearty embrace. His lanky arms wrapped tightly around the couple. Ylva could smell the spice mingled with floral notes that scented his skin and hair.

"The Light will guide you," Elior whispered.

"The Darkness will fear you," they replied as was the custom of the Four Realms.

He released the embrace. Joy spread in a grin over his countenance. Then he was gone, vanished as though he had never been there at all.

Vǫrðr and Shura barked beside Ylva—confirming Elior's words—that his presence had not been her imagination. She giggled at their happy faces and scratched their ears. Her guardians, her wardens, the companions Lys had given her would always be a reminder that the Light would not forsake them.

Ylva leaned her head on Rohan's shoulder. "Shall we return to the celebration, my king?"

He smiled down at her and kissed the top of her head. "Of course, my Wolf Queen."

THE END.

"Guard your heart above all else,
for it determines the course of your life."
Proverbs 4:23 NLT

ACKNOWLEDGMENTS

Writing a book is hard, y'all. There are so many hours and so many tears that were poured into this story. I am grateful to the people in my life that support and encourage me through every part of the process.

Thank you to my husband and daughters for graciously giving me the space to write, and for believing in me when I had trouble believing in myself.

Thank you to the best intern/assistant ever! Katie you rock all the socks. Thanks for listening to me rant and process. Thanks for eating Triscuits and watching true crime shows with me when I needed a break. Thanks for making me feel way cooler than I actually am.

Thank you, Victoria and Aly for being my friends and supporters and for always having my back through this author thing. I value you both more than I can express.

Thank you, Team LiveChosen for being the best squad ever. You make being an author fun and I am so grateful for each and every one of you.

Thank you, Blue Ink Press. I am honored to have found a

publishing home with a team that believes in me and invests in me the way you do.

Thanks to my mom and dad. You taught me to be brave. You taught me to put Jesus first. I never doubt that you are in my corner.

Thank you, readers. I am always in awe that anyone would take time to read my stories. I hope that even a handful of my words are as meaningful to you as you are to me.

Thank you, Jesus. Thank you for your love and grace. Thank you for being the Light that fights the darkness in my own heart and mind. Thank you for writing my life into a beautiful story... one I hope always points to you.

With love,
    Tabitha

ABOUT THE AUTHOR

Tabitha Caplinger gets way too emotionally invested in the lives of fictional characters, whether it's obsessing over a book or tv show, or getting lost creating her own worlds. Tabitha is the author of The Chronicle of the Three Trilogy, a Christian urban fantasy, and a lover of good stories and helping others live chosen. When she's not writing book words, she's reheating her coffee, binging a new show or teaching God's Word to students. Tabitha, her husband and two beautifully sassy daughters desire to be Jesus with skin on for those around them. They live to love others...and for Marvel movies.

CPSIA information can be obtained
at www.ICGtesting.com
Printed in the USA
LVHW030108311220
675430LV00010B/1907

9 781948 449083